THE EXHAM CYCLE

ROBERT M. PRICE, EDITOR

THE EXHAM CYCLE

JAMES GEORGE FRAZER
SABINE M. BARING-GOULD
EDGAR ALLEN POE
FIONA MACLEOD
IRVIN S. COBB
MICHAEL HARRISON
H. P. LOVECRAFT
PETER H. CANNON
ROBERT M. PRICE

EDITED AND INTRODUCED BY ROBERT M. PRICE

COVER ART BY JASON C. ECKHARDT.

2020
Exham Priory
Selma, North Carolina
United States of America

The Exham Cycle is published by Exham Priory, an imprint of Mindvendor

The Golden Bough: A Study in Comparative Religion by James George Frazer (New York and London: Macmillan and Co., 1894). Portions used in this volume include by chapter: XXXIV, "The Myth and Ritual of Attis;" XXXV, "Attis as a God of Vegetation;" XXXVI, "Human Representatives of Attis;" XXVII, "Oriental Religions in the West." This work is in the public domain. *Curious Myths of the Middle Ages* by Sabine M. Baring-Gould, (Boston, 1867). Portions used in this volume include "Bishop Hatto" and "S. Patrick's Purgatory." This work is in the public domain. "*Ligeia*" by Edgar Allen Poe, (Baltimore, 1838). This work is in the public domain. "The Sin-Eater" by Fiona Macleod (pen name of William Sharp) (Chicago: Stone and Kimball, 1895). This work is in the public domain. "The Unbroken Chain" by Irvin S. Cobb appeared in *On an Island That Cost $24.00* (New York: George H. Doran Company, 1926). "The Rats in the Walls" by H.P. Lovecraft first appeared in *Weird Tales*, March 1924. This work is in the public domain. "Some Very Odd Happenings at Kibblesham Manor House" copyright © 1969 by Michael Harrison (pen name of Maurice Desmond Rohan), first appeared in *The Magazine of Fantasy and Science Fiction* [v36 #4, #215, April 1969], reprinted here by kind permission of literary executor J. M. Gibson. "Cats, Rats, and Bertie Wooster" © 1990 by Peter H. Cannon, first appeared in *Crypt of Cthulhu #72* (vol. 9, no. 5, Roodmas, 1990). It appears here by the kind permission of the author. "Exham Priory" copyright © 1990 by Robert M. Price, first appeared in *Crypt of Cthulhu 72* (vol. 9, no. 5, Roodmas 1990).

Introductions copyright © 2020 by Robert M. Price.

Cover art copyright © by Jason C. Eckhardt. Rat illustration by Gordon Johnson. Cover design by Qarol Price

ISBN: 978-0-9991537-6-5

Dedicated to the memory of

Wilum Hopfrog Pugmire,
avatar of liminality.

CONTENTS

❖ ❖ ❖

‮ℰ‬The Rat Race‮ℛ‬

AN INTRODUCTION

*It was the eldritch scurrying of those fiend-born rats, always questing
for new horrors, and determined to lead me on even unto those
grinning caverns of earth's centre where Nyarlathotep, the mad
faceless god, howls blindly in the darkness to the piping of two
amorphous idiot flute-players.*

H.P. Lovecraft, *"The Rats in the Walls"*

COMING REPULSIONS

TEAPOT CONTROVERSY HAS ALWAYS SWIRLED about this story,
whether, on the admittedly slender basis of the lines just quoted,
"The Rats in the Walls" should be enumerated among Lovecraft's
"tales of the Cthulhu Mythos." Only here, near to the end, does
Nyarlathotep receive mention. There is no intimation that the de la
Poers or their fiendish forbears from under the earth were relatives
to Nyarlathotep or his worshippers, or anything else connected to
him. Indeed, one might say that, having unveiled the horrors of
Exham Priory and of the cumulative degenerates of various origins,
nations, and tribes, the plunge of the cascading rats into the planet
center is the transit for the narrator into the final horror against
which the squealing pig-men, the cannibalistic aristocrats, and the
self-castrating Attys fanatics pale into comparison. "You ain't seen
nothin' yet," Lovecraft means to warn us in this passage, and this
means that Nyarlathotep is not the subject of "The Rats in the

9

Walls," not in any manner analogous to Cthulhu in "The Call of Cthulhu" or even to Yog-Sothoth in "The Dunwich Horror." This story is a signpost telling us, "You are now leaving Lovecraft's spectral tales. Next stop, his Mythos stories."

We can see in this passage how Lovecraft himself has only the vaguest notion of the Mythos that will later blossom forth in noxious luxuriance. Notice that he has not so much combined associations of Nyarlathotep with those of Azathoth as fashioned a crude prototype of an Old One which he will streamline and refine, selecting out traits for two or three Old Ones before he is done. Ultimately HPL is thinking of Lord Dunsany's cosmic dreamer Mana Yood Sushai who ever sleeps, lulled by the efforts of a pair of tireless drummers whose percussion, like the ticking of a grandfather clock, keeps him drowsy. When he awakens, this dream of a world will end. The element of an age-long slumber whose conclusion marks Armageddon Lovecraft used for Great Cthulhu, asleep in R'lyeh. The element of the twin musicians (though their original use has been forgotten—they do not keep anyone asleep anymore—has been appropriated for Nyarlathotep and Azathoth. There is a similar ambiguity, it seems to me, between two sonnets in *Fungi from Yuggoth*. Which one is the being whom the interpreting demon figure clubs over the head? To whom does the poem's title "Nyarlathotep" refer? The oblivious Master or the contemptuous servant? I give up. But there is no answer. Lovecraft never systematized his lore, certainly not this early in the game.

EXHAM PRIORITY

THOUGH THE CHIEF LITERARY SOURCE of "The Rats in the Walls" can be found in Poe's "Ligeia," we also detect a species of Neo-Platonic metaphysical horror characteristic of one of Lovecraft's other "gods of fiction" (the *real* "Old Ones"), Arthur Machen. What is it that the hell-spawn Helen Vaughan tempts men to behold, destroying in them any hope or any will to continue? Apparently, it is the secret origin of all things in pre-creation Chaos. If things were first Chaos, they are essentially Chaos. Helen herself (whose spectacular passage from this plane so strikingly anticipates that of Wilbur Whateley) metamorphoses, as she dies, from one evolutionary form to another, all the way back, till there is no defining form at all. And, as in Greek Mythology, a being with no one, stable form, has no real form at all. "As a foulness shall ye know them."

The same thing happens at the end of "The Rats in the Walls" when narrator de la Poer suffers a mental breakdown. Only he does not merely crash into a psychic heap; no, he regresses toward ever more bestial, less civilized ancestral, albeit human, forms. He has "made the inner as the outer" as the Gospel of Thomas tells us to do, adjusting the microcosm of his own soul, with its awakening ancestral memory, to the successive stages of inhabitation of the complex beneath Exham Priory as he explores them. But he is not imitating what he sees. Instead, he is dropping layer after layer of disguise, dropping layer after layer of civilized, humanized *veneer*, to get down to the *real thing*, the chaos that civilization seeks to confine within a suit of clothes. This was one of the chief points of difference between his own thought and that of Robert E. Howard, HPL's friend, colleague, and correspondent. Howard offered his characters Conan and King Kull as fine examples of the Noble Savage, Howard taking Burroughs's Tarzan as his exemplar. Howard considered civilization as inherently jaded and decadent. Lovecraft, on the other hand, regarded raw humanity as a set of stones that, with difficulty, had been made to serve as the rough-hewn building blocks for civilization's Tower of Babel. Howard depicted civilization as he saw it in the Conan tale "Red Nails," while Lovecraft portrayed "natural man" in "The Rats in the Walls."

Taint So

HOW ARE WE SUPPOSED TO UNDERSTAND the hereditary taint of the de la Poers? The narrator, as we have seen, appears to be overcome by a flood of ancestral memory. Perhaps this has something to do with the cannibalistic practices of his clan. If they had been in the habit of new generations devouring their forbears, some might suggest that each generation absorbed genetic matter containing memory data, though it sounds bogus to me. Especially since there is no way the cannibalism had continued into the narrator's generation. He had certainly never partaken. But the major alternative explanation would seem to have the same weakness. We are told that Exham Priory had been the site of nefarious practices since time immemorial and that every successive wave of new inhabitants, though they added a new top floor to the house, so to speak, would soon be sucked into the aboriginal culture, members of which must have carefully made themselves known, intermingling with the come-lately Celts, Romans, etc. We would have to envision in broad terms a pattern like that seen in China, where wave after wave of conquerors assimilated Chinese culture rather than imposing their own. But, again, how would this have affected poor de la Poer? There is no hint either that his gathering, with the help of Captain Norrys, of the local lore could so affect him, or that he already had latent psychosis that was only brought out into the open by learning the lore of the place (like Jack Torrance in Stephen King's *The Shining*).

Jack Torrance and his fate supply an important possibility. As I read King's novel, though Jack was already dangerously unstable, it was his son, not he himself, who possessed psychic potency and placed him in danger while at the Overlook. The hotel was not only the habitat of lingering ghosts, imprisoned there to relive their awful crimes (apparently an orgy of murder, to begin with); it had its own ghostly sentience, its own "shine." The ghosts tried to have Jack murder his son so they might add him to their number and feed off his spiritual force. Jack was assimilated to the drama that the Overlook always sought to replay. He became a character. When Jack is talking with the spectral Mr. Grady, and the latter tells him, "You've always been the caretaker here," he doesn't mean Jack himself. After all, we know quite well the previous caretaker who murdered his family was Mr. Grady. What the Grady ghost means is that it is Jack's turn to take the role. And that is what I suggest the narrator of "The Rats in the Walls" does. He, too, is stalked by ghosts, those of Bishop Hatto's rats, who have lured him down into

12

the bowels below the Priory, where he finds the stage where the past is to be replayed, for only so can the devilish ghosts who linger there be rejuvenated, if only temporarily. When he trails off into Cymric gibberish, he is not voicing his own ancient memories, now reawakened; he is rather mouthing the lines assigned him by the "shining" of the place.

Keep in mind, too, that the de la Poer line seems to have experienced nothing extraordinary after relocating to Virginia. A blood contagion would not have been so easily silenced by a change of place. It all starts up again only once a de la Poer goes back to Exham Priory. It is the place that is the magnet and catalyst of evil.

The main weakness of my theory is that it can have been no accident that narrator de la Poer was the scion of the spent de la Poer line, and that Norrys was a descendent of the "flabby beasts" once bred as livestock on the estate. Does not this fact imply that the characters are some kind of reincarnations of their ancestors? No, I think not. After all, we never hear that Norrys experiences any psychic alteration, only that his plump form starts de la Poer a-drooling! The fact that de la Poer played the lead role, in the position of one of his ancestors, is poetic justice. It is only he whom the ghosts of the Priory want, only he to whom they reveal themselves. Only he can hear them rushing through the walls, but not because he has inherited some unique de la Poer talent/curse of hearing them. No, it is because they want *him*.

Robert M. Price
Hour of the curious bulging of the wall paper,
May 15, 2009

13

FROM

THE GOLDEN BOUGH

JAMES GEORGE FRAZER

SIR JAMES GEORGE FRAZER (1854-1941) is most famous as the author of *The Golden Bough*, an encyclopedic compendium of worldwide folklore giving special prominence to the role of the myth of the dying and rising god. The first edition was published in 1890, followed by various, much longer editions until it reached thirteen volumes. (The Lovecraftian reader is inevitably reminded of the ever-growing *Revelations of Glaaki*.) Frazer was one of the earliest anthropologists. He traveled in Greece and Italy but no farther. For him, the world of the colonial frontier was as alien as that of the remote past, and his evidence for both was of the same kind: fragmentary and documentary, for he employed both the writings of ancient historians and reports of modern missionaries. Some recent critics of Frazer hesitate to trust his conclusions, fearing that such generalizing syntheses produce artificial results. But I for one prefer Frazer's approach to that of modern participant observers who fully analyze the ways of a single tribe and then start generalizing.

Attis was one of the major dying-and-rising savior deities of the Mediterranean world, having originated in Phrygia (in Asia Minor) and made his way to Rome via the orgiastic cult of Attis and Cybele. (Lovecraft was wrong in claiming that their cult was at first "vainly forbidden" to Romans; rather, their religion was welcomed in at the instruction of the Delphic Oracle who prescribed it as a cure for current troubles in the city.) Frazer's theory was that all such religions were survivals of primordial matriarchy. The Queen represented the fertility of nature, her childbearing symbolic of the annual harvest. But, as everyone knows, vegetation dies every year, nature's power spent. This failure was due to the wearing out of the king's virility, so he had to be sacrificed, to be replaced by another (in whose person he was symbolically resurrected), every New Year. This made possible the renewal of the seasons. Before long, the king would yield the throne for a single day, and a nobody or a condemned criminal would be elected the King for a Day or Fool King. Guess which day? Once he was feted, then sacrificed, the old king would go through the motions as his own resurrection/successor. In many cultures, the whole process was eventually transformed into pure symbolism, using edible effigies, perhaps bread and juice as the god-king's body and blood. But the rites of Attis remained bloody, entailing genital mutilation. This Lovecraft naturally abhorred and therefore saw as the

15

perfect complement to the ancient diabolisms of his imaginary Exham orgiasts. He had certainly read of these matters in Frazer's *The Golden Bough*, which he mentions so frequently as next to the *Necronomicon* on the shelves of his doomed scholarly protagonists.

Frazer's theories may be found bodied forth in appropriately mysterious trappings in two films: *The Eye of the Devil* (1967), starring David Niven, Deborah Kerr, Sharon Tate, and Donald Pleasance, and the better known *The Wicker Man*, with Edward Woodward, Christopher Lee, and Britt Ekland (1973). Also worth your time as Frazerian works are L. Sprague de Camp's trilogy, *The Goblin Tower*, *The Clocks of Iraz*, and *The Unbeheaded King*. Fans of the screen epic *Excalibur* will certainly want to read another scholarly book, about the Grail Mythos, Jessie Weston's *From Ritual to Romance*, which illuminates the myths of the Chapel Perilous, the Fisher King, etc., with light from Frazer's torch.

ℰℭ

XXXIV. THE MYTH AND RITUAL OF ATTIS

ANOTHER OF THOSE GODS whose supposed death and resurrection struck such deep roots into the faith and ritual of Western Asia is Attis. He was to Phrygia what Adonis was to Syria. Like Adonis, he appears to have been a god of vegetation, and his death and resurrection were annually mourned and rejoiced over at a festival in spring. The legends and rites of the two gods were so much alike that the ancients themselves sometimes identified them. Attis was said to have been a fair young shepherd or herdsman beloved by Cybele, the Mother of the Gods, a great Asiatic goddess of fertility, who had her chief home in Phrygia. Some held that Attis was her son. His birth, like that of many other heroes, is said to have been miraculous. His mother, Nana, was a virgin, who conceived by putting a ripe almond or a pomegranate in her bosom. Indeed in the Phrygian cosmogony an almond figured as the father of all things, perhaps because its delicate lilac blossom is one of the first heralds of the spring, appearing on the bare boughs before the leaves have opened. Such tales of virgin mothers are relics of an age of childish ignorance when men had not yet recognized the intercourse of the sexes as the true cause of offspring. Two different accounts of the death of Attis were current. According to the one he was killed by a boar, like Adonis. According to the other he unmanned himself under a pine-tree, and bled to death on the spot. The latter is said to have been the local story told by the people of Pessinus, a great seat of the worship of Cybele, and the whole legend of which the story forms a part is stamped with a character of rudeness and savagery that speaks strongly for its antiquity. Both tales might claim the support of custom, or rather both were probably invented to explain certain customs observed by the worshippers. The story of the self-mutilation of Attis is clearly an attempt to account for the self-mutilation of his priests, who regularly castrated themselves on entering the service of the goddess. The story of his death by the boar may have been told to explain why his worshippers, especially the people of Pessinus, abstained from eating swine. In like manner the worshippers of Adonis abstained from pork, because a boar had killed their god. After his death Attis is said to have been changed into a pine-tree.

The worship of the Phrygian Mother of the Gods was adopted by the Romans in 204 B.C. towards the close of their long struggle with Hannibal. For their drooping spirits had been opportunely cheered by a prophecy, alleged to be drawn from that convenient farrago of nonsense, the Sibylline Books, that the foreign invader would be driven from Italy if the great Oriental goddess were brought to Rome. Accordingly ambassadors were despatched to her sacred city Pessinus in Phrygia. The small black stone which embodied the mighty divinity was entrusted to them and conveyed to Rome, where it was received with great respect and installed in the temple of Victory on the Palatine Hill. It was the middle of April when the goddess arrived, and she went to work at once. For the harvest that year was such as had not been seen for many a long day, and in the very next year Hannibal and his veterans embarked for Africa. As he looked his last on the coast of Italy, fading behind him in the distance, he could not foresee that Europe, which had repelled the arms, would yet yield to the gods of the Orient. The vanguard of the conquerors had already encamped in the heart of

Italy before the rearguard of the beaten army fell sullenly back from its shores.

We may conjecture, though we are not told, that the Mother of the Gods brought with her the worship of her youthful lover or son to her new home in the West. Certainly the Romans were familiar with the Galli, the emasculated priests of Attis, before the close of the Republic. These unsexed beings, in their Oriental costume, with little images suspended on their breasts, appear to have been a familiar sight in the streets of Rome, which they traversed in procession, carrying the image of the goddess and chanting their hymns to the music of cymbals and tambourines, flutes and horns, while the people, impressed by the fantastic show and moved by the wild strains, flung alms to them in abundance, and buried the image and its bearers under showers of roses. A further step was taken by the Emperor Claudius when he incorporated the Phrygian worship of the sacred tree, and with it probably the orgiastic rites of Attis, in the established religion of Rome. The great spring festival of Cybele and Attis is best known to us in the form in which it was celebrated at Rome; but as we are informed that the Roman ceremonies were also Phrygian, we may assume that they differed hardly, if at all, from their Asiatic original. The order of the festival seems to have been as follows.

On the twenty-second day of March, a pine-tree was cut in the woods and brought into the sanctuary of Cybele, where it was treated as a great divinity. The duty of carrying the sacred tree was entrusted to a guild of Tree-bearers. The trunk was swathed like a corpse with woollen bands and decked with wreaths of violets, for violets were said to have sprung from the blood of Attis, as roses and anemones from the blood of Adonis; and the effigy of a young man, doubtless Attis himself, was tied to the middle of the stem. On the second day of the festival, the twenty-third of March, the chief ceremony seems to have been a blowing of trumpets. The third day, the twenty-fourth of March, was known as the Day of Blood: the Archigallus or highpriest drew blood from his arms and presented it as an offering. Nor was he alone in making this bloody sacrifice. Stirred by the wild barbaric music of clashing cymbals, rumbling drums, droning horns, and screaming flutes, the inferior clergy whirled about in the dance with waggling heads and streaming hair, until, rapt into a frenzy of excitement and insensible to pain, they gashed their bodies with potsherds or slashed them with knives in order to bespatter the altar and the sacred tree with their flowing blood. The ghastly rite probably formed part of the mourning for Attis and may have been intended to strengthen him for the resurrection. The Australian aborigines cut themselves in like manner over the graves of their friends for the purpose, perhaps, of enabling them to be born again. Further, we may conjecture, though we are not expressly told, that it was on the same Day of Blood and for the same purpose that the novices sacrificed their virility. Wrought up to the highest pitch of religious excitement they dashed the severed portions of themselves against the image of the cruel goddess. These broken instruments of fertility were afterwards reverently wrapt up and buried in the earth or in subterranean chambers sacred to Cybele, where, like the offering of blood, they may have been deemed instrumental in recalling Attis to life and hastening the general resurrection of nature, which was then bursting into leaf and blossom in the vernal sunshine. Some confirmation of this conjecture is furnished by the savage story that the mother of Attis conceived by putting in her bosom a pomegranate sprung from the severed genitals of a man-monster named Agdestis, a sort of double of Attis.

If there is any truth in this conjectural explanation of the custom, we can readily understand why other Asiatic goddesses of fertility were served in like manner by eunuch priests. These feminine deities required to receive from their male ministers, who personated the divine lovers, the means of discharging their beneficent functions: they had themselves to be impregnated by the life-giving energy before they could transmit it to the world. Goddesses thus ministered to by eunuch priests were the great Artemis of Ephesus and the great Syrian Astarte of Hierapolis, whose sanctuary, frequented by swarms of pilgrims and enriched by the offerings of Assyria and Babylonia, of Arabia and Phoenicia, was perhaps in the days of its glory the most popular in the East. Now the unsexed priests of this Syrian goddess resembled those of Cybele so closely that some people took them to be the same. And the mode in which they dedicated themselves to the religious life was similar. The greatest festival of the year at Hierapolis fell at the beginning of spring, when multitudes thronged to the sanctuary from Syria and the regions round about. While the flutes played, the drums beat, and the eunuch priests slashed themselves with knives, the religious excitement gradually spread like a wave among the crowd of onlookers, and many a one did that which he little thought to do when he came as a holiday spectator to the festival. For man after man, his veins throbbing with the music, his eyes fascinated by the sight of the streaming blood, flung his garments from him, leaped forth with a shout, and seizing one of the swords which stood ready for the purpose, castrated himself on the spot. Then he ran through the city, holding the bloody pieces in his hand, till he threw them into one of the houses which he passed in his mad career. The household thus honoured had to furnish him with a suit of female attire and female ornaments, which he wore for the rest of his life. When the tumult of emotion had subsided, and the man had come to himself again, the irrevocable sacrifice must often have been followed by passionate sorrow and lifelong regret. This revulsion of natural human feeling after the frenzies of a fanatical religion is powerfully depicted by Catullus in a celebrated poem.

The parallel of these Syrian devotees confirms the view that in the similar worship of Cybele the sacrifice of virility took place on the Day of Blood at the vernal rites of the goddess, when the violets, supposed to spring from the red drops of her wounded lover, were in bloom among the pines. Indeed the story that Attis unmanned himself under a pine-tree was clearly devised to explain why his priests did the same beside the sacred violet-wreathed tree at his festival. At all events, we can hardly doubt that the Day of Blood witnessed the mourning for Attis over an effigy of him which was afterwards buried. The image thus laid in the sepulchre was probably the same which had hung upon the tree. Throughout the period of mourning the worshippers fasted from bread, nominally because Cybele had done so in her grief for the death of Attis, but really perhaps for the same reason which induced the women of Harran to abstain from eating anything ground in a mill while they wept for Tammuz. To partake of bread or flour at such a season might have been deemed a wanton profanation of the bruised and broken body of the god. Or the fast may possibly have been a preparation for a sacramental meal.

But when night had fallen, the sorrow of the worshippers was turned to joy. For suddenly a light shone in the darkness: the tomb was opened: the god had risen from the dead; and as the priest touched the lips of the weeping mourners with balm, he softly whispered in their ears the glad tidings of salvation. The resurrection of the god was hailed by his disciples as a promise that they too would issue triumphant from the corruption of the grave. On the morrow, the twenty-fifth day of March, which was reckoned the vernal equinox, the divine resurrection was celebrated with a wild outburst of glee. At Rome, and probably elsewhere, the celebration took the form of a carnival. It was the Festival of Joy (*Hilaria*). A universal licence prevailed. Every man might say and do what he pleased. People went about the streets in disguise. No dignity was too high or too sacred for the humblest citizen to assume with impunity. In the reign of Commodus a band of conspirators thought to take advantage of the masquerade by dressing in the uniform of the Imperial Guard, and so, mingling with the crowd of merrymakers, to get within stabbing distance of the emperor. But the plot miscarried. Even the stern Alexander Severus used to relax so far on the joyous day as to admit a pheasant to his frugal board. The next day, the twenty-sixth of March, was given to repose, which must have been much needed after the varied excitements and fatigues of the preceding days. Finally, the Roman festival closed on the twenty-seventh of March with a procession to the brook Almo. The silver image of the goddess, with its face of jagged black stone, sat in a waggon drawn by oxen. Preceded by the nobles walking barefoot, it moved slowly, to the loud music of pipes and tambourines, out by the Porta Capena, and so down to the banks of the Almo, which flows into the Tiber just below the walls of Rome. There the high-priest, robed in purple, washed the waggon, the image, and the other sacred objects in the water of the stream. On returning from their bath, the wain and the oxen were strewn with fresh spring flowers. All was mirth and gaiety. No one thought of the blood that had flowed so lately. Even the eunuch priests forgot their wounds.

Such, then, appears to have been the annual solemnisation of the death and resurrection of Attis in spring. But besides these public rites, his worship is known to have comprised certain secret or mystic ceremonies, which probably aimed at bringing the worshipper, and especially the novice, into closer communication with his god. Our information as to the nature of these mysteries and the date of their celebration is unfortunately very scanty, but they seem to have included a sacramental meal and a baptism of blood. In the sacrament the novice became a partaker of the mysteries by eating out of a drum and drinking out of a cymbal, two instruments of music which figured prominently in the thrilling orchestra of Attis. The fast which accompanied the mourning for the dead god may perhaps have been designed to prepare the body of the communicant for the reception of the blessed sacrament by purging it of all that could defile by contact the sacred elements. In the baptism the devotee, crowned with gold and wreathed with fillets, descended into a pit, the mouth of which was covered with a wooden grating. A bull, adorned with garlands of flowers, its forehead glittering with gold leaf, was then driven on to the grating and there stabbed to death with a consecrated spear. Its hot reeking blood poured in torrents through the apertures, and was received with devout eagerness by the worshipper on every part of his person and garments, till he emerged from the pit, drenched, dripping, and scarlet from head to foot, to receive the homage, nay the adoration, of his fellows as one who had been born again to eternal life and had washed away his sins in the blood of the bull. For some time afterwards the fiction of a new birth was kept up by dieting him on milk like a new-born babe. The regeneration of the worshipper took place at the same time as the regeneration of his god, namely at the vernal equinox. At Rome the new birth and the remission of sins by the shedding of bull's blood appear to have been carried out above all at the sanctuary of the Phrygian goddess on the Vatican Hill, at or near the spot where the great basilica of St. Peter's now stands; for many inscriptions relating to the rites were found when the church was being enlarged in 1608 or 1609. From the Vatican as a centre this barbarous system of superstition seems to have spread to other parts of the Roman empire. Inscriptions found in Gaul and Germany prove that provincial sanctuaries modelled their ritual on that of the Vatican. From the same source we learn that the testicles as well as the blood of the bull played an important part in the ceremonies. Probably they were regarded as a powerful charm to promote fertility and hasten the new birth.

◆

XXXV. ATTIS AS A GOD OF VEGETATION

THE ORIGINAL CHARACTER OF ATTIS as a tree-spirit is brought out plainly by the part which the pine-tree plays in his legend, his ritual, and his monuments. The story that he was a human being transformed into a pine-tree is only one of those transparent attempts at rationalising old beliefs which meet us so frequently in mythology. The bringing in of the pine-tree from the woods, decked with violets and woollen bands, is like bringing in the May-tree or Summer-tree in modern folk-custom; and the effigy which was attached to the pine-tree was only a duplicate representative of the tree-spirit Attis. After being fastened to the tree, the effigy was kept for a year and then burned. The same thing appears to have been sometimes done with the May-pole; and in like manner the effigy of the corn-spirit, made at harvest, is often preserved till it is replaced by a new effigy at next year's harvest. The original intention of such customs was no doubt to maintain the spirit of vegetation in life throughout the year. Why the Phrygians should have worshipped the pine above other trees we can only guess. Perhaps the sight of its changeless, though sombre, green cresting the ridges of the high hills above the fading splendour of the autumn woods in the valleys may have seemed to their eyes to mark it out as the seat of a diviner life, of something exempt from the sad vicissitudes of the seasons, constant and eternal as the sky which stooped to meet it. For the same reason, perhaps, ivy was sacred to Attis; at all events, we read that his eunuch priests were tattooed with a pattern of ivy leaves.

Another reason for the sanctity of the pine may have been its usefulness. The cones of the stone-pine contain edible nut-like seeds, which have been used as food since antiquity, and are still eaten, for example, by the poorer classes in Rome. Moreover, a wine was brewed from these seeds, and this may partly account for the orgiastic nature of the rites of Cybele, which the ancients compared to those of Dionysus. Further, pine-cones were regarded as symbols or rather instruments of fertility. Hence at the festival of the Thesmophoria they were thrown, along with pigs and other agents or emblems of fecundity, into the sacred vaults of Demeter for the purpose of quickening the ground and the wombs of women.

Like tree-spirits in general, Attis was apparently thought to wield power over the fruits of the earth or even to be identical with the corn. One of his epithets was "very fruitful": he was addressed as the "reaped green (or yellow) ear of corn"; and the story of his sufferings, death, and resurrection was interpreted as the ripe grain wounded by the reaper, buried in the granary, and coming to life again when it is sown in the ground. A statue of him in the Lateran Museum at Rome clearly indicates his relation to the fruits of the earth, and particularly to the corn; for it represents him with a bunch of ears of corn and fruit in his hand, and a wreath of pine-cones, pomegranates, and other fruits on his head, while from the top of his Phrygian cap ears of corn are sprouting. On a stone urn, which contained the ashes of an Archigallus or high-priest of Attis, the same idea is expressed in a slightly different way. The top of the urn is adorned with ears of corn carved in relief, and it is surmounted by the figure of a cock, whose tail consists of ears of corn. Cybele in like manner was conceived as a goddess of fertility who could make or mar the fruits of the earth; for the people of Augustodunum (Autun) in Gaul used to cart her image about in a waggon for the good of the fields and vineyards, while they danced and sang before it, and we have seen that in Italy an unusually fine harvest was attributed to the recent arrival of the Great Mother. The bathing of the image of the goddess in a river may well have been a rain-charm to ensure an abundant supply of moisture for the crops.

◆

XXXVI. HUMAN REPRESENTATIVES OF ATTIS

FROM INSCRIPTIONS IT APPEARS THAT BOTH at Pessinus and Rome the high-priest of Cybele regularly bore the name of Attis. It is therefore a reasonable conjecture that he played the part of his namesake, the legendary Attis, at the annual festival. We have seen that on the Day of Blood he drew blood from his arms, and this may have been an imitation of the self-inflicted death of Attis under the pine-tree. It is not inconsistent with this supposition that Attis was also represented at these ceremonies by an effigy; for instances can be shown in which the divine being is first represented by a living person and afterwards by an effigy, which is then burned or otherwise destroyed. Perhaps we may go a step farther and conjecture that this mimic killing of the priest, accompanied by a real effusion of his blood, was in Phrygia, as it has been elsewhere, a substitute for a human sacrifice which in earlier times was actually offered.

A reminiscence of the manner in which these old representatives of the deity were put to death is perhaps preserved in the famous story of Marsyas. He was said to be a Phrygian satyr or Silenus, according to others a shepherd or herdsman, who played sweetly on the flute. A friend of Cybele, he roamed the country with the disconsolate goddess to soothe her grief for the death of Attis. The composition of the Mother's Air, a tune played on the flute in honour of the Great Mother Goddess, was attributed to him by the people of Celaenae in Phrygia. Vain of his skill, he challenged Apollo to a musical contest, he to play on the flute and Apollo on the lyre. Being vanquished, Marsyas was tied up to a pine-tree and flayed or cut limb from limb either by the victorious Apollo or by a Scythian slave. His skin was shown at Celaenae in historical times. It hung at the foot of the citadel in a cave from which the river Marsyas rushed with an impetuous and noisy tide to join the Maeander. So the Adonis bursts full-born from the precipices of the Lebanon; so the blue river of Ibreez leaps in a crystal jet from the red rocks of the Taurus; so the stream, which now rumbles deep underground, used to gleam for a moment on its passage from darkness to darkness in the dim light of the Corycian cave. In all these copious fountains, with their glad promise of fertility and life, men of old saw the hand of God and worshipped him beside the rushing river with the music of its tumbling waters in their ears. At Celaenae, if we can trust tradition, the piper Marsyas, hanging in his cave, had a soul for harmony even in death; for it is said that at the sound of his native Phrygian melodies the skin of the dead satyr used to thrill, but that if the musician struck up an air in praise of Apollo it remained deaf and motionless.

In this Phrygian satyr, shepherd, or herdsman who enjoyed the friendship of Cybele, practised the music so characteristic of her rites, and died a violent death on her sacred tree, the pine, may we not detect a close resemblance to Attis, the favourite shepherd or herdsman of the goddess, who is himself described as a piper, is said to have perished under a pine-tree, and was annually represented by an effigy hung, like Marsyas, upon a pine? We may conjecture that in old days the priest who bore the name and played the part of Attis at the spring festival of Cybele was regularly hanged or otherwise slain upon the sacred tree, and that this barbarous custom was afterwards mitigated into the form in which it is known to us in later times, when the priest merely drew blood from his body under the tree and attached an effigy instead of himself to its trunk. In the holy grove at Upsala men and animals were sacrificed by being hanged upon the sacred trees. The human victims dedicated to Odin were regularly put to death by hanging or by a combination of hanging and stabbing, the man being strung up to a tree or a gallows and then wounded with a spear. Hence Odin was called the Lord of the Gallows or the God of the Hanged, and he is represented sitting under a gallows tree. Indeed he is said to have been sacrificed to himself in the ordinary way, as we learn from the weird verses of the *Havamal*, in which the god describes how he acquired his divine power by learning the magic runes:

> *"I know that I hung on the windy tree*
> *For nine whole nights,*

26

Wounded with the spear, dedicated to Odin,
Myself to myself."

The Bagobos of Mindanao, one of the Philippine Islands, used annually to sacrifice human victims for the good of the crops in a similar way. Early in December, when the constellation Orion appeared at seven o'clock in the evening, the people knew that the time had come to clear their fields for sowing and to sacrifice a slave. The sacrifice was presented to certain powerful spirits as payment for the good year which the people had enjoyed, and to ensure the favour of the spirits for the coming season. The victim was led to a great tree in the forest; there he was tied with his back to the tree and his arms stretched high above his head, in the attitude in which ancient artists portrayed Marsyas hanging on the fatal tree. While he thus hung by the arms, he was slain by a spear thrust through his body at the level of the armpits. Afterwards the body was cut clean through the middle at the waist, and the upper part was apparently allowed to dangle for a little from the tree, while the under part wallowed in blood on the ground. The two portions were finally cast into a shallow trench beside the tree. Before this was done, anybody who wished might cut off a piece of flesh or a lock of hair from the corpse and carry it to the grave of some relation whose body was being consumed by a ghoul. Attracted by the fresh corpse, the ghoul would leave the mouldering old body in peace. These sacrifices have been offered by men now living.

In Greece the great goddess Artemis herself appears to have been annually hanged in effigy in her sacred grove of Condylea among the Arcadian hills, and there accordingly she went by the name of the Hanged One. Indeed a trace of a similar rite may perhaps be detected even at Ephesus, the most famous of her sanctuaries, in the legend of a woman who hanged herself and was thereupon dressed by the compassionate goddess in her own divine garb and called by the name of Hecate. Similarly, at Melite in Phthia, a story was told of a girl named Aspalis who hanged herself, but who appears to have been merely a form of Artemis. For after her death her body could not be found, but an image of her was discovered standing beside the image of Artemis, and the people bestowed on it the title of Hecaerge or Far-shooter, one of the regular epithets of the goddess. Every year the virgins sacrificed a young goat to the image by hanging it, because Aspalis was said to have hanged herself. The sacrifice may have been a substitute for hanging an image or a human representative of Artemis. Again, in Rhodes the fair Helen was worshipped under the title of Helen of the Tree, because the queen of the island had caused her handmaids, disguised as Furies, to string her up to a bough. That the Asiatic Greeks sacrificed animals in this fashion is proved by coins of Ilium, which represent an ox or cow hanging on a tree and stabbed with a knife by a man, who sits among the branches or on the animal's back. At Hierapolis also the victims were hung on trees before they were burnt. With these Greek and Scandinavian parallels before us we can hardly dismiss as wholly improbable the conjecture that in Phrygia a man-god may have hung year by year on the sacred but fatal tree.

◆

XXXVII. ORIENTAL RELIGIONS IN THE WEST

THE WORSHIP OF THE GREAT MOTHER OF THE GODS and her lover or son was very popular under the Roman Empire. Inscriptions prove that the two received divine honours, separately or conjointly, not only in Italy, and especially at Rome, but also in the provinces, particularly in Africa, Spain, Portugal, France, Germany, and Bulgaria. Their worship survived the establishment of Christianity by Constantine; for Symmachus records the recurrence of the festival of the Great Mother, and in the days of Augustine her effeminate priests still paraded the streets and squares of Carthage with whitened faces, scented hair, and mincing gait, while, like the mendicant friars of the Middle Ages, they begged alms from the passers-by. In Greece, on the other hand, the bloody orgies of the Asiatic goddess and her consort appear to have found little favour. The barbarous and cruel character of the worship, with its frantic excesses, was doubtless repugnant to the good taste and humanity of the Greeks, who seem to have preferred the kindred but gentler rites of Adonis. Yet the same features which shocked and repelled the Greeks may have positively attracted the less refined Romans and barbarians of the West. The ecstatic frenzies, which were mistaken for divine inspiration, the mangling of the body, the theory of a new birth and the remission of sins through the shedding of blood, have all their origin in savagery, and they naturally appealed to peoples in whom the savage instincts were still strong. Their true character was indeed often disguised under a decent veil of allegorical or philosophical interpretation, which probably sufficed to impose upon the rapt and enthusiastic worshippers, reconciling even the more cultivated of them to things which otherwise must have filled them with horror and disgust.

The religion of the Great Mother, with its curious blending of crude savagery with spiritual aspirations, was only one of a multitude of similar Oriental faiths which in the later days of paganism spread over the Roman Empire, and by saturating the European peoples with alien ideals of life gradually undermined the whole fabric of ancient civilisation. Greek and Roman society was built on the conception of the subordination of the individual to the community, of the citizen to the state; it set the safety of the commonwealth, as the supreme aim of conduct, above the safety of the individual whether in this world or in the world to come. Trained from infancy in this unselfish ideal, the citizens devoted their lives to the public service and were ready to lay them down for the common good; or if they shrank from the supreme sacrifice, it never occurred to them that they acted otherwise than basely in preferring their personal existence to the interests of their country. All this was changed by the spread of Oriental religions which inculcated the communion of the soul with God and its eternal salvation as the only objects worth living for, objects in comparison with which the prosperity and even the existence of the state sank into insignificance. The inevitable result of this selfish and immoral doctrine was to withdraw the devotee more and more from the public service, to concentrate his thoughts on his own spiritual emotions, and to breed in him a contempt for the present life which he regarded merely as a probation for a better and an eternal. The saint and the recluse, disdainful of earth and rapt in ecstatic

contemplation of heaven, became in popular opinion the highest
ideal of humanity, displacing the old ideal of the patriot and hero
who, forgetful of self, lives and is ready to die for the good of his
country. The earthly city seemed poor and contemptible to men
whose eyes beheld the City of God coming in the clouds of heaven.
Thus the centre of gravity, so to say, was shifted from the present to
a future life, and however much the other world may have gained,
there can be little doubt that this one lost heavily by the change. A
general disintegration of the body politic set in. The ties of the state
and the family were loosened: the structure of society tended to
resolve itself into its individual elements and thereby to relapse into
barbarism; for civilisation is only possible through the active cooperation of the citizens and their willingness to subordinate their
private interests to the common good. Men refused to defend their
country and even to continue their kind. In their anxiety to save
their own souls and the souls of others, they were content to leave
the material world, which they identified with the principle of evil,
to perish around them. This obsession lasted for a thousand years.
The revival of Roman law, of the Aristotelian philosophy, of ancient
art and literature at the close of the Middle Ages, marked the return
of Europe to native ideals of life and conduct, to saner, manlier
views of the world. The long halt in the march of civilisation was
over. The tide of Oriental invasion had turned at last. It is ebbing
still.

Among the gods of eastern origin who in the decline of the
ancient world competed against each other for the allegiance of the
West was the old Persian deity Mithra. The immense popularity of
his worship is attested by the monuments illustrative of it which
have been found scattered in profusion all over the Roman Empire.
In respect both of doctrines and of rites the cult of Mithra appears
to have presented many points of resemblance not only to the
religion of the Mother of the Gods but also to Christianity. The
similarity struck the Christian doctors themselves and was explained
by them as a work of the devil, who sought to seduce the souls of
men from the true faith by a false and insidious imitation of it. So
to the Spanish conquerors of Mexico and Peru many of the native
heathen rites appeared to be diabolical counterfeits of the Christian

sacraments. With more probability the modern student of comparative religion traces such resemblances to the similar and independent workings of the mind of man in his sincere, if crude, attempts to fathom the secret of the universe, and to adjust his little life to its awful mysteries. However that may be, there can be no doubt that the Mithraic religion proved a formidable rival to Christianity, combining as it did a solemn ritual with aspirations after moral purity and a hope of immortality. Indeed the issue of the conflict between the two faiths appears for a time to have hung in the balance. An instructive relic of the long struggle is preserved in our festival of Christmas, which the Church seems to have borrowed directly from its heathen rival. In the Julian calendar the twenty-fifth of December was reckoned the winter solstice, and it was regarded as the Nativity of the Sun, because the day begins to lengthen and the power of the sun to increase from that turning-point of the year. The ritual of the nativity, as it appears to have been celebrated in Syria and Egypt, was remarkable. The celebrants retired into certain inner shrines, from which at midnight they issued with a loud cry, "The Virgin has brought forth! The light is waxing!" The Egyptians even represented the new-born sun by the image of an infant which on his birthday, the winter solstice, they brought forth and exhibited to his worshippers. No doubt the Virgin who thus conceived and bore a son on the twenty-fifth of December was the great Oriental goddess whom the Semites called the Heavenly Virgin or simply the Heavenly Goddess; in Semitic lands she was a form of Astarte. Now Mithra was regularly identified by his worshippers with the Sun, the Unconquered Sun, as they called him; hence his nativity also fell on the twenty-fifth of December. The Gospels say nothing as to the day of Christ's birth, and accordingly the early Church did not celebrate it. In time, however, the Christians of Egypt came to regard the sixth of January as the date of the Nativity, and the custom of commemorating the birth of the Saviour on that day gradually spread until by the fourth century it was universally established in the East. But at the end of the third or the beginning of the fourth century the Western Church, which had never recognised the sixth of January as the day of the Nativity, adopted the twenty-fifth of December as the true date, and in time its decision was accepted also by the Eastern Church. At Antioch the change was not introduced till about the year 375 A.D.

What considerations led the ecclesiastical authorities to institute the festival of Christmas? The motives for the innovation are stated with great frankness by a Syrian writer, himself a Christian. "The reason," he tells us, "why the fathers transferred the celebration of the sixth of January to the twenty-fifth of December was this. It was a custom of the heathen to celebrate on the same twenty-fifth of December the birthday of the Sun, at which they kindled lights in token of festivity. In these solemnities and festivities the Christians also took part. Accordingly when the doctors of the Church perceived that the Christians had a leaning to this festival, they took counsel and resolved that the true Nativity should be solemnised on that day and the festival of the Epiphany on the sixth of January. Accordingly, along with this custom, the practice has prevailed of kindling fires till the sixth." The heathen origin of Christmas is plainly hinted at, if not tacitly admitted, by Augustine when he exhorts his Christian brethren not to celebrate that solemn day like the heathen on account of the sun, but on account of him who made the sun. In like manner Leo the Great rebuked the pestilent belief that Christmas was solemnised because of the birth of the new sun, as it was called, and not because of the nativity of Christ.

Thus it appears that the Christian Church chose to celebrate the birthday of its Founder on the twenty-fifth of December in order to transfer the devotion of the heathen from the Sun to him who was called the Sun of Righteousness. If that was so, there can be no intrinsic improbability in the conjecture that motives of the same sort may have led the ecclesiastical authorities to assimilate the Easter festival of the death and resurrection of their Lord to the festival of the death and resurrection of another Asiatic god which fell at the same season. Now the Easter rites still observed in Greece, Sicily, and Southern Italy bear in some respects a striking resemblance to the rites of Adonis, and I have suggested that the Church may have consciously adapted the new festival to its heathen predecessor for the sake of winning souls to Christ. But this adaptation probably took place in the Greek-speaking rather than in the Latin-speaking parts of the ancient world; for the worship of Adonis, while it flourished among the Greeks, appears to have made little impression on Rome and the West. Certainly it never formed part of the official Roman religion. The place which it might have taken in the affections of the vulgar was already occupied by the similar but more barbarous worship of Attis and the Great Mother. Now the death and resurrection of Attis were officially celebrated at Rome on the twenty-fourth and twenty-fifth of March, the latter being regarded as the spring equinox, and therefore as the most appropriate day for the revival of a god of vegetation who had been dead or sleeping throughout the winter. But according to an ancient and widespread tradition Christ suffered on the twenty-fifth of March, and accordingly some Christians regularly celebrated the Crucifixion on that day without any regard to the state of the moon. This custom was certainly observed in Phrygia, Cappadocia, and Gaul, and there seem to be grounds for thinking that at one time it was followed also in Rome. Thus the tradition which placed the death of Christ on the twenty-fifth of March was ancient and deeply rooted. It is all the more remarkable because astronomical considerations prove that it can have had no historical foundation. The inference appears to be inevitable that the passion of Christ must have been arbitrarily referred to that date in order to harmonise with an older festival of the spring equinox. This is the view of the learned ecclesiastical historian Mgr. Duchesne, who points out that the death of the Saviour was thus made to fall upon the very day on which, according to a widespread belief, the world had been created. But the resurrection of Attis, who combined in himself the characters of the divine Father and the divine Son, was officially celebrated at Rome on the same day. When we remember that the festival of St. George in April has replaced the ancient pagan festival of the Parilia; that the festival of St. John the Baptist in June has succeeded to a heathen midsummer festival of water: that the festival of the Assumption of the Virgin in August has ousted the festival of Diana; that the feast of All Souls in November is a continuation of an old heathen feast of the dead; and that the Nativity of Christ himself was assigned to the winter solstice in December because that day was deemed the Nativity of the Sun; we can hardly be thought rash or unreasonable in conjecturing that the other cardinal festival of the Christian church—the solemnisation of Easter—may have been in like manner, and from like motives of edification, adapted to a similar celebration of the Phrygian god Attis at the vernal equinox.

At least it is a remarkable coincidence, if it is nothing more, that the Christian and the heathen festivals of the divine death and resurrection should have been solemnised at the same season and in the same places. For the places which celebrated the death of Christ at the spring equinox were Phrygia, Gaul, and apparently Rome, that is, the very regions in which the worship of Attis either originated or struck deepest root. It is difficult to regard the coincidence as purely accidental. If the vernal equinox, the season at which in the temperate regions the whole face of nature testifies to a fresh outburst of vital energy, had been viewed from of old as the time when the world was annually created afresh in the resurrection of a god, nothing could be more natural than to place the resurrection of the new deity at the same cardinal point of the year. Only it is to be observed that if the death of Christ was dated on the twenty-fifth of March, his resurrection, according to Christian tradition, must have happened on the twenty-seventh of March, which is just two days later than the vernal equinox of the Julian calendar and the resurrection of Attis. A similar displacement of two days in the adjustment of Christian to heathen celebrations occurs in the festivals of St. George and the Assumption of the Virgin. However, another Christian tradition, followed by Lactantius and perhaps by the practice of the Church in Gaul, placed the death of Christ on the twenty-third and his resurrection on the twenty-fifth of March. If that was so, his resurrection coincided exactly with the resurrection of Attis.

In point of fact it appears from the testimony of an anonymous Christian, who wrote in the fourth century of our era, that Christians and pagans alike were struck by the remarkable coincidence between the death and resurrection of their respective deities, and that the coincidence formed a theme of bitter controversy between the adherents of the rival religions, the pagans contending that the resurrection of Christ was a spurious imitation of the resurrection of Attis, and the Christians asserting with equal warmth that the resurrection of Attis was a diabolical counterfeit of the resurrection of Christ. In these unseemly bickerings the heathen took what to a superficial observer might seem strong ground by arguing that their god was the older and therefore presumably the original, not the counterfeit, since as a general rule an original is older than its copy. This feeble argument the Christians easily rebutted. They admitted, indeed, that in point of time Christ was the junior deity, but they triumphantly demonstrated his real seniority by falling back on the subtlety of Satan, who on so important an occasion had surpassed himself by inverting the usual order of nature.

Taken altogether, the coincidences of the Christian with the heathen festivals are too close and too numerous to be accidental. They mark the compromise which the Church in the hour of its triumph was compelled to make with its vanquished yet still dangerous rivals. The inflexible Protestantism of the primitive missionaries, with their fiery denunciations of heathendom, had been exchanged for the supple policy, the easy tolerance, the comprehensive charity of shrewd ecclesiastics, who clearly perceived that if Christianity was to conquer the world it could do so only by relaxing the too rigid principles of its Founder, by widening a little the narrow gate which leads to salvation. In this respect an instructive parallel might be drawn between the history of Christianity and the history of Buddhism. Both systems were in their origin essentially ethical reforms born of the generous ardour, the lofty aspirations, the tender compassion of their noble Founders, two of those beautiful spirits who appear at rare intervals on earth like beings come from a better world to support and guide our weak and erring nature. Both preached moral virtue as the means of accomplishing what they regarded as the supreme object of life, the eternal salvation of the individual soul, though by a curious antithesis the one sought that salvation in a blissful eternity, the other in a final release from suffering, in annihilation. But the austere ideals of sanctity which they inculcated were too deeply opposed not only to the frailties but to the natural instincts of humanity ever to be carried out in practice by more than a small

35

number of disciples, who consistently renounced the ties of the family and the state in order to work out their own salvation in the still seclusion of the cloister. If such faiths were to be nominally accepted by whole nations or even by the world, it was essential that they should first be modified or transformed so as to accord in some measure with the prejudices, the passions, the superstitions of the vulgar. This process of accommodation was carried out in after ages by followers who, made of less ethereal stuff than their masters, were for that reason the better fitted to mediate between them and the common herd. Thus as time went on, the two religions, in exact proportion to their growing popularity, absorbed more and more of those baser elements which they had been instituted for the very purpose of suppressing. Such spiritual decadences are inevitable. The world cannot live at the level of its great men. Yet it would be unfair to the generality of our kind to ascribe wholly to their intellectual and moral weakness the gradual divergence of Buddhism and Christianity from their primitive patterns. For it should never be forgotten that by their glorification of poverty and celibacy both these religions struck straight at the root not merely of civil society but of human existence. The blow was parried by the wisdom or the folly of the vast majority of mankind, who refused to purchase a chance of saving their souls with the certainty of extinguishing the species.

CURIOUS MYTHS OF THE MIDDLE AGES

SABINE M. BARING-GOULD

WHAT A PROLIFIC MAN! Sabine Baring-Gould (1824-1934), like M.R. James, was like one of the scholarly protagonists of either man's ghost stories: ecclesiastic, antiquarian, fiction writer, expert in old manuscripts and biblical apocrypha. In fact, one might almost be excused for confusing the two men and their works, so close are the parallels. For James's *Ghost Stories of an Antiquary* Baring-Gould could boast his own *A Book of Ghosts* (1904). With James's *Old Testament Legends* and *Lost Apocrypha of the Old Testament* we might compare Baring-Gould's *Legends of Old Testament Characters* (1871) and *Lost and Hostile Gospels* (1874). In fact, Baring-Gould was the author of over 1,200 separate literary works! I relish the fact that he was the author of both the hymn "Onward Christian Soldiers" and *The Book of Were-Wolves* (1865). Now that's my kind of clergyman!

Lovecraft called Baring-Gould's *Curious Myths of the Middle Ages* "that curious body of medieval lore which the late Mr. Baring-Gould so effectively assembled in book form." Steven J. Mariconda ("Baring-Gould and the Ghouls" in *The Horror of It All: Encrusted Gems from the Crypt of Cthulhu*, Starmont/Borgo, 1990, pp. 42-48) first pointed out the great influence this book had upon HPL's "The Rats in the Walls." As to the motif of the rampaging rats themselves, Lovecraft plainly derived it from Baring-Gould's chapter on "Bishop Hatto," a ruler cut from pretty much the same cloth as Prince Prospero in Poe's "The Masque of the Red Death." The originally quite distinct notion of the underground world, as well as some specific descriptive details of it, Lovecraft borrowed from the chapter, "S. Patrick's Purgatory." Reading of that legend, the modern Christian may find quaint the notion that a shallow, accessible cavern in the earth's crust might function as an "antechamber of hell," but then one may be equally surprised to discover that the original notion of a fiery, subterranean hell was based on the surface-visible magma pits and fumaroles of ancient Sicily (see Peter Kingsley, *Ancient Philosophy, Mystery, and Magic: Empedocles and Pythagorean Tradition*, Oxford University Press, 1995, pp. 79-87, 193).

❧ BISHOP HATTO ❧

Of the many who yearly visit the Rhine, and bring away with them reminiscences of tottering castles and desecrated convents, whether they take interest or not in the legends inseparably attached to these ruins, none, probably, have failed to learn and remember the famous story of God's judgment on the wicked Bishop Hatto, in the quaint Mäusethurm, erected on a little rock in midstream.

At the close of the tenth century lived Hatto, once abbot of Fulda, where he ruled the monks with great prudence for twelve years, and afterwards Bishop of Mayence.

In the year 970, Germany suffered from famine.
"The summer and autumn had been so wet,
 That in winter the corn was growing yet.
 'Twas a piteous sight to see all around
 The corn lie rotting on the ground.

"Every day the starving poor
 Crowded around Bishop Hatto's door,
 For he had a plentiful last year's store;
 And all the neighbourhood could tell
 His granaries were furnish'd well."

Wearied by the cries of the famishing people, the Bishop appointed a day, whereon he undertook to quiet them. He bade all who were without bread, and the means to purchase it at its then high rate repair to his great barn. From all quarters, far and near, the poor hungry folk flocked into Kaub, and were admitted into the barn, till it was as full of people as it could be made to contain.

38

"Then, when he saw it could hold no more,
Bishop Hatto he made fast the door,
And while for mercy on Christ they call,
He set fire to the barn, and burnt them all.

"'I'faith, 'tis an excellent bonfire!' quoth he,
'And the country is greatly obliged to me
For ridding it, in these times forlorn,
Of rats that only consume the corn.'

"So then to his palace returned he,
And he sat down to supper merrily,
And he slept that night like an innocent man;
But Bishop Hatto never slept again.

"In the morning, as he enter'd the hall
Where his picture hung against the wall,
A sweat, like death, all over him came,
For the rats had eaten it out of the frame."

Then there came a man to him from his farm, with a countenance pale with fear, to tell him that the rats had devoured all the corn in his granaries. And presently there came another servant, to inform him that a legion of rats was on its way to his palace. The Bishop looked from his window, and saw the road and fields dark with the moving multitude; neither hedge nor wall impeded their progress, as they made straight for his mansion. Then, full of terror, the prelate fled by his postern, and, taking a boat, was rowed out to his tower in the river,

"—— and barr'd
All the gates secure and hard.

"He laid him down, and closed his eyes;
But soon a scream made him arise.
He started, and saw two eyes of flame
On his pillow, from whence the screaming came.

39

"He listen'd and look'd—it was only the cat;
But the Bishop he grew more fearful for that,
For she sat screaming, mad with fear,
At the army of rats that were drawing near.

"For they have swum over the river so deep,
And they have climb'd the shores so steep,
And now by thousands up they crawl
To the holes and windows in the wall.

"Down on his knees the Bishop fell,
And faster and faster his beads did tell,
As louder and louder, drawing near,
The saw of their teeth without he could hear

"And in at the windows, and in at the door,
And through the walls by thousands they pour,
And down from the ceiling, and up through the floor,
From the right and the left, from behind and before,
From within and without, from above and below,
And all at once to the Bishop they go.

"They have whetted their teeth against the stones,
And now they pick the Bishop's bones;
They gnaw'd the flesh from every limb,
For they were sent to do judgment on him."

It is satisfactory to know that popular fiction has maligned poor
Bishop Hatto, who was not by any means a hard-hearted and wicked
prelate. Wolfius[1], who tells the story on the authority of Honorius
Augustodunensis (d. 1152), Marianus Scotus (d. 1086), and
Grithemius (d. 1516), accompanying it with the curious picture
which is reproduced on the opposite page, says, "This is regarded by
many as a fable, yet the tower, taking its name from the mice, exists
to this day in the river Rhine." But this is no evidence, as there is

40

documentary proof that the tower was erected as a station for collecting tolls on the vessels which passed up and down the river.

The same story is told of other persons and places. Indeed, Wolfius reproduces his picture of Hatto in the mouse-tower, to do

BISHOP HATTO.
FROM JOB. WOLFLI LECT. MEMORAB. LAVINGÆ (1600).

service as an illustration of the dreadful death of Widerolf, Bishop of Strasburg (997), who, in the seventeenth year of his episcopate, on July 17th, in punishment for having suppressed the convent of Seltzen on the Rhine, was attacked and devoured by mice or rats[2]. The same fate is also attributed to Bishop Adolf of Cologne, who died in 1112[3].

The story comes to us from Switzerland. A Freiherr von Güttingen possessed three castles between Constance and Arbon, in the

Canton of Thurgau, namely, Güttingen, Moosburg, and Oberburg. During a famine, he collected the poor of his territory into a great barn, and there consumed them, mocking their cries by exclamations of "Hark! how the rats and mice are squeaking." Shortly after, he was attacked by an army of mice, and fled to his castle of Güttingen in the waters of the Lake of Constance; but the vermin pursued him to his retreat, and devoured him. The castle then sank into the lake, and its ruins are distinguishable when the water is clear and unruffled[4]. In Austria, a similar legend is related of the mouse tower at Holzölster, with this difference only, that the hard-hearted nobleman casts the poor people into a dungeon and starves them to death, instead of burning them[5].

Between Inning and Seefeld in Bavaria is Wörthsee, called also the Mouse-lake. There was once a Count of Seefeld, who in time of famine put all his starving poor in a dungeon, jested at their cries, which he called the squeaking of mice, and was devoured by these animals in his tower in the lake, to which he fled from them, although he suspended his bed by iron chains from the roof[6].

A similar story is told of the Mäuseschloss in the Hirschberger lake. A Polish version occurs in old historical writers.

Martinus Gallus, who wrote in 1110, says that King Popiel, having been driven from his kingdom, was so tormented by mice, that he fled to an island whereon was a wooden tower, in which he took refuge; but the host of mice and rats swam over and ate him up. The story is told more fully by Majolus[7]. When the Poles murmured at the bad government of the king, and sought redress, Popiel summoned the chief murmurers to his palace, where he pretended that he was ill, and then poisoned them. After this the corpses were flung by his orders into the lake Gopolo. Then the king held a banquet of rejoicing at having freed himself from these troublesome complainers. But during the feast, by a strange metamorphosis (mira quadam metamorphosi), an enormous number of mice issued from the bodies of his poisoned subjects, and rushing on the palace, attacked the king and his family. Popiel took refuge within a circle of fire, but the mice broke through the flaming ring; then he fled with his wife and child to a castle in the sea, but was followed by the animals and devoured.

42

A Scandinavian legend is to this effect[8]. King Knut the Saint was murdered by the Earl Asbjorn, in the church of S. Alban, in Odense, during an insurrection of the Jutes, in 1086. Next year the country suffered severely from famine, and this was attributed to Divine vengeance for the murder of the king. Asbjorn was fallen upon by rats, and eaten up.

William of Malmesbury tells this story[9]: "I have heard a person of the utmost veracity relate, that one of the adversaries of Henry IV. (of Germany), a weak and factious man, while reclining at a banquet, was on a sudden so completely surrounded by mice as to be unable to escape. So great was the number of these little animals, that there could scarcely be imagined more in a whole province. It was in vain that they were attacked with clubs and fragments of the benches which were at hand; and though they were for a long time assailed by all, yet they wreaked their deputed curse on no one else; pursuing him only with their teeth, and with a kind of dreadful squeaking. And although he was carried out to sea about a javelin's cast by the servants, yet he could not by these means escape their violence; for immediately so great a multitude of mice took to the water, that you would have sworn the sea was strewed with chaff. But when they began to gnaw the planks of the ship, and the water, rushing through the chinks, threatened inevitable shipwreck, the servants turned the vessel to the shore. The animals, then also swimming close to the ship, landed first. Thus the wretch, set on shore, and soon after entirely gnawed in pieces, satiated the dreadful hunger of the mice.

"I deem this the less wonderful, because it is well known that in Asia, if a leopard bite any person, a party of mice approach directly. But if, by the care of servants driving them off, the destruction can be avoided during nine days, then medical assistance, if called in, may be of service. My informant had seen a person wounded after this manner, who, despairing of safety on shore, proceeded to sea, and lay at anchor; when, immediately, more than a thousand mice swam out, wonderful to relate, in the rinds of pomegranates, the insides of which they had eaten; but they were drowned through the loud shouting of the sailors."

Albertus Trium-Fontium tells the same story under the year 1083, quoting probably from William of Malmesbury.

Giraldus Cambrensis (d. 1220), in his "Itinerary," relates a curious story of a youth named Siscillus Esceir-hir, or Long-shanks, who was attacked in his bed by multitudes of toads, and who fled from them to the top of a tree, but was pursued by the reptiles, and his flesh picked from his bones. "And in like manner," he adds, "we read of how by the secret, but never unjust, counsel of God a certain man was persecuted by the larger sort of mice which are commonly called rats[10]."

And Thietmar of Merseburg (b. 976, d. 1018) says, that there was once a certain knight who, having appropriated the goods of S. Clement, and refused to make restitution, was one day attacked by an innumerable host of mice, as he lay in bed. At first he defended himself with a club, then with his sword, and, as he found himself unable to cope with the multitude, he ordered his servants to put him in a box, and suspend this by a rope from the ceiling, and as soon as the mice were gone, to liberate him. But the animals pursued him even thus, and when he was taken down, it was found that they had eaten the flesh and skin off his bones. And it became manifest to all how obnoxious to God is the sin of sacrilege[11].

Cæsarius of Heisterbach (Dist. ii. c. 31) tells a tale of a usurer in Cologne, who, moved with compunction for his sins, confessed to a priest, who bade him fill a chest with bread, as alms for the poor attached to the church of S. Gereon. Next morning the loaves were found transformed into toads and frogs. "Behold," said the priest, "the value of your alms in the sight of God!" To which the terrified usurer replied, "Lord, what shall I do?" And the priest answered, "If you wish to be saved, lie this night naked amidst these reptiles." Wondrous contrition. He, though he recoiled from such a couch, preferred to lie among worms which perish, rather than those which are eternal; and he cast himself nude upon the creatures. Then the priest went to the box, shut it, and departed; which, when he opened it on the following day, he found to contain nothing save human bones.

It will be seen from these versions of the Hatto myth, how prevalent among the Northern nations was the idea of men being devoured by vermin. The manner of accounting for their death differs, but all the stories agree in regarding that death as mysterious.

I believe the origin of these stories to be a heathen human sacrifice made in times of famine. That such sacrifice took place among the Scandinavian and Teutonic peoples is certain. Tacitus tells us that the Germans sacrificed men. Snorro Sturlesson (d. 1241) gives us an instance of the Swedes offering their king to obtain abundant crops[12]

"Donald took the heritage after his father Visbur, and ruled over the land. As in his time there was a great famine and distress, the Swedes made great offerings of sacrifice at Upsala. The first autumn they sacrificed oxen, but the succeeding season was not improved by it. The following autumn they sacrificed men, but the succeeding year was rather worse. The third autumn, when the offer of sacrifices should begin, a great multitude of Swedes came to Upsala; and now the chiefs held consultations with each other, and all agreed that the times of scarcity were on account of their king Donald, and they resolved to offer him for good seasons, and to assault and kill him, and sprinkle the altar of the gods with his blood. And they did so." So again with Olaf the Tree-feller: "There came dear times and famine, which they ascribed to their king, as the Swedes used always to reckon good or bad crops for or against their kings. The Swedes took it amiss that Olaf was sparing in his sacrifices, and believed the dear times must proceed from this cause. The Swedes therefore gathered together troops, made an expedition against King Olaf, surrounded his house, and burnt him in it, giving him to Odin as a sacrifice for good crops."

Saxo Grammaticus says that in the reign of King Snio of Denmark there was a famine. The "Chronicon Regum Danicorum" tells a curious story about this Snio being devoured by vermin, sent to destroy him by his former master the giant Lae. Probably Snio was sacrificed, like Donald and Olaf, to obtain good harvests.

The manner in which human sacrifices were made was very different. Sometimes the victims were precipitated off a rock, sometimes hung, at other times they were sunk in a bog. It seems probable to me that the manner in which an offering was made for plenty, was by exposure to rats, just as M. Du Chaillu tells us, an African tribe place their criminals in the way of ants to be devoured by them. The peculiar death of Ragnar Lodbrog, who was sentenced by Ella of Northumberland to be stung to death by serpents in a dungeon, was somewhat similar. Offerings to rats and mice are still prevalent among the peasantry in certain parts of Germany, if we may credit Grimm and Wolf; and this can only be a relic of heathenism, for the significance of the act is lost.

In Mark it is said that the Elves appear in Yuletide as mice, and cakes are laid out for them. In Bohemia, on Christmas eve, the remainder of the supper is given them with the words, "Mice! eat of these crumbs, and leave the wheat."

If I am correct in supposing that the Hatto myth points to sacrifices of chieftains and princes in times of famine, and that the manner of offering the sacrifice was the exposure of the victim to rats, then it is not to be wondered at, that, when the reason of such a sacrifice was forgotten, the death should be accounted as a judgment of God for some crime committed by the sufferer, as hardheartedness, murder, or sacrilege. Both Giraldus Cambrensis and William of Malmesbury are, however, sadly troubled to find a cause.

Rats and mice have generally been considered sacred animals. Among the Scandinavian and Teutonic peoples they were regarded as the souls of the dead.

In the article on the Piper of Hameln, I mentioned that Prætorius gives a story of a woman's soul leaving her body in the shape of a red mouse. According to Bohemian belief, one must not go to sleep thirsty, or the soul will leave the body in search of drink. Three labourers once lost their way in a wood. Parched with thirst, they sought, but in vain, for a spring of water. At last one of them lay down and fell asleep, but the others continuing their search, discovered a fountain. They drank, and then returned to their comrade. He still slept, and they observed a little white mouse run out of his mouth, go to the spring, drink, and return to his mouth. They woke him and said, "You are such an idle fellow, that instead of going yourself after water, you send your soul. We will have nothing more to do with you."

A miller in the Black Forest, after having cut wood, lay down and slept. A servant saw a mouse run out of him. He and his companions went in pursuit. They scared the little creature away, little thinking it was the soul of the miller, and they were never able to rouse him again. Paulus Diaconus relates of King Gunthram that his soul left his body in the shape of a serpent; and Hugh Miller, in his "Schools and Schoolmasters," tells a Scottish story of two companions, one of whom slept whilst the other watched. He who was awake saw a bee come out of the mouth of the sleeper, cross a stream of water on a straw, run into a hole, and then return and disappear into the mouth of his friend. These are similar stories, but the bee and the serpent have taken the place of the mouse. The idea that the soul is like a mouse, lies at the root of several grotesque stories, as that told by Luther, in his "Table-Talk," of a woman giving birth to a rat, and that of a mother harassed by the clamour of her children, wishing they were mice, and finding this inconsiderate wish literally fulfilled.

The same idea has passed into Christian iconography. According to the popular German belief, the souls of the dead spend the first night after they leave the body with S. Gertrude, the second with S. Michael, and the third in their destined habitation. S. Gertrude is regarded as the patroness of fleeting souls, the saint who is the first to shelter the spirits when they begin their wandering. As the patroness of souls, her symbol is a mouse. Various stories have been invented to account for this symbol. Some relate that a maiden span on her festival, and the mice ate through her clew as a punishment. A prettier story is that, when she prayed, she was so absorbed that the mice ran about her, and up her pastoral staff, without attracting her attention. Another explanation is that the mouse is a symbol of the evil spirit, which S. Gertrude overcame[13]. But S. Gertrude occupies the place of the ancient Teutonic goddess Holda or Perchta, who was the receiver of the souls of maidens and children, and who still exists as the White Lady, not unfrequently, in German legends, transforming herself, or those whom she decoys into her home, into white mice.

It is not unlikely that the saying, "Rats desert a falling house," applied originally to the crumbling ruin of the body from which the soul fled. In the Hatto and Popiel legends it is evident that the rats are the souls of those whom the Bishop and the King murdered.

The rats of Bingen issue from the flames in which the poor people are being consumed. The same is said of the rats which devoured the Freiherr of Güttingen. The rats mira metamorphosi come from the corpses of those poisoned by Popiel.

There is a curious Icelandic story, written in the twelfth century, which bears a striking resemblance to those of Hatto, Widerolf, &c., but in which the rats make no appearance.

In the tenth century Iceland suffered severely from a bad year, so that there was a large amount of destitution throughout the country; and, unless something were done by the wealthy bonders to relieve it, there was a certainty of many poor householders perishing during the approaching winter. Then Svathi, a heathen chief, stepped forward and undertook to provide for a considerable number of sufferers. Accordingly, the poor starving wretches assembled at his door, and were ordered by him to dig a large pit in his tun, or home meadow. They complied with alacrity, and in the evening they were gathered into a barn, the door was locked upon them, and it was explained to them that on the following morning they were to be buried alive in the pit of their own digging.

"You will at once perceive," said Svathi, "that if a number of you be put out of your misery, the number of mouths wanting food will be reduced, and there will be more victuals for those who remain."

There was truth in what Svathi said; but the poor wretches did not view the matter in the same light as he, nor appreciate the force of his argument; and they spent the night howling with despair. Thorwald of Asi, a Christian, who happened to be riding by towards dawn, heard the outcries, and went to the barn to inquire into their signification. When he learned the cause of their distress, he liberated the prisoners, and bade them follow him to Asi. Before long, Svathi became aware that his victims had escaped, and set off in pursuit. However, he was unable to recover them, as Thorwald's men were armed, and the poor people were prepared to resist with the courage of despair. Thus the golden opportunity was lost, and he was obliged to return home, bewailing the failure of his scheme. As he dashed up to his house, blinded with rage, and regardless of what was before him, the horse fell with him into the pit which the poor folk had dug, and he was killed by the fall. He was buried in it next day, along with his horse and hound[14].

In all likelihood this Svathi was sacrificed in time of famine, and the legend may describe correctly the manner in which he was offered to the gods, viz. by burial alive.

In this story, as in Snorro's account of Donald, we have a sacrifice of human beings, taken from a low rank, offered first, and then the chief himself sacrificed.

The god to whom these human oblations were made, seems to have been Odin. In the "Herverar Saga" is an account of a famine in Jutland, to obtain relief from which, the nobles and farmers consulted whom to sacrifice, and they decided that the king's son was the most illustrious person they could present to Odin. But the king, to save his son, fought with another king, and slew him and his son, and with their blood smeared the altar of Odin, and thus appeased the god[15].

Now, Odin was the receiver of the souls of men, as Freya, or the German Holda, took charge of those of women. Odin appears as the wild huntsman, followed by a multitude of souls; or, as the Piper of Hameln, leading them into the mountain where he dwells.

Freya, or Holda, leads an army of mice, and Odin a multitude of rats.

As a rat or soul god, it is not unlikely that sacrifices to him may have been made by the placing of the victim on an island infested by water-rats, there to be devoured. The manner in which sacrifices were made has generally some relation to the nature of the god to whom they were made. Thus, as Odin was a wind-god, men were hung in his honour. Most of the legends we are considering point to islands as the place where the victim suffered, and islands, we know, were regarded with special sanctity by the Northern nations. Rügen and Heligoland in the sea were sacred from a remote antiquity, and probably lakes had as well their sacred islets, to which the victim was rowed out, his back broken, and on which he was left to become the prey of the rats.

We find rats and mice regarded as sacred animals in other Aryan mythologies. Thus the mouse was the beast of the Indian Rudra.

"This portion belongs to thee, O Rudra, with thy sister Ambika," is the wording of a prayer in the Yajur-Veda; "may it please you. This portion belongs to thee, O Rudra, whose animal is the mouse[16]." In later mythology it became the attribute of Ganeça, who was represented as riding upon a rat; but Ganeça is simply an hypostasis for Rudra.

Apollo was called Smintheus, as has been stated already. On some of the coins of Argos, in place of the god, is figured his symbol, the mouse[17]. In the temple at Chrisa was a statue of Apollo, with a mouse at his feet[18]; and tame mice were kept as sacred to the god. [19]

Among Semitic nations the mouse was also sacred.

Herodotus gives a curious legend relating to the destruction of the host of Sennacherib before Jerusalem. Isaiah simply says, "Then the angel of the Lord went forth, and smote in the camp of the Assyrians a hundred and fourscore and five thousand: and when they arose early in the morning, behold, they were all dead corpses[20]." How they were slain he does not specify, but as the army was threatened with a "hot blast," and a "destroying wind," it is rendered probable that they were destroyed by a hot wind. But the story of Herodotus is very different. He received it from the Egyptian priests, who claimed the miracle, of which they had but an imperfect knowledge, for one of their gods, and transferred the entire event to their own country. "After Amyrtæus reigned the priest of Vulcan, whose name was Sethon; he held in no account and despised the military caste of the Egyptians, as not having need of their services; and accordingly, among other indignities, he took away their lands; to each of whom, under former kings, twelve chosen acres had been assigned. After this, Sennacherib, king of the Arabians and Assyrians, marched a large army against Egypt; whereupon the Egyptian warriors refused to assist him; and the priest being reduced to a strait, entered the temple, and bewailed before the image the calamities he was in danger of suffering. While he was lamenting, sleep fell upon him; and it appeared to him in a vision that the god stood by and encouraged him, assuring him that he should suffer nothing disagreeable in meeting the Arabian army, for he would himself send assistants to him. Confiding in this vision, he took with him such of the Egyptians as were willing to follow him, and encamped in Pelusium, for there the entrance into Egypt is; but none of the military caste followed him, but tradesmen, mechanics, and sutlers. When they arrived there, a number of field-mice, pouring in upon their enemies, devoured their quivers and their bows, and, moreover, the handles of their shields; so that on the next day, when they fled bereft of their arms, many of them fell. And to this day, a stone statue of this king stands in the temple of Vulcan, with a mouse in his hand, and an inscription to the following effect: 'Whoever looks on me, let him revere the gods[21].'"

Among the Babylonians the mouse was sacrificed and eaten as a religious rite, but in connexion with what god does not transpire[22]. And the Philistines, who, according to Hitzig, were a Pelasgic and therefore Aryan race, after having suffered from the retention of the ark, were told by their divines to 'make images of your mice that mar the land; and ye shall give glory unto the God of Israel." Therefore they made five golden mice as an offering to the Lord[23]. This indicates the mouse as having been the symbol among the Philistines of a deity whom they identified with the God of Israel.

Original footnotes

1. Wolfii Lect. Memorab. Centenarii xvi. Lavingæ, 1600, tom. i. p. 343.

2. Id. tom. i. p. 270. See also Königshofen's Chronik. Königshofen was priest of Strasbourg (b. 1360, d. 1420). His German Chronicle contains the story of Bishop Widerolf and the mice.

3. San-Marte, Germania, viii. 77.

4. Zeitschrift f. Deut. Myth. iii. p. 307.

5. Vernaleken, Alpensagen, p. 328.

6. Zeitschrift f. Deut. Myth. i. p. 452.

7. Majolus, Dierum Came. p. 793.

8. Afzelius, Sagohäfder (2nd ed.), ii. p. 132.

9. William of Malmesbury, book iii., Bohn's trans., p. 313.

10. Girald. Cambr. Itin. Cambriæ, lib. xi. c. 2. 11. Thietmar, Ep. Merseburg. Chronici libri viii., lib. vi; c. 30.

12. Snorro Sturlesson, Heimskringla, Saga i. c. 18, 47.

13. Die Attribute der Heiligen. Hanover, 1843, p. 114.

14. Younger Olaf's Saga Trygvas., cap. 225.

15. Herverar Saga, cap. xi

16. Yajur-Veda, iii. 57.

17. Otfr. Müller, Dorier, i. p. 285.

18. Strabo, xiii. i.

19. Ælian, Hist. Animal, xii. 15.

20. Isa. xxxvii. 36.

21. Herod. Euterpe, c. 141, Trans. Bohn.

22. Movers, Phönizier, i. p. 219. Cf. Isa. lxvi. 17.

23. 1 Sam. vi. 4, 5

◆

❧S. PATRICK'S PURGATORY☙

IN THAT CHARMING MEDIEVAL ROMANCE, Fortunatus and his Sons, which, by the way, is a treasury of Popular Mythology, is an account of a visit paid by the favoured youth to that cave of mystery in Lough Derg, the Purgatory of S. Patrick.

Fortunatus, we are told, had heard in his travels of how two days' journey from the town, Valdric, in Ireland, was a town, Vernic, where was the entrance to the Purgatory; so thither he went with many servants. He found a great abbey, and behind the altar of the church a door, which led into the dark cave which is called the Purgatory of S. Patrick. In order to enter it, leave had to be obtained from the abbot; consequently, Leopold, servant to Fortunatus, betook himself to that worthy, and made known to him that a nobleman from Cyprus desired to enter the mysterious cavern.

The abbot at once requested Leopold to bring his master to supper with him. Fortunatus bought a large jar of wine, and sent it as a present to the monastery, and followed at the meal time.

"Venerable sir!" said Fortunatus, "I understaid the Purgatory of S. Patrick is here; is it so?"

The abbot replied, "It is so indeed. Many hundred years ago, this place, where stand the abbey and the town, was a howling wilderness. Not far off, however, lived a venerable hermit, Patrick by name, who often sought the desert for the purpose of therein exercising his austerities. One day he lighted on this cave, which is of vast extent. He entered it, and wandering on in the dark, lost his way, so that he could no more find how to return to the light of day. After long ramblings through the gloomy passages, he fell on his knees, and besought Almighty God, if it were His will, to deliver him from the great peril wherein he lay. Whilst Patrick thus prayed, he was aware of piteous cries issuing from the depths of the cave, just such as would be the wailings of souls in Purgatory. The hermit rose from his orison, and by God's mercy found his way back to the surface, and from that day exercised greater austerities, and after his death he was numbered with the saints. Pious people, who had heard the story of Patrick's adventure in the cave, built this cloister on the site."

Then Fortunatus asked whether all who ventured into the place heard likewise the howls of the tormented souls.

The abbot replied, "Some have affirmed that they have heard a bitter crying and piping therein whilst others have heard and seen nothing. No one, however, has penetrated, as yet, to the furthest limits of the cavern."

Fortunatus then asked permission to enter, and the abbot cheerfully consented, only stipulating that his guest should keep near the entrance, and not ramble too far, as some who had ventured in had never returned.

Next day, early, Fortunatus received the Blessed Sacrament with his trusty Leopold; the door of the Purgatory was unlocked, each was provided with a taper, and then with the blessing of the abbot they were left in total darkness, and the door bolted behind them. Both wandered on in the cave, hearing faintly the chanting of the monks in the church, till the sound died away. They traversed several passages, lost their way, their candles burned out, and they sat down in despair on the ground, a prey to hunger, thirst, and fear.

The monks waited in the church hour after hour; and the visitors of the Purgatory had not returned. Day declined, vespers were sung, and still there was no sign of the two who in the morning had passed from the church into the cave. Then the servants of Fortunatus began to exhibit anger, and to insist on their master being restored to them. The abbot was frightened, and sent for an old man who had once penetrated far into the cave, with a ball of twine, the end attached to the door handle. This man volunteered to seek Fortunatus, and providentially his search was successful. After this the abbot refused permission to any one to visit the cave.

In the reign of Henry II. lived Henry of Saltrey, who wrote a history of the visit of a Knight Owen to the Purgatory of S. Patrick, which gained immense popularity. Henry was a monk of the Benedictine Abbey of Saltrey, in Huntingdonshire, and received his story from Gilbert, Abbot of Louth, who is said by some to have also published a written account of the extraordinary visions of Owen [1]. This account was soon translated into other languages, and spread the fable through mediaeval Europe. It was this work of Henry of Saltrey which first made known the virtues of the mysterious cave of Lough Derg. Marie of France translated it into French metre, but hers was not the only version in that tongue; in English there are two versions. In one of these, "Owayne Miles," H. S. Cotton. Calig. A. ii., fol. 89, the origin of the purgatory is thus described:~

Holy byschoppes some tyme ther were, That tawgte me of Goddes lore. In Irlonde preched Seyn Patryke, In that londe was non hym lyke: He prechede Goddes worde full wyde, And tolde men what shullde betyde. Fyrste he preched of Heven blysse, Who ever go thyder may ryght nowgt mysse: Sethen he preched of Hell pyne, Howe wo them ys that cometh therinne: And then he preched of purgatory, As he fonde in hisstory, But yet the folke of the contré Beleved not that hit mygth be; And seyed, hut gyf hit were so, That eny non myth hymself go, And Se alle that. and come ageyn, Then wolde they beleve fayn."

Vexed at the obstinacy of his hearers, S. Patrick besought the Almighty to make the truth manifest to the unbelievers; whereupon

"God spakke to Saynt Patryke tho By nam, and badde hym with Hym go He ladde hym ynte a wyldernesse, Wher was no reste more ne lesse, And shewed that he might se late the erthe a pryvé entré: Hit was yn a depe dyches ende. 'What mon,' He sayde, 'that wylle hereyn werde, And dwelle theryn a day and a nyght, And hold his byleve and ryght, And come ageyn that he ne dwelle, Mony a mervayle he may of telle. And alle tho that doth thys pylgrymage, I shalle hem graunt for her wage, Whether he be sqwyer or knave, Other purgatorye shalle he non have.'"

Thereupon S. Patrick, "he ne stynte ner day ne night," till he had built there a "fayr abbey," and stocked it with pious canons. Then he made a door to the cave, and locked the door, and gave the key to the keeping of the prior[2]. The Knight Owain, who had served under King Stephen, had lived a life of violence and dissolution; but filled with repentance, he sought by way of penance S. Patrick's Purgatory. Fifteen days he spent in preliminary devotions and alms-deeds, and then he heard mass, was washed with holy water, received the Holy Sacrament, and followed the sacred relics in procession, whilst the priests sang for him the Litany, "as lowde as they mygth crye." Then Sir Owain was locked in the cave, and he groped his way onward in darkness, till he reached a glimmering light; this brightened, and he came out into an underground land, where was a great hall and cloister, in which were men with shaven heads and white garments. These men informed the knight how he was to protect himself against the assaults of evil spirits. After having received this instruction, he heard "grete dynn," and

"Then come ther develes on every syde, Wykked gostes, I wote, fro Helle, So mony that no tonge mygte telle They fylled the hows yn two rowes; Some grenned on hym and some mad mowes."

He then visits the different places of torment. In one, the souls are nailed to the ground with glowing hot brazen nails; in another, they are fastened to the soil by their hair, and are bitten by fiery reptiles. In another, again, they are hung over fires by those members which had sinned, whilst others are roasted on spits. In one place were pits in which were molten metals. In these pits were men and women, some up to their chins, others to their breasts, others to their hams. The knight was pushed by the devils into one of these pits, and was dreadfully scalded, but he cried to the Saviour, and escaped. Then he visited a lake where souls were tormented with great cold; and a river of pitch, which he crossed on a frail and narrow bridge. Beyond this bridge was a wall of glass, in which opened a beautiful gate, which conducted into Paradise. This place so delighted him that he would fain have remained in it had he been suffered, but he was bidden return to earth and finish there his penitence. He was put into a shorter and pleasanter way back to the cave than that by which he had come; and the prior found the knight next morning at the door, waiting to be let out, and full of his adventures. He afterwards went on a pilgrimage to the Holy Land, and ended his life in piety. "Explycit Owayne [3]"

Marie's translation is in three thousand verses; Legrand d'Aussy has given the analysis of it in his "Fabliaux," tom. iv

Giraldus Cambrensis, in his topography of Ireland, alludes to the Purgatory. He places the island of Lough Derg among one of the marvels of the country. According to him it is divided into two parts, whereof one is fair and agreeable, and contains a church, whilst the other is rough and uncultivated, and a favourite haunt of devils. In the latter part of the island, he adds, there were nine caves, in any one of which, if a person were bold enough to pass the night, he would be so tormented by the demons, that he would be fortunate if he escaped with life; and he says, it is reported that a night so spent relieved the sufferer from having to undergo the torments of purgatory hereafter[4].

In the ancient Office of S. Patrick occurred the following verse:-

"Hie est doctor benevolus, Hibernicorum apostolus, Cui loca purgatoria Ostendit Dei gratia."

Joscelin, in his life of the saint, repeats the fable. Henry de Knyghton, in his history, however, asserts that it was not the Apostle of Ireland, but an abbot Patrick, to whom the revelation of purgatory was made; and John of Brompton says the same. Alexander Neckham calls it S. Brandan's Purgatory. Cæsar of Heisterhach, in the beginning of the 13th century, says, "If any one doubt of purgatory, let him go to Scotland (i. e. Ireland), and enter the Purgatory of S. Patrick, and his doubts will be dispelled[5]." "This recommendation," says Mr. Wright, in his interesting and all but exhaustive essay on the myth, "was frequently acted upon in that, and particularly in the following century, when pilgrims from all parts of Europe, some of them men of rank and wealth, repaired to this abode of superstition. On the patent rolls in the Tower of London, under the year 1358, we have an instance of testimonials given by the king (Edward III.) on the same day, to two distinguished foreigners, one a noble Hungarian, the other a Lombard, Nicholas de Beccarus, of their having faithfully performed this pilgrimage. And still later, in 1397, we find King Richard II. granting a safe conduct to visit the same place, to Raymond, Viscount of Perilhos, knight of Rhodes, and chamberlain of the King of France, with twenty men and thirty horses. Raymond de Perilhos, on his return to his native country, wrote a narrative of what he had seen, in the dialect of the Limousan of which a Latin version was printed by O'Sullivan, in his 'Historia Catholica Iberniæ'"[6] This work is simply the story of Owain slightly altered.

Froissart tells us of a conversation he had with one Sir William Lisle, who had been in the Purgatory. "I asked him of what sort was the cave that is in Ireland, called S. Patrick's Purgatory, and if that were true which was related of it. He replied that there certainly was such a cave, for he and another English knight had been there whilst the king was at Dublin, and said that they entered the cave, and were shut in as the sun set, and that they remained there all night, and left it next morning at sunrise. And then I asked if he had seen the strange sights and visions spoken of. Then he said that when he and his companion had passed the gate of the Purgatory of S. Patrick, that they had descended as though into a cellar, and that a hot vapour rose towards them, and so affected their heads, that they were obliged to sit down on the stone steps. And after sitting there awhile they felt heavy with sleep, and so fell asleep, and slept all night. Then I asked if they knew where they were in their sleep, and what sort of dreams they had had; he answered that they had been oppressed with many fancies and wonderful dreams, different from those they were accustomed to in their chambers; and in the morning when they went out, in a short while they had clean forgotten their dreams and visions; wherefore he concluded that the whole matter was fancy."

The next to give us an account of his descent into S. Patrick's Purgatory, is William Staunton of Durham, who went down into the cave on the Friday next after the feast of Holyrood, in the year 1409. Mr. Wright has quoted the greater portion of his vision from a manuscript in the British Museum; I have only room for a few extracts, which I shall modernize, as the original spelling is somewhat perplexing.

"I was put in by the Prior of S. Matthew, of the same Purgatory, with procession and devout prayers of the prior, and the convent gave me an orison to bless me with, and to write the first word in my forehead, the which prayer is this, 'Jhesu Christe, Fili Dei vivi, miserere mihi peccatori.' And the prior taught me to say this prayer when any spirit, good or evil, appeared unto me, or when I heard any noise that I should be afraid of." When left in the cave, William fell asleep, and dreamed that he saw coming to him S. John of Bridlington and S. Ive, who undertook to conduct him through the scenes of mystery. After they had proceeded a while, William was found to be guilty of a trespass against Holy Church, of which he had to be purged before he could proceed much further. Of this trespass he was accused by his sister who appeared in the way. "I make my complaint unto you against my brother that here standeth; for this man that standeth hereby loved me, and I loved him, and either of us would have had the other according to God's law, as Holy Church teaches, and I should have gotten of me three souls to God, but my brother hindered us from marrying." S. John of Bridlington then turned to William, and asked him why he did not allow the two who loved one another to be married. "I tell thee there is no man that hindereth man or woman from being united in the bond of God, though the man be a shepherd and all his ancestors, and the woman be come of kings or of emperors, or if the man he come of never so high kin, and the woman of never so low kin, if they love one another, but he sinneth in Holy Church against God and his deed, and therefore he shall have much pain and tribulations." Being assoiled of this crying sin, S. John takes William to a fire "grete and styngkyng," in which he sees people burning in their gay clothes. "I saw some with collars of gold about their necks, and some of silver, and some men I saw with gay girdles of silver and gold, and harnessed with horns about their necks, some with no jagges on their clothes, than whole cloth, others full of jingles and bells of silver all over set, and some with long pokes on their sleeves, and women with gowns trailing behind them a long space, and some with chaplets on their heads of gold and pearls and other precious stones. And I looked on him that I saw first in pain, and saw the collars, and gay girdles, and baldrics burning, and the fiends dragging him by two fingermits. And I saw the jagges that men were clothed in turn all to adders, to dragons, and to toads, and 'many other orrible bestes' sucking them, and biting them, and stinging them with all their might, and through every jingle I saw fiends smite burning nails of fire into their flesh. I also saw fiends drawing down the skin of their shoulders like to pokes, and cutting them off; and drawing them to the heads of those they cut them from, all burning as fire. And then I saw the women that had side trails behind them, and the side trails cut off by the fiends and burned on their head; and some took of the cutting all burning and stopped therewith their mouths, their noses, and their ears. I saw also their gay chaplets of gold and pearls and precious stones, turned into nails of iron, burning, and fiends with burning hammers smiting them into their heads." These were proud and vain people. Then he saw another fire, where the fiends were putting out people's eyes, and pouring molten brass and lead into the sockets, and tearing off their arms, and the nails of their feet and hands, and soldering them on again. This was the doom of swearers. William saw other fires wherein the devils were executing tortures varied and horrible on their unfortunate victims. We need follow him no further.

At the end of the fifteenth century the Purgatory in Lough Derg was destroyed, by orders of the pope, on hearing the report of a monk of Eymstadt in Holland, who had visited it, and had satisfied himself that there was nothing in it more remarkable than in any ordinary cavern. The Purgatory was closed on S. Patrick's day, 1497; but the belief in it was not so speedily banished from popular superstition. Calderon made it the subject of one of his dramas; and it became the subject of numerous popular chap-books in France and Spain, where during last century it occupied in the religious belief of the people precisely the same position which is assumed by the marvellous visions of heaven and hell sold by hawkers in England at the present day, one of which, probably founded on the old S. Patrick's Purgatory legend, I purchased the other day, and found it to be a publication of very modern date.

Unquestionably, the story of S. Patrick's Purgatory is founded on the ancient Hell-descents prevalent in all heathen nations; Herakles, Orpheus, Odysseus, in Greek Mythology, Æneas, in Roman, descend to the nether world, and behold sights very similar to those described in the Christian legends just quoted. Among the Finns, Wainomoinen goes down into Pohjola, the land of darkness and fear; and the Esths tell of Kalewa plunging into a mysterious cave which led him to the abode of the foul fiend, where he visited his various courts, and whence he ravished his daughters. A still more striking myth is that of the ancient Quiches, contained in their sacred book, the Popol-Vuh; in which the land of Xibalba contains mansions nearly as unpleasant as the fields and lakes of S. Patrick's Purgatory. One is the house of gloom, another of men with sharp swords, another of heat, one of cold, one of the mansions is haunted by bloodsucking bats, another is the den of ferocious tigers[7]. Odin, in Northern Mythology, has mansions of cold and heat[8]; and Hell's abode is thus described:~ "In Nifiheim she possesses a habitation protected by exceedingly high walls and strongly barred gates. Her hall is called Elvidnir; Hunger is her table; Starvation, her knife; Delay, her man; Slowness, her maid; Precipice, her threshold; Care, her bed; and Burning Anguish forms the hangings of her apartment[9]." Into this the author of the Solarliod, in the Elder Edda, is supposed to have descended. This curious poem is attributed by some to Soemund the Wise (d. 1131), and is certainly not later. The composition exhibits a strange mixture of Christianity and Heathenism, whence it would seem that the poet's own religion was in a transition state:

"The sun I saw, true star of day, Sink in its roaring home; but Hell's grated doors On the other side I heard heavily creaking.

In the Norn's seat nine days sat I, Thence was I mounted on a horse: There the giantess's sun shone grimly Through the dripping clouds of heaven.

Without and within, I seemed to traverse All the seven nether worlds; up and down, I sought an easier way Where I might have the readiest paths."

He comes to a torrent about which flew "scorched birds, which were souls, numerous as flies." Then the wind dies away, and he comes to a land where the waters do not flow. There false-faced women grind earth for food.

"Gory stones these dark women Turned sorrowfully; out of their breasts Hung bleeding hearts, faint with much affliction."

He saw men with faces bloody, and heathen stars above their heads, painted with deadly characters; men who had envied others had bloody runes cut in their breasts. Covetous men went to Castle

Covetous dragging weights of lead, murderers were consumed by venomous serpents, sabbath-breakers were nailed by their hands to hot stones. Proud men were wrapped in flame, slanderers had their eyes plucked out by Hell's ravens.

"All the horrors thou wilt not get to know Which Hell's inmates suffer. Pleasant sins end in painful penalties Pains ever follow pleasure[10]."

Among the Greeks a descent into the cave of Trophonius occupied much the same place in their popular Mysticism that the Purgatory of S. Patrick assumed among Christians. Lustral rites, somewhat similar, preceded the descent, and the results were not unlike[11].

It is worthy of remark that the myth of S. Patrick's Purgatory originated among the Kelts, and the reason is not far to seek. In ancient Keltic Mythology the nether world was divided into three circles, corresponding with Purgatory, Hell, and Heaven and over Hell was cast a bridge, very narrow, which souls were obliged to traverse if they hoped to reach the mansions of light. This was—

"The Brig O' Dread, na brader than a thread."

And the Purgatory under consideration is a reflex of old Druidic teaching. Thus in an ancient Breton ballad Tina passes through the lake of pain, on which float the dead, white robed, in little boats. She then wades through valleys of blood[12].

As this myth has been exhaustively treated by Mr. Thomas Wright (S. Patrick's Purgatory; by T. Wright, London, 1844), it shall detain us no longer. I differ from him, however, as to its origin. He attributes it to monkish greed; but I have no hesitation in asserting that it is an example of the persistency of heathen myths, colouring and influencing Mediaeval Christianity. We will only refer the reader for additional information to the *Purgatoire de Saint Patrice; légende du xii' Siècle*, 1842; a reprint by M. Prosper Tarbé of a MS. in the library at Rheims; a Mémoire by M. Paul Lacroix in the *Mélanges historiques*, published by M. Champollion Figeac, vol. iii.; the poem of Marie de France in the edition of her works, Paris, 1820, vol. ii.; an *Histoire de la Vie et du Purgatoire de S. Patrice*, par R. P. François

Bouillon, 0. S. F., Paris, 1651, Rouen, 1696; and also *Le Monde Enchanté*, par M. Ferdinand Denys, Paris, 1845, pp. 157—174.

1Biograph. Brit. Lit.; Anglo-Norm. Period, p.3212 Wright, S. Patrick's Purgatory, p. 65.

3 Wright, Op. cit., cap. iii.

4 Girald. Camhr. Topog. Hiberniæ, cap. V.

5 Cæsar. Heist. De Miracubs sui Temporis, lib. xii., cap 38. Ap. Wright.

6 Wright, Op. cit., p.135.

7 Popul-Vuh: Brasseur de Bouboorg, Paris, 1861; lib. ii. 7-I4.

8 Hrolf's Saga Kráka cap. 39; in Fornm. Sögur I., pp. 77-79.

9 Prose Edda, c. 33.

10 Edda of Sœmund, tr. by Thorpe, Part I., p.117.

11 Pausanias, ix. C. 39-4O, and Plutarch., De genio Socrat.

12 Lehrbuch der Religionsgeschichte: Band II I., Die Kelten, p. 29.

LIGEIA

EDGAR ALLAN POE

MUCH OF THE ATMOSPHERIC DETAIL in "The Rats in the Walls" stems from Poe's "Ligeia." Lovecraft's narrator, de la Poer, has sought relief from mourning his son by buying and reappointing an ancient abbey in England. It is conspicuously hung with tapestries. Is it coincidence that in "Ligeia" we also have the narrator purchase an old English abbey and move into it to divert himself from his grief after the death of a loved one, the lady Ligeia? Both abbeys are even said to evidence a composite workmanship recalling the many eras in which the structure was built and rebuilt. Poe's is said to possess a ceiling "of gloomy-looking oak, ... excessively lofty, vaulted, and elaborately fretted with the wildest and most grotesque specimens of a semi-Gothic, semi-Druidical device." Other rooms show "an endless succession of the ghastly forms which belong to the superstition of the Norman, or arise in the guilty slumbers of the monk." Lovecraft even lists several of the very same historical-architectural associations, including "Druidical or ante-Druidical" remains.

"The phantasmagoric effect," Poe's narrator recalls, "was vastly heightened by the artificial introduction of a strong continual current of wind behind the draperies, giving a hideous and uneasy animation to the whole." Sounds familiar! Moving arras? In the days of his second wife Rowena's decline she seems possessed of hallucinations which no one else is able to see. "She partly arose, and spoke in an earnest low whisper of sounds which she had heard but which I could not hear, of motions which she saw but which I could not perceive. The wind was rushing hurriedly behind the tapestries," and the narrator puts the sounds and motions down to this, but Rowena will not believe it. "She spoke again, and now more frequently, of the sounds - of the slight sounds - and of the unusual motions among the tapestries." I think it is obvious that here we read the origin of de la Poer's horrified sight of the moving arras in his chamber, as well as of the scratching of the rats in the walls which only he can hear.

ಚಿಂ

And the will therein lieth, which dieth not. Who knoweth the mysteries of the will, with its vigor? For God is but a great will pervading all things by nature of its intentness. Man doth not yield himself to the angels, nor unto death utterly, save only through the weakness of his feeble will.

Joseph Glanvill

I CANNOT, FOR MY SOUL, remember how, when, or even precisely where, I first became acquainted with the lady Ligeia. Long years have since elapsed, and my memory is feeble through much suffering. Or, perhaps, I cannot *now* bring these points to mind, because, in truth, the character of my beloved, her rare learning, her singular yet placid cast of beauty, and the thrilling and enthralling eloquence of her low musical language, made their way into my heart by paces so steadily and stealthily progressive that they have been unnoticed and unknown. Yet I believe that I met her first and most frequently in some large, old, decaying city near the Rhine. Of her family ~ I have surely heard her speak. That it is of a remotely ancient date cannot be doubted. Ligeia! Ligeia!

Buried in studies of a nature more than all else adapted to deaden impressions of the outward world, it is by that sweet word alone ~ by Ligeia ~ that I bring before mine eyes in fancy the image of her who is no more. And now, while I write, a recollection flashes upon me that I have *never known* the paternal name of her who was my friend and my betrothed, and who became the partner of my studies, and finally the wife of my bosom. Was it a playful charge on the part of my Ligeia? or was it a test of my strength of affection, that I should institute no inquiries upon this point? or was it rather a caprice of my own ~ a wildly romantic offering on the shrine of the most passionate devotion? I but indistinctly recall the fact itself ~ what wonder that I have utterly forgotten the circumstances which originated or attended it? And, indeed, if ever that spirit which is entitled *Romance* ~ if ever she, the wan and the misty-winged *Ashtophet* of idolatrous Egypt, presided, as they tell, over marriages ill-omened, then most surely she presided over mine.

There is one dear topic, however, on which my memory fails me not. It is the *person* of Ligeia. In stature she was tall, somewhat slender, and, in her latter days, even emaciated. I would in vain attempt to portray the majesty, the quiet ease, of her demeanor, or the incomprehensible lightness and elasticity of her footfall. She came and departed as a shadow. I was never made aware of her entrance into my closed study save by the dear music of her low sweet voice, as she placed her marble hand upon my shoulder. In beauty of face no maiden ever equalled her. It was the radiance of an opium-dream ~ an airy and spirit-lifting vision more wildly divine than the phantasies which hovered about the slumbering souls of the daughters of Delos. Yet her features were not of that regular mould which we have been falsely taught to worship in the classical labors of the heathen. 'There is no exquisite beauty,' says Bacon, Lord Verulam, speaking truly of all the forms and *genera* of beauty, 'without some *strangeness* in the proportion.' Yet, although I saw that the features of Ligeia were not of a classic regularity ~ although I perceived that her loveliness was indeed 'exquisite,' and felt that there was much of 'strangeness' pervading it, yet I have tried in vain to detect the irregularity and to trace home my own perception of 'the strange.' I examined the contour of the lofty and pale forehead ~ it was faultless ~ how cold indeed that word when applied to a majesty so divine! ~ the skin rivalling the purest ivory, the commanding extent and repose, the gentle prominence of the regions above the temples; and then the raven-black, the glossy, the luxuriant and naturally-curling tresses, setting forth the full force of the Homeric epithet, 'hyacinthine!' I looked at the delicate outlines of the nose ~ and nowhere but in the graceful medallions of the Hebrews had I beheld a similar perfection. There were the same luxurious smoothness of surface, the same scarcely perceptible tendency to the aquiline, the same harmoniously curved nostrils speaking the free spirit. I regarded the sweet mouth. Here was indeed the triumph of all things heavenly ~ the magnificent turn of the short upper lip ~ the soft, voluptuous slumber of the under ~ the dimples which sported, and the color which spoke ~ the teeth glancing back, with a brilliancy almost startling, every ray of the holy light which fell upon them in her serene and placid, yet most exultingly radiant of all smiles. I scrutinized the formation of the chin ~ and here, too, I found the gentleness of breadth, the softness and the majesty, the fullness and the spirituality, of the Greek ~ the contour which the god Apollo revealed but in a dream, to Cleomenes, the son of the Athenian. And then I peered into the large eyes of Ligeia.

For eyes we have no models in the remotely antique. It might have been, too, that in these eyes of my beloved lay the secret to which Lord Verulam alludes. They were, I must believe, far larger than the ordinary eyes of our own race. They were even fuller than the fullest of the gazelle eyes of the tribe of the valley of Nourjahad. Yet it was only at intervals ~ in moments of intense excitement ~ that this peculiarity became more than slightly noticeable in Ligeia. And at such moments was her beauty ~ in my heated fancy thus it appeared perhaps ~ the beauty of beings either above or apart from the earth ~ the beauty of the fabulous Houri of the Turk. The hue of the orbs was the most brilliant of black, and, far over them, hung jetty lashes of great length. The brows, slightly irregular in outline, had the same tint. The 'strangeness,' however, which I found in the eyes, was of a nature distinct from the formation, or the color, or the brilliancy of the features, and must, after all, be referred to the *expression*. Ah, word of no meaning! behind whose vast latitude of mere sound we intrench our ignorance of so much of the spiritual. The expression of the eyes of Ligeia! How for long hours have I pondered upon it! How have I, through the whole of a midsummer night, struggled to fathom it! What was it ~ that something more profound than the well of Democritus ~ which lay far within the pupils of my beloved? What *was* it? I was possessed with a passion to discover. Those eyes! those large, those shining, those divine orbs! they became to me twin stars of Leda, and I to them devoutest of astrologers.

There is no point, among the many incomprehensible anomalies of the science of mind, more thrillingly exciting than the fact ~ never, I believe, noticed in the schools ~ that, in our endeavors to recall to memory something long forgotten, we often find ourselves *upon the very verge* of remembrance, without being able, in the end, to remember. And thus how frequently, in my intense scrutiny of Ligeia's eyes, have I felt approaching the full knowledge of their expression ~ felt it approaching ~ yet not quite be mine ~ and so at length entirely depart! And (strange, oh strangest mystery of all!) I found, in the commonest objects of the universe, a circle of analogies to that expression. I mean to say that, subsequently to the period when Ligeia's beauty passed into my spirit, there dwelling as in a shrine, I derived, from many existences in the material world, a sentiment such as I felt always aroused within me by her large and luminous orbs. Yet not the more could I define that sentiment, or analyze, or even steadily view it. I recognized it, let me repeat, sometimes in the survey of a rapidly-growing vine ~ in the contemplation of a moth, a butterfly, a chrysalis, a stream of running water. I have felt it in the ocean; in the falling of a meteor. I have felt it in the glances of unusually aged people. And there are one or two stars in heaven ~ (one especially, a star of the sixth magnitude, double and changeable, to be found near the large star in Lyra) in a telescopic scrutiny of which I have been made aware of the feeling. I have been filled with it by certain sounds from stringed instruments, and not unfrequently by passages from books. Among innumerable other instances, I well remember something in a volume of Joseph Glanvill, which (perhaps merely from its quaintness ~ who shall say?) never failed to inspire me with the sentiment; ~ 'And the will therein lieth, which dieth not. Who knoweth the mysteries of the will, with its vigor? For God is but a great will pervading all things by nature of its intentness. Man doth not yield him to the angels, nor unto death utterly, save only through the weakness of his feeble will.'

Length of years, and subsequent reflection, have enabled me to trace, indeed, some remote connection between this passage in the English moralist and a portion of the character of Ligeia. An *intensity* in thought, action, or speech, was possibly, in her, a result, or at least an index, of that gigantic volition which, during our long intercourse, failed to give other and more immediate evidence of its existence. Of all the women whom I have ever known, she, the outwardly calm, the ever-placid Ligeia, was the most violently a prey to the tumultuous vultures of stern passion. And of such passion I could form no estimate, save by the miraculous expansion of those eyes which at once so delighted and appalled me ~ by the almost magical melody, modulation, distinctness and placidity of her very low voice ~ and by the fierce energy (rendered doubly effective by contrast with her manner of utterance) of the wild words which she habitually uttered.

I have spoken of the learning of Ligeia: it was immense ~ such as I have never known in woman. In the classical tongues was she deeply proficient, and as far as my own acquaintance extended in regard to the modern dialects of Europe, I have never known her at fault. Indeed upon any theme of the most admired, because simply the most abstruse of the boasted erudition of the academy, have I *ever* found Ligeia at fault? How singularly ~ how thrillingly, this one point in the nature of my wife has forced itself, at this late period only, upon my attention! I said her knowledge was such as I have never known in woman ~ but where breathes the man who has traversed, and successfully, *all* the wide areas of moral, physical, and mathematical science? I saw not then what I now clearly perceive, that the acquisitions of Ligeia were gigantic, were astounding; yet I was sufficiently aware of her infinite supremacy to resign myself, with a childlike confidence, to her guidance through the chaotic world of metaphysical investigation at which I was most busily occupied during the earlier years of our marriage. With how vast a triumph ~ with how vivid a delight ~ with how much of all that is ethereal in hope ~ did I *feel*, as she bent over me in studies but little sought ~ but less known ~ that delicious vista by slow degrees expanding before me, down whose long, gorgeous, and all untrodden path, I might at length pass onward to the goal of a wisdom too divinely precious not to be forbidden!

How poignant, then, must have been the grief with which, after some years, I beheld my well-grounded expectations take wings to themselves and fly away! Without Ligeia I was but as a child groping benighted. Her presence, her readings alone, rendered vividly luminous the many mysteries of the transcendentalism in which we were immersed. Wanting the radiant lustre of her eyes, letters, lambent and golden, grew duller than Saturnian lead. And now those eyes shone less and less frequently upon the pages over which I pored. Ligeia grew ill. The wild eyes blazed with a too ~ too glorious effulgence; the pale fingers became of the transparent waxen hue of the grave, and the blue veins upon the lofty forehead swelled and sank impetuously with the tides of the most gentle emotion. I saw that she must die ~ and I struggled desperately in spirit with the grim Azrael. And the struggles of the passionate wife were, to my astonishment, even more energetic than my own. There had been much in her stern nature to impress me with the belief that, to her, death would have come without its terrors; ~ but not so. Words are impotent to convey any just idea of the fierceness of resistance with which she wrestled with the Shadow. I groaned in anguish at the pitiable spectacle. I would have soothed ~ I would have reasoned; but, in the intensity of her wild desire for life, ~ for life ~ *but* for life ~ solace and reason were alike the uttermost of folly. Yet not until the last instance, amid the most convulsive writhings of her fierce spirit, was I shaken by the external placidity of her demeanor. Her voice grew more gentle ~ grew more low ~ yet I would not wish to dwell upon the wild meaning of the quietly uttered words. My brain reeled as I hearkened entranced, to a melody more than mortal ~ to assumptions and aspirations which mortality had never before known.

That she loved me I should not have doubted; and I might have been easily aware that, in a bosom such as hers, love would have reigned no ordinary passion. But in death only, was I fully impressed with the strength of her affection. For long hours, detaining my hand, would she pour out before me the overflowing of a heart whose more than passionate devotion amounted to idolatry. How had I deserved to be so blessed by such confessions? ~ how had I deserved to be so cursed with the removal of my beloved in the hour of her making them? But upon this subject I cannot bear to dilate. Let me say only, that in Ligeia's more than womanly abandonment to a love, alas! all unmerited, all unworthily bestowed, I at length recognized the principal of her longing with so wildly earnest a desire for the life which was now fleeing so rapidly away. It is this wild longing ~ it is this eager vehemence of desire for life ~ but for life ~ that I have no power to portray ~ no utterance capable of expressing.

At high noon on the night in which she departed, beckoning me, peremptorily, to her side, she bade me repeat certain verses composed by herself not many days before. I obeyed her. ~ They were these:

Lo! 'tis a gala night
Within the lonesome latter years!
An angel throng, bewinged, bedight
In veils, and drowned in tears,
Sit in a theatre, to see
A play of hopes and fears,
While the orchestra breathes fitfully
The music of the spheres.

Mimes, in the form of God on high,
Mutter and mumble low,
And hither and thither fly ~
Mere puppets they, who come and go
At bidding of vast formless things
That shift the scenery to and fro,
Flapping from out their Condor wings
Invisible Wo!

That motley drama! ~ oh, be sure
It shall not be forgot!
With its Phantom chased forever more,
By a crowd that seize it not,
Through a circle that ever returneth in
To the self-same spot,
And much of Madness and more of Sin
And Horror the soul of the plot.

But see, amid the mimic rout,

A crawling shape intrude!
A blood-red thing that writhes from out
The scenic solitude!

It writhes! ~ it writhes! ~ with mortal pangs
The mimes become its food,
And the seraphs sob at vermin fangs
In human gore imbued.

Out ~ out are the lights ~ out all!
And over each quivering form,
The curtain, a funeral pall,
Comes down with the rush of a storm,

And the angels, all pallid and wan,
Uprising, unveiling, affirm
That the play is the tragedy, "Man,"
And its hero the Conqueror Worm.

'O God!' half shrieked Ligeia, leaping to her feet and extending her arms aloft with a spasmodic movement, as I made an end of these lines ~ 'O God! O Divine Father! shall these things be undeviatingly so? ~ shall this Conqueror be not once conquered? Are we not part and parcel in Thee? Who ~ who knoweth the mysteries of the will with its vigor? Man doth not yield him to the angels, *nor unto death utterly*, save only through the weakness of his feeble will.'

And now, as if exhausted with emotion, she suffered her white arms to fall, and returned solemnly to her bed of death. And as she breathed her last sighs, there came mingled with them a low murmur from her lips. I bent to them my ear and distinguished, again, the concluding words of the passage in Glanvill ~ '*Man doth not yield him to the angels, nor unto death utterly, save only through the weakness of his feeble will.*'

She died; ~ and I, crushed into the very dust with sorrow, could no longer endure the lonely desolation of my dwelling in the dim and decaying city by the Rhine. I had no lack of what the world calls wealth. Ligeia had brought me far more, very far more than ordinarily falls the lot of mortals. After a few months, therefore, of weary and aimless wandering, I purchased, and put in some repair, an abbey, which I shall not name, in one of the wildest and least frequented portions of fair England. The gloomy and dreary grandeur of the building, the almost savage aspect of the domain, the many melancholy and time-honored memories connected with both, had much in unison with the feelings of utter abandonment which had driven me into that remote and unsocial region of the country. Yet although the external abbey, with its verdant decay hanging about it, suffered but little alteration, I gave way, with a child-like perversity, and perchance with a faint hope of alleviating my sorrows, to a display of more than regal magnificence within. ~ For such follies, even in childhood, I had imbibed a taste and now they came back to me as in the dotage of grief. Alas, I feel how much even of incipient madness might have been discovered in the gorgeous and fantastic draperies, in the solemn carving of Egypt, in the wild cornices and furniture, in the Bedlam patterns of the carpets of tufted gold! I had become a bounden slave in the trammels of opium, and my labors and my orders had taken a coloring from my dreams. But these absurdities I must not pause to detail. Let me speak only of that one chamber, ever accursed, whither in a moment of mental alienation, I led from the altar as my bride ~ as the successor of the unforgotten Ligeia ~ the fair-haired and blue-eyed Lady Rowena Trevanion, of Tremaine.

There is no individual portion of the architecture and decoration of that bridal chamber which is not now visibly before me. Where were the souls of the haughty family of the bride, when, through thirst of gold, they permitted to pass the threshold of an apartment so bedecked, a maiden and daughter so beloved? I have said that I minutely remember the details of the chamber ~ yet I am sadly forgetful on topics of deep moment ~ and here there was no system, no keeping, in the fantastic display, to take hold upon the memory. The room lay in a high turret of the castellated abbey, was pentagonal in shape, and of capacious size. Occupying the whole southern face of the pentagon was the sole window ~ an immense sheet of unbroken glass from Venice ~ a single pane, and tinted of a leaden hue, so that the rays of either the sun or moon, passing through it, fell with a ghastly lustre on the objects within. Over the upper portion of this huge window, extended the trellice-work of an aged vine, which clambered up the massy walls of the turret. The ceiling, of gloomy-looking oak, was excessively lofty, vaulted, and elaborately fretted with the wildest and most grotesque specimens of a semi-Gothic, semi-Druidical device. From out the most central recess of this melancholy vaulting, depended, by a single chain of gold with long links, a huge censer of the same metal, Saracenic in pattern, and with many perforations so contrived that there writhed in and out of them, as if endued with a serpent vitality, a continual succession of parti-colored fires.

Some few ottomans and golden candelabra, of Eastern figure, were in various stations about ~ and there was the couch, too ~ the bridal couch ~ of an Indian model, and low, and sculptured of solid ebony, with a pall-like canopy above. In each of the angles of the chamber stood on end a gigantic sarcophagus of black granite, from the tombs of the kings over against Luxor, with their aged lids full of immemorial sculpture. But in the draping of the apartment lay, alas! the chief phantasy of all. The lofty walls, gigantic in height ~ even unproportionably so ~ were hung from summit to foot, in vast folds, with a heavy and massive-looking tapestry ~ tapestry of a material which was found alike as a carpet on the floor, as a covering for the ottomans and the ebony bed, as a canopy for the bed, and as the gorgeous volutes of the curtains which partially shaded the window. The material was the richest cloth of gold. It was spotted all over, at irregular intervals, with arabesque figures, about a foot in diameter, and wrought upon the cloth in patterns of the most jetty black. But these figures partook of the true character of the arabesque only when regarded from a single point of view. By a contrivance now common, and indeed traceable to a very remote period of antiquity, they were made changeable in aspect. To one entering the room, they bore the appearance of simple monstrosities; but upon a farther advance, this appearance gradually departed; and step by step, as the visiter moved his station in the chamber, he saw himself surrounded by an endless succession of the ghastly forms which belong to the superstition of the Norman, or arise in the guilty slumbers of the monk. The phantasmagoric effect was vastly heightened by the artificial introduction of a strong continual current of the wind behind the draperies ~ giving a hideous and uneasy animation to the whole.

In halls such as these ~ in a bridal chamber such as this ~ I passed, with the Lady of Tremaine, the unhallowed hours of the first month of our marriage ~ passed them with but little disquietude. That my wife dreaded the fierce moodiness of my temper ~ that she shunned me and loved me but little ~ I could not help perceiving; but it gave me rather pleasure than otherwise. I loathed her with a hatred belonging more to demon than to man. My memory flew back, (oh, with what intensity of regret!) to Ligeia, the beloved, the august, the beautiful, the entombed. I revelled in recollections of her purity, of her wisdom, of her lofty, her ethereal nature, of her passionate, her idolatrous love. Now, then, did my spirit fully and freely burn with more than all the fires of her own. In the excitement of my opium dreams (for I was habitually fettered in the shackles of the drug) I would call aloud upon her name, during the silence of the night, or among the sheltered recesses of the glens by day, as if, through the wild eagerness, the solemn passion, the consuming ardor of my longing for the departed, I could restore her to the pathway she had abandoned ~ ah, *could* it be forever? ~ upon the earth.

About the commencement of the second month of the marriage, the Lady Rowena was attacked with sudden illness, from which her recovery was slow. The fever which consumed her rendered her nights uneasy; and in her perturbed state of half-slumber, she spoke of sounds, and of motions, in and about the chamber of the turret, which I concluded had no origin save in the distemper of her fancy, or perhaps in the phantasmagoric influences of the chamber itself. She became at length convalescent ~ finally well. Yet but a brief period elapsed, ere a second more violent disorder again threw her upon a bed of suffering; and from this attack her frame, at all times feeble, never altogether recovered. Her illnesses were, after this epoch, of alarming character, and of more alarming recurrence, defying alike the knowledge and the great exertions of her physicians. With the increase of the chronic disease which had thus, apparently, taken too sure hold upon her constitution to be eradicated by human means, I could not fail to observe a similar increase in the nervous irritation of her temperament, and in her excitability by trivial causes of fear. She spoke again, and now more frequently and pertinaciously, of the sounds ~ of the slight sounds ~ and of the unusual motions among the tapestries, to which she had formerly alluded.

One night, near the closing in of September, she pressed this distressing subject with more than usual emphasis upon my attention. She had just awakened from an unquiet slumber, and I had been watching, with feelings half of anxiety, half of vague terror, the workings of her emaciated countenance. I sat by the side of her ebony bed, upon one of the ottomans of India. She partly arose, and spoke, in an earnest low whisper, of sounds which she *then* heard, but which I could not hear ~ of motions which she *then* saw, but which I could not perceive. The wind was rushing hurriedly behind the tapestries, and I wished to show her (what, let me confess it, I could not *all* believe) that those almost inarticulate breathings, and those very gentle variations of the figures upon the wall, were but the natural effects of that customary rushing of the wind. But a deadly pallor, overspreading her face, had proved to me that my exertions to reassure her would be fruitless. She appeared to be fainting, and no attendants were within call. I remembered where was deposited a decanter of light wine which had been ordered by her physicians, and hastened across the chamber to procure it. But, as I stepped beneath the light of the censer, two circumstances of a startling nature attracted my attention. I had felt that some palpable although invisible object had passed lightly by my person; and I saw that there lay upon the golden carpet, in the very middle of the rich lustre thrown from the censer, a shadow ~ a faint, indefinite shadow of angelic aspect ~ such as might be fancied for the shadow of a shade. But I was wild with the excitement of an immoderate dose of opium, and heeded these things but little, nor spoke of them to Rowena. Having found the wine, I recrossed the chamber, and poured out a goblet-ful, which I held to the lips of the fainting lady. She had now partially recovered, however, and took the vessel herself, while I sank upon an ottoman near me, with my eyes fastened upon her person. It was then that I became distinctly aware of a gentle foot-fall upon the carpet, and near the couch; and in a second thereafter, as Rowena was in the act of raising the wine to her lips, I saw, or may have dreamed that I saw, fall within the goblet, as if from some invisible spring in the atmosphere of the room, three or four large drops of a brilliant and ruby colored fluid. If this I saw ~ not so Rowena. She swallowed the wine unhesitatingly, and I forbore to speak to her of a circumstance which must, after all, I considered, have been but the suggestion of a vivid imagination, rendered morbidly active by the terror of the lady, by the opium, and by the hour.

Yet I cannot conceal it from my own perception that, immediately subsequent to the fall of the ruby-drops, a rapid change for the worse took place in the disorder of my wife; so that, on the third subsequent night, the hands of her menials prepared her for the tomb, and on the fourth, I sat alone, with her shrouded body, in that fantastic chamber which had received her as my bride. ~ Wild visions, opium-engendered, flitted, shadow-like, before me. I gazed with unquiet eye upon the sarcophagi in the angles of the room, upon the varying figures of the drapery, and upon the writhing of the parti-colored fires in the censer overhead. My eyes then fell, as I called to mind the circumstances of a former night, to the spot beneath the glare of the censer where I had seen the faint traces of the shadow. It was there, however, no longer; and breathing with greater freedom, I turned my glances to the pallid and rigid figure upon the bed. Then rushed back upon me a thousand memories of Ligeia ~ and then came back upon my heart, with the turbulent violence of a flood, the whole of that unutterable woe with which I had regarded *her* thus enshrouded. The night waned; and still, with a bosom full of bitter thoughts of the one only and supremely beloved, I remained gazing upon the body of Rowena.

It might have been midnight, or perhaps earlier, or later, for I had taken no note of time, when a sob, low, gentle, but very distinct, startled me from my revery. ~ I *felt* that it came from the bed of ebony ~ the bed of death. I listened in an agony of superstitious terror ~ but there was no repetition of the sound. I strained my vision to detect any motion in the corpse ~ but there was not the slightest perceptible. Yet I could not have been deceived. I *had* heard the noise, however faint, and my soul was awakened within me. I resolutely and perseveringly kept my attention riveted upon the body. Many minutes elapsed before any circumstance occurred tending to throw light upon the mystery. At length it became evident that a slight, a very feeble, and barely noticeable tinge of color had flushed up within the cheeks, and along the sunken small veins of the eyelids. Through a species of unutterable horror and awe, for which the language of mortality has no sufficiently energetic expression, I felt my heart cease to beat, my limbs grow rigid where I sat. Yet a sense of duty finally operated to restore my self-possession. I could no longer doubt that we had been precipitate in our preparations ~ that Rowena still lived. It was necessary that some immediate exertion be made; yet the turret was altogether apart from the portion of the abbey tenanted by the servants ~ there were none within call ~ I had no means of summoning them to my aid without leaving the room for many minutes ~ and this I could not venture to do. I therefore struggled along in my endeavors to call back the spirit still hovering. In a short period it was certain, however, that a relapse had taken place; the color disappeared from both eyelid and cheek, leaving a wanness even more than that of marble; the lips became doubly shrivelled and pinched up in the ghastly expression of death; a repulsive clamminess and coldness overspread rapidly the surface of the body; and all the usual rigorous stiffness immediately supervened. I fell back with a shudder upon the couch from which I had been so startlingly aroused, and again gave myself up to passionate waking visions of Ligeia.

An hour thus elapsed when (could it be possible?) I was a second time aware of some vague sound issuing from the region of the bed. I listened ~ in extremity of horror. The sound came again ~ it was a sigh. Rushing to the corpse, I saw ~ distinctly saw ~ a tremor upon the lips. In a minute afterward they relaxed, disclosing a bright line of the pearly teeth. Amazement now struggled in my bosom with the profound awe which had hitherto reigned there alone. I felt that my vision grew dim, that my reason wandered; and it was only by a violent effort that I at length succeeded in nerving myself to the task which duty thus once more had pointed out. There was now a partial glow upon the forehead and upon the cheek and throat; a perceptible warmth pervaded the whole frame; there was even a slight pulsation at the heart. The lady *lived*; and with redoubled ardor I betook myself to the task of restoration. I chafed and bathed the temples and the hands, and used every exertion which experience, and no little medical reading, could suggest. But in vain. Suddenly, the color fled, the pulsation ceased, the lips resumed the expression of the dead, and, in an instant afterward, the whole body took upon itself the icy chilliness, the livid hue, the intense rigidity, the sunken outline, and all the loathsome peculiarities of that which has been, for many days, a tenant of the tomb.

And again I sunk into visions of Ligeia ~ and again, (what marvel that I shudder while I write?) *again* there reached my ears a low sob from the region of the ebony bed. But why shall I minutely detail the unspeakable horrors of that night? Why shall I pause to relate how, time after time, until near the period of the gray dawn, this hideous drama of revification was repeated; how each terrific relapse was only into a sterner and apparently more irredeemable death; how each agony wore the aspect of a struggle with some invisible foe; and how each struggle was succeeded by I know not what of wild change in the personal appearance of the corpse? Let me hurry to a conclusion.

The greater part of the fearful night had worn away, and she who had been dead, once again stirred ~ and now more vigorously than hitherto, although arousing from a dissolution more appalling in its utter hopelessness than any. I had long ceased to struggle or to move, and remained sitting rigidly upon the ottoman, a helpless prey to a whirl of violent emotions, of which extreme awe was perhaps the least terrible, the least consuming. The corpse, I repeat, stirred, and now more vigorously than before. The hues of life flushed up with unwonted energy into the countenance ~ the limbs relaxed ~ and, save that the eyelids were yet pressed heavily together, and that the bandages and draperies of the grave still imparted their charnel character to the figure, I might have dreamed that Rowena had indeed shaken off, utterly, the fetters of Death. But if this idea was not, even then, altogether adopted, I could at least doubt no longer, when, arising from the bed, tottering, with feeble steps, with closed eyes, and with the manner of one bewildered in a dream, the thing that was enshrouded advanced boldly and palpably into the middle of the apartment.

I trembled not ~ I stirred not ~ for a crowd of unutterable fancies connected with the air, the stature, the demeanor of the figure, rushing hurriedly through my brain, had paralyzed ~ had chilled me into stone. I stirred not ~ but gazed upon the apparition. There was a mad disorder in my thoughts ~ a tumult unappeasable. Could it, indeed, be the *living* Rowena who confronted me? Could it indeed be Rowena *at all* ~ the fair-haired, the blue-eyed Lady Rowena Trevanion of Tremaine? Why, *why* should I doubt it? The bandage lay heavily about the mouth ~ but then might it not be the mouth of the breathing Lady of Tremaine? And the cheeks ~ there were the roses as in her noon of life ~ yes, these might indeed be the fair cheeks of the living Lady of Tremaine. And the chin, with its dimples, as in health, might it not be hers? ~ *but had she then grown taller since her malady?* What inexpressible madness seized me with that thought? One bound, and I had reached her feet! Shrinking from my touch, she let fall from her head, unloosened, the ghastly cerements which had confined it, and there streamed forth, into the rushing atmosphere of the chamber, huge masses of long and dishevelled hair; *it was blacker than the raven wings of the midnight!* And now slowly opened the eyes of the figure which stood before me. 'Here then, at least,' I shrieked aloud, 'can I never ~ can I never be mistaken ~ these are the full, and the black, and the wild eyes ~ of my lost love ~ of the lady ~ of the LADY LIGEIA.'

THE SIN-EATER

FIONNA MACLEOD

THIS TRULY EERIE TALE INVOLVES one of the many folk variations of Christian soteriology. One might have thought that the definitive atonement of Christ on the cross would have settled matters for the repentant sinner. Throughout the Christian centuries, however, people have thought they needed to supplement the salvation wrought by Christ. This is because of a strategic loophole in the theory. Christian thinkers as well as popular believers have never been able to deliver a single answer to the question of what one must do to get in on the atonement. Granted that the Son of God did all he had to do upon Mount Calvary (Golgotha), what do *we* need to do in order for his salvation to avail for us? Do we need to believe in it, period? Must we believe in it and then try our best to please God through subsequent good deeds and spiritual works? Christ's atonement was, to be sure, an act of grace, but do we need to get our heads on straight before we can sincerely accept it? Or is that very repentant disposition also kindled within us by God's initiative? And if the bottom line is to do one's best, well, that is what religion has told us since time immemorial, so why did Christ "die for sins"? What new element did he introduce? Most Christians seem to think that Jesus Christ was like a doctor who discovered the cure for AIDS. But he did not simply cure everyone of AIDS. He only made it possible. And traditional Christian salvation doctrine saw Jesus as the one who made salvation possible at last, but not the one who actually saved the human race. But if he were really "the savior," doesn't that mean he *did* it, not that he made it possible, leaving the rest of the process to you? That is the claim of Universalists: Christ died to save humanity, *and it worked.* This would render unnecessary bizarre gimmicks like the "Sin-Eater." It's as if he gobbles up the sins that would otherwise have given you such heartburn in Purgatory.

One cannot read very far into "The Sin-Eater" without pausing over the place name "Duninch"! But of course HPL's interest in regional dialects of English was uppermost. He appreciated the author's use of it here, and he even borrowed snatches of it, out of context, knowing few readers would ever know the difference.

When old Sheen Macarthur crosses herself and chants:

> "*Crois nan naoi aingeal leam*

81

'*O mhuhlach mo chinu Gu craican mo bhonn.*"

It translates as:

> *The cross of the nine angels be about me,*
> *From the top of my head,*
> *To the soles of my feet.*

When the Sin-Eater himself later enumerates blessings he does not plan to use: *A chuid do Pharas da!* means: "His share of heaven be his!" *Gu'n gleidheadh Dia thu* means, "May God preserve you!" And *Gu'n beannaic-headh Dia an tigh!"* means "God's blessing on this house!" He intends rather to say *Droch caoidh ort!* ("Bad moan on you!", i.e., May ill befall you!") and *Gaoth gun direadh ort!* ("Wind without direction on you!," i.e., "Drift till you drown!") and *Dia ad aghaidh 's ad aodaun ~ agus bas dunach ort! Dhonas 's dholas ort, agus leat-sa!* ("God against thee and in thy face, and may a woeful death be yours! Evil and sorrow to you and yours!"). It is this last which de la Poer hears himself growling at poor Captain Norrys.

This story appeared initially in *The Sin-Eater and Other Tales* (1895).

SIN.

Taste this bread, this substance: tell me
Is it bread or flesh?

[The Senses approach.]

THE SMELL.
Its smell
Is the smell of bread.

SIN.

Touch, come. Why tremble?
Say what's this thou touchest?

THE TOUCH.

82

Bread.

SIN.

Sight, declare what thou discernest
In this object.

THE SIGHT.

Bread alone.

CALDERON,
Los Encantos de la Culpa.

A WET WIND OUT OF THE SOUTH mazed and mooned through the sea-mist that hung over the Ross. In all the bays and creeks was a continuous weary lapping of water. There was no other sound anywhere.

Thus was it at daybreak: it was thus at noon: thus was it now in the darkening of the day. A confused thrusting and falling of sounds through the silence betokened the hour of the setting. Curlews wailed in the mist: on the seething limpet-covered rocks the skuas and terns screamed, or uttered hoarse, rasping cries. Ever and again the prolonged note of the oyster-catcher shrilled against the air, as an echo flying blindly along a blank wall or cliff. Out of weedy places, wherein the tide sobbed with long, gurgling moans, came at intervals the barking of a seal.

Inland, by the hamlet of Contullich, there is a reedy tarn called the Loch-a-chaoruinn. By the shores of this mournful water a man moved. It was a slow, weary walk that of the man Neil Ross. He had come from Duninch, thirty miles to the eastward, and had not rested foot, nor eaten, nor had word of man or woman, since his going west an hour after dawn.

At the bend of the loch nearest the clachan he came upon an old woman carrying peat. To his reiterated question as to where he was, and if the tarn were Feur-Lochan above Fionnaphort that is on the strait of Iona on the west side of the Ross of Mull, she did not at first make any answer. The rain trickled down her withered brown face, over which the thin grey locks hung limply. It was only in the deep-set eyes that the flame of life still glimmered, though that dimly.

The man had used the English when first he spoke, but as though mechanically. Supposing that he had not been understood, he repeated his question in the Gaelic.

After a minute's silence the old woman answered him in the native tongue, but only to put a question in return.

"I am thinking it is a long time since you have been in Iona?"

The man stirred uneasily.

"And why is that, mother?" he asked, in a weak voice hoarse with damp and fatigue; "how is it you will be knowing that I have been in Iona at all?"

"Because I knew your kith and kin there, Neil Ross."

"I have not been hearing that name, mother, for many a long year. And as for the old face o' you, it is unbeknown to me."

"I was at the naming of you, for all that. Well do I remember the day that Silis Macallum gave you birth; and I was at the house on the croft of Ballyrona when Murtagh Ross that was your father laughed. It was an ill laughing that."

"I am knowing it. The curse of God on him!"

"'Tis not the first, nor the last, though the grass is on his head three years agone now."

"You that know who I am will be knowing that I have no kith or kin now on Iona?"

"Ay; they are all under grey stone or running wave. Donald your brother, and Murtagh your next brother, and little Silis, and your mother Silis herself, and your two brothers of your father, Angus and Ian Macallum, and your father Murtagh Ross, and his lawful childless wife, Dionaid, and his sister Anna one and all, they lie beneath the green wave or in the brown mould. It is said there is a curse upon all who live at Ballyrona. The owl builds now in the rafters, and it is the big sea-rat that runs across the fireless hearth."

"It is there I am going."

"The foolishness is on you, Neil Ross."

84

"Now it is that I am knowing who you are. It is old Sheen Macarthur I am speaking to."

"*Tha mise* ... it is I."

"And you will be alone now, too, I am thinking, Sheen?"

"I am alone. God took my three boys at the one fishing ten years ago; and before there was moonrise in the blackness of my heart my man went. It was after the drowning of Anndra that my croft was taken from me. Then I crossed the Sound, and shared with my widow sister Elsie McVurie: till *she* went: and then the two cows had to go: and I had no rent: and was old."

In the silence that followed, the rain dribbled from the sodden bracken and dripping loneroid. Big tears rolled slowly down the deep lines on the face of Sheen. Once there was a sob in her throat, but she put her shaking hand to it, and it was still.

Neil Ross shifted from foot to foot. The ooze in that marshy place squelched with each restless movement he made. Beyond them a plover wheeled, a blurred splatch in the mist, crying its mournful cry over and over and over. It was a pitiful thing to hear: ah, bitter loneliness, bitter patience of poor old women. That he knew well. But he was too weary, and his heart was nigh full of its own burthen. The words could not come to his lips. But at last he spoke.

"*Tha mo chridhe goirt*," he said, with tears in his voice, as he put his hand on her bent shoulder; "my heart is sore."

She put up her old face against his.

"'*S tha e ruidhinn mo chridhe*," she whispered; "it is touching my heart you are."

After that they walked on slowly through the dripping mist, each dumb and brooding deep.

"Where will you be staying this night?" asked Sheen suddenly, when they had traversed a wide boggy stretch of land; adding, as by an afterthought "Ah, it is asking you were if the tarn there were Feur Lochan. No; it is Loch-a-chaoruinn, and the clachan that is near is Contullich."

"Which way?"

"Yonder: to the right."

"And you are not going there?"

"No. I am going to the steading of Andrew Blair. Maybe you are for knowing it? It is called the Baile-na-Chlais-nambuidheag."

"I do not remember. But it is remembering a Blair I am. He was Adam, the son of Adam, the son of Robert. He and my father did many an ill deed together."

"Ay, to the Stones be it said. Sure, now, there was, even till this weary day, no man or woman who had a good word for Adam Blair."

"And why that . . . why till this day?"

"It is not yet the third hour since he went into the silence."

Neil Ross uttered a sound like a stifled curse. For a time he trudged wearily on.

"Then I am too late," he said at last, but as though speaking to himself. "I had hoped to see him face to face again, and curse him between the eyes. It was he who made the farm in the hollow of the yellow flowers. Murtagh Ross break his troth to my mother, and marry that other woman, barren at that, God be praised! And they say ill of him, do they?"

"Ay, it is evil that is upon him. This crime and that, God knows; and the shadow of murder on his brow and in his eyes. Well, well, 'tis ill to be speaking of a man in corpse, and that near by. 'Tis Himself only that knows, Neil Ross."

"Maybe ay and maybe no. But where is it that I can be sleeping this night, Sheen Macarthur?"

"They will not be taking a stranger at the farm this night of the nights, I am thinking. There is no place else for seven miles yet, when there is the clachan, before you will be coming to Fionnaphort. There is the warm byre, Neil, my man; or, if you can bide by my peats, you may rest, and welcome, though there is no bed for you, and no food either save some of the porridge that is over."

"And that will do well enough for me, Sheen; and Himself bless you for it."

And so it was.

After old Sheen Macarthur had given the wayfarer food, poor food at that, but welcome to one nigh starved, and for the heartsome way it was given, and because of the thanks to God that was upon it before even spoon was lifted she told him a lie. It was the good lie of tender love.

"Sure now, after all, Neil, my man," she said, "it is sleeping at the farm I ought to be, for Maisie Macdonald, the wise woman, will be sitting by the corpse, and there will be none to keep her company. It is there I must be going; and if I am weary, there is a good bed for me just beyond the dead-board, which I am not minding at all. So, if it is tired you are sitting by the peats, lie down on my bed there, and have the sleep; and God be with you."

With that she went, and soundlessly, for Neil Ross was already asleep, where he sat on an upturned *claar*, with his elbows on his knees, and his flame-lit face in his hands.

The rain had ceased; but the mist still hung over the land, though in thin veils now, and these slowly drifting seaward. Sheen stepped wearily along the stony path that led from her bothy to the farmhouse. She stood still once, the fear upon her, for she saw three or four blurred yellow gleams moving beyond her, eastward, along the dyke. She knew what they were ~ the corpse-lights that on the night of death go between the bier and the place of burial. More than once she had seen them before the last hour, and by that token had known the end to be near.

Good Catholic that she was, she crossed herself, and took heart. Then, muttering –

"*Crois nan naoi aingeal leam*
'*O mhuhlach mo chinu*
Gu craican mo bhonn."

she went on her way fearlessly.

When she came to the White House, she entered by the milk-shed that was between the byre and the kitchen. At the end of it was a paved place, with washing-tubs. At one of these stood a girl that served in the house, an ignorant lass called Jessie McFall, out of Oban. She was ignorant, indeed, not to know that to wash clothes with a newly dead body near by was an ill thing to do. Was it not a matter for the knowing that the corpse could hear, and might rise up in the night and clothe itself in a clean white shroud?

She was still speaking to the lassie when Maisie Macdonald, the deid-watcher, opened the door of the room behind the kitchen to see who it was that was come. The two old women nodded silently. It was not till Sheen was in the closed room, midway in which something covered with a sheet lay on a board, that any word was spoken.

"*Duit sith mor*, Beann Macdonald."

"And deep peace to you, too, Sheen; and to him that is there."

"*Och, ochone, misc 'n diugh*; 'tis a dark hour this.'"

"Ay; it is bad. Will you have been hearing or seeing anything?"

"Well, as for that, I am thinking I saw lights moving betwixt here and the green place over there."

"The corpse-lights?"

"Well, it is calling them that they are."

"I *thought* they would be out. And I have been hearing the noise of the planks the cracking of the boards, you know, that will be used for the coffin to-morrow."

A long silence followed. The old women had seated themselves by the corpse, their cloaks over their heads. The room was fireless, and was lit only by a tall wax death-candle, kept against the hour of the going.

At last Sheen began swaying slowly to and fro, crooning low the while. "I would not be for doing that, Sheen Macarthur," said the deid-watcher in a low voice, but meaningly; adding, after a moment's pause, "*The mice have all left the house.*"

Sheen sat upright, a look half of terror half of awe in her eyes.

"God save the sinful soul that is hiding," she whispered.

Well she knew what Maisie meant. If the soul of the dead be a lost soul it knows its doom. The house of death is the house of sanctuary; but before the dawn that follows the death-night the soul must go forth, whosoever or whatsoever wait for it in the homeless, shelterless plains of air around and beyond. If it be well with the soul, it need have no fear: if it be not ill with the soul, it may fare forth with surety; but if it be ill with the soul, ill will the going be. Thus is it that the spirit of an evil man cannot stay, and yet dare not go; and so it strives to hide itself in secret places anywhere, in dark channels and blind walls; and the wise creatures that live near man smell the error, and flee. Maisie repeated the saying of Sheen; then, after a silence, added "Adam Blair will not lie in his grave for a year and a day because of the sins that are upon him; and it is knowing that, they are, here. He will be the Watcher of the Dead for a year and a day."

"Ay, sure, there will be dark prints in the dawn-dew over yonder."

Once more the old women relapsed into silence. Through the night there was a sighing sound. It was not the sea, which was too far off to be heard save in a day of storm. The wind it was, that was dragging itself across the sodden moors like a wounded thing, moaning and sighing.

Out of sheer weariness, Sheen twice rocked forward from her stool, heavy with sleep. At last Maisie led her over to the niche-bed opposite, and laid her down there, and waited till the deep furrows in the face relaxed somewhat, and the thin breath laboured slow across the fallen jaw.

"Poor old woman," she muttered, heedless of her own grey hairs and greyer years; "a bitter, bad thing it is to be old, old and weary. 'Tis the sorrow, that. God keep the pain of it!"

As for herself, she did not sleep at all that night, but sat between the living and the dead, with her plaid shrouding her. Once, when Sheen gave a low, terrified scream in her sleep, she rose, and in a loud voice cried, "*Sheeach-ad*! Away with you!" And with that she lifted the shroud from the dead man, and took the pennies off the eyelids, and lifted each lid; then, staring into these filmed wells, muttered an ancient incantation that would compel the soul of Adam Blair to leave the spirit of Sheen alone, and return to the cold corpse that was its coffin till the wood was ready.

The dawn came at last. Sheen slept, and Adam Blair slept a deeper sleep, and Maisie stared out of her wan, weary eyes against the red and stormy flares of light that came into the sky.

When, an hour after sunrise, Sheen Macarthur reached her bothy, she found Neil Ross, heavy with slumber, upon her bed. The fire was not out, though no flame or spark was visible; but she stooped and blew at the heart of the peats till the redness came, and once it came it grew. Having done this, she kneeled and said a rune of the morning, and after that a prayer, and then a prayer for the poor man Neil. She could pray no more because of the tears. She rose and put the meal and water into the pot for the porridge to be ready against his awaking. One of the hens that was there came and pecked at her ragged skirt. "Poor beastie," she said. "Sure, that will just be the way I am pulling at the white robe of the Mother o' God. 'Tis a bit meal for you, cluckie, and for me a healing hand upon my tears. O, och, ochone, the tears, the tears!"

It was not till the third hour after sunrise of that bleak day in that winter of the winters, that Neil Ross stirred and arose. He ate in silence. Once he said that he smelt the snow coming out of the north. Sheen said no word at all. After the porridge, he took his pipe, but there was no tobacco. All that Sheen had was the pipeful she kept against the gloom of the Sabbath. It was her one solace in the long weary week. She gave him this, and held a burning peat to his mouth, and hungered over the thin, rank smoke that curled upward.

It was within half-an-hour of noon that, after an absence, she returned.

"Not between you and me, Neil Ross," she began abruptly, "but just for the asking, and what is beyond. Is it any money you are having upon you?"

"No."

"Nothing?"

"Nothing."

"Then how will you be getting across to Iona? It is seven long miles to Fionnaphort, and bitter cold at that, and you will be needing food, and then the ferry, the ferry across the Sound, you know."

"Ay, I know."

"What would you do for a silver piece, Neil, my man?"

"You have none to give me, Sheen Macarthur; and, if you had, it would not be taking it I would."

"Would you kiss a dead man for a crown-piece, a crown-piece of five good shillings?"

Neil Ross stared. Then he sprang to his feet.

"It is Adam Blair you are meaning, woman! God curse him in death now that he is no longer in life!"

Then, shaking and trembling, he sat down again, and brooded against the dull red glow of the peats.

But, when he rose, in the last quarter before noon, his face was white.

"The dead are dead, Sheen Macarthur. They can know or do nothing. I will do it. It is willed. Yes, I am going up to the house there. And now I am going from here. God Himself has my thanks to you, and my blessing too. They will come back to you. It is not forgetting you I will be. Good-bye."

"Good-bye, Neil, son of the woman that was my friend. A south wind to you! Go up by the farm. In the front of the house you will see what you will be seeing. Maisie Macdonald will be there. She will tell you what's for the telling. There is no harm in it, sure: sure, the dead are dead. It is praying for you I will be, Neil Ross. Peace to you!"

"And to you, Sheen."

And with that the man went.

When Neil Ross reached the byres of the farm in the wide hollow, he saw two figures standing as though awaiting him, but separate, and unseen of the other. In front of the house was a man he knew to be Andrew Blair; behind the milk-shed was a woman he guessed to be Maisie Macdonald.

It was the woman he came upon first.

"Are you the friend of Sheen Macarthur?" she asked in a whisper, as she beckoned him to the doorway.

"I am."

"I am knowing no names or anything. And no one here will know you, I am thinking. So do the thing and begone."

"There is no harm to it?"

"None."

"It will be a thing often done, is it not?"

"Ay, sure."

"And the evil does not abide?"

"No. The ... the ... person ... the person takes them away, and . . ."

"*Them?*"

91

"For sure, man! Them . . . the sins of the corpse. He takes them away; and are you for thinking God would let the innocent suffer for the guilty? No ... the person ... the Sin-Eater, you know . . . takes them away on himself, and one by one the air of heaven washes them away till he, the Sin-Eater, is clean and whole as before."

"But if it is a man you hate ... if it is a corpse that is the corpse of one who has been a curse and a foe ... if ..."

"Sst! Be still now with your foolishness. It is only an idle saying, I am thinking. Do it, and take the money and go. It will be hell enough for Adam Blair, miser as he was, if he is for knowing that five good shillings of his money are to go to a passing tramp because of an old, ancient silly tale."

Neil Ross laughed low at that. It was for pleasure to him.

"Hush wi' ye! Andrew Blair is waiting round there. Say that I have sent you round, as I have neither bite nor bit to give."

Turning on his heel, Neil walked slowly round to the front of the house. A tall man was there, gaunt and brown, with hairless face and lank brown hair, but with eyes cold and grey as the sea.

"Good day to you, an' good faring. Will you be passing this way to anywhere?"

"Health to you. I am a stranger here. It is on my way to Iona I am. But I have the hunger upon me. There is not a brown bit in my pocket. I asked at the door there, near the byres. The woman told me she could give me nothing, not a penny even, worse luck, nor, for that, a drink of warm milk. 'Tis a sore land this."

"You have the Gaelic of the Isles. Is it from Iona you are?"

"It is from the Isles of the West I come."

"From Tiree ? . . . from Coll?"

"No."

"From the Long Island ... or from Uist . . . or maybe from Benbecula?"

"No."

"Oh well, sure it is no matter to me. But may I be asking your name?"

"Macallum."

"Do you know there is a death here, Macallum?"

"If I didn't, I would know it now, because of what lies yonder."

Mechanically Andrew Blair looked round. As he knew, a rough bier was there, that was made of a dead-board laid upon three milking-stools. Beside it was a *claar*, a small tub to hold potatoes. On the bier was a corpse, covered with a canvas sheeting that looked like a sail.

"He was a worthy man, my father," began the son of the dead man, slowly; "but he had his faults, like all of us. I might even be saying that he had his sins, to the Stones be it said. You will be knowing, Macallum, what is thought among the folk . . . that a stranger, passing by, may take away the sins of the dead, and that, too, without any hurt whatever . . . any hurt whatever."

"Ay, sure."

"And you will be knowing what is done?"

"Ay."

"With the bread . . . and the water . . . ?"

"Ay."

"It is a small thing to do. It is a Christian thing. I would be doing it myself, and that gladly, but the ... the ... passer-by who . . ."

"It is talking of the Sin-Eater you are?"

"Yes, yes, for sure. The Sin-Eater as he is called and a good Christian act it is, for all that the ministers and the priests make a frowning at it. The Sin-Eater must be a stranger. He must be a stranger, and should know nothing of the dead man above all, bear him no grudge."

At that Neil Ross's eyes lightened for a moment.

"And why that?"

"Who knows? I have heard this, and I have heard that. If the Sin - Eater was hating the dead man he could take the sins and fling them into the sea, and they would be changed into demons of the air that would harry the flying soul till Judgment-Day."

"And how would that thing be done?"

The man spoke with flashing eyes and parted lips, the breath coming swift. Andrew Blair looked at him suspiciously; and hesitated, before, in a cold voice, he spoke again.

"That is all folly, I am thinking, Macallum. Maybe it is all folly, the whole of it. But, see here, I have no time to be talking with you. If you will take the bread and the water you shall have a good meal if you want it, and . . . and . . . yes, look you, my man, I will be giving you a shilling too, for luck."

"I will have no meal in this house, Anndramhic-Adam; nor will I do this thing unless you will be giving me two silver half-crowns. That is the sum I must have, or no other."

"Two half-crowns! Why, man, for one half-crown ..."

"Then be eating the sins o' your father yourself, Andrew Blair! It is going I am."

"Stop, man! Stop, Macallum. See here: I will be giving you what you ask."

"So be it. Is the ... Are you ready?"

"Ay, come this way."

With that the two men turned and moved slowly towards the bier. In the doorway of the house stood a man and two women; farther in, a woman; and at the window to the left, the serving-wench, Jessie McFall, and two men of the farm. Of those in the doorway, the man was Peter, the half-witted youngest brother of Andrew Blair; the taller and older woman was Catreen, the widow of Adam, the second brother; and the thin, slight woman, with staring eyes and drooping mouth, was Muireall, the wife of Andrew. The old woman behind these was Maisie Macdonald.

Andrew Blair stooped and took a saucer out of the *claar*. This he put upon the covered breast of the corpse. He stooped again, and brought forth a thick square piece of new-made bread. That also he placed upon the breast of the corpse. Then he stooped again, and with that he emptied a spoonful of salt alongside the bread.

"I must see the corpse," said Neil Ross simply.

"It is not needful, Macallum."

"I must be seeing the corpse, I tell you and for that, too, the bread and the water should be on the naked breast."

"No, no, man; it ..." But here a voice, that of Maisie the wise woman, came upon them, saying that the man was right, and that the eating of the sins should be done in that way and no other.

With an ill grace the son of the dead man drew back the sheeting. Beneath it, the corpse was in a clean white shirt, a death-gown long ago prepared, that covered him from his neck to his feet, and left only the dusky yellowish face exposed.

While Andrew Blair unfastened the shirt and placed the saucer and the bread and the salt on the breast, the man beside him stood staring fixedly on the frozen features of the corpse. The new laird had to speak to him twice before he heard.

"I am ready. And you, now? What is it you are muttering over against the lips of the dead?"

"It is giving him a message I am. There is no harm in that, sure?"

"Keep to your own folk, Macallum. You are from the West you say, and we are from the North. There can be no messages between you and a Blair of Strathmore, no messages for you to be giving."

"He that lies here knows well the man to whom I am sending a message" and at this response Andrew Blair scowled darkly. He would fain have sent the man about his business, but he feared he might get no other.

"It is thinking I am that you are not a Macallum at all. I know all of that name in Mull, Iona, Skye, and the near isles. What will the name of your naming be, and of your father, and of his place?"

Whether he really wanted an answer, or whether he sought only to divert the man from his procrastination, his question had a satisfactory result.

"Well, now, it's ready I am, Anndra Mhic-Adam."

With that, Andrew Blair stooped once more and from the *claar* brought a small jug of water. From this he filled the saucer.

"You know what to say and what to do, Macallum."

There was not one there who did not have a shortened breath because of the mystery that was now before them, and the fearfulness of it. Neil Ross drew himself up, erect, stiff, with white, drawn face. All who waited, save Andrew Blair, thought that the moving of his lips was because of the prayer that was slipping upon them, like the last lapsing of the ebb-tide. But Blair was watching him closely, and knew that it was no prayer which stole out against the blank air that was around the dead.

Slowly Neil Ross extended his right arm. He took a pinch of the salt and put it in the saucer, then took another pinch and sprinkled it upon the bread. His hand shook for a moment as he touched the saucer. But there was no shaking as he raised it towards his lips, or when he held it before him when he spoke.

"With this water that has salt in it, and has lain on thy corpse, O Adam mhic Anndra mhic Adam Mior, I drink away all the evil that is upon thee ..."

There was throbbing silence while he paused.

"... And may it be upon me and not upon thee, if with this water it cannot flow away."

Thereupon, he raised the saucer and passed it thrice round the head of the corpse sun-ways; and, having done this, lifted it to his lips and drank as much as his mouth would hold. Thereafter he poured the remnant over his left hand, and let it trickle to the ground. Then he took the piece of bread. Thrice, too, he passed it round the head of the corpse sun-ways.

He turned and looked at the man by his side, then at the others, who watched him with beating hearts. With a loud clear voice he took the sins.

"*Thoir dhomh do ciontachd, O Adam mhic Anndra Mhic Adam Mior!* Give me thy sins to take away from thee! Lo, now, as I stand here, I break this bread that has lain on thee in corpse, and I am eating it, I am, and in that eating I take upon me the sins of thee, O man that was alive and is now white with the stillness!"

Thereupon Neil Ross broke the bread and ate of it, and took upon himself the sins of Adam Blair that was dead. It was a bitter swallowing, that. The remainder of the bread he crumbled in his hand, and threw it on the ground, and trod upon it. Andrew Blair gave a sigh of relief. His cold eyes lightened with malice.

"Be off with you, now, Macallum. We are wanting no tramps at the farm here, and perhaps you had better not be trying to get work this side of Iona; for it is known as the Sin-Eater you will be, and that won't be for the helping, I am thinking! There: there are the two half-crowns for you . . . and may they bring you no harm, you that are Scapegoat now!"

The Sin-Eater turned at that, and stared like a hill-bull. Scapegoat! Ay, that's what he was. Sin-Eater, Scapegoat! Was he not, too, another Judas, to have sold for silver that which was not for the selling? No, no, for sure Maisie Macdonald could tell him the rune that would serve for the easing of this burden. He would soon be quit of it.

Slowly he took the money, turned it over, and put it in his pocket.

"I am going, Andrew Blair," he said quietly, "I am going now. I will not say to him that is there in the silence, *A chuid do Pharas da!* nor will I say to you, *Gu'n gleidheadh Dia thu*, nor will I say to this dwelling that is the home of thee and thine, *Gu'n beannaic-headh Dia an tigh!*"

Here there was a pause. All listened. Andrew Blair shifted uneasily, the furtive eyes of him going this way and that, like a ferret in the grass.

"But, Andrew Blair, I will say this: when you fare abroad, *Droch caoidh ort!* and when you go upon the water, *Gaoth gun direadh ort!* Ay, ay, Anndra-mhic-Adam, *Dia ad aghaidh 's ad aodaun ~ agus bas dunach ort! Dhonas 's dholas ort, agus leat-sa!*"

The bitterness of these words was like snow in June upon all there. They stood amazed. None spoke. No one moved. Neil Ross turned upon his heel, and, with a bright light in his eyes, walked away from the dead and the living. He went by the byres, whence he had come. Andrew Blair remained where he was, now glooming at the corpse, now biting his nails and staring at the damp sods at his feet.

When Neil reached the end of the milk-shed he saw Maisie Macdonald there, waiting.

"These were ill sayings of yours, Neil Ross," she said in a low voice, so that she might not be overheard from the house.

"So, it is knowing me you are."

"Sheen Macarthur told me."

"I have good cause."

"That is a true word. I know it."

---

*(i) Droch caoidh ort! "May a fatal accident happen to you" (lit. " bad moan on you "). (2) Gaoth gun direadh ort ! "May you drift to your drowning " (lit. "wind without direction on you"). (3) Dia ad aghaidh, etc., "God against thee and in thy face . . . and may a death of woe be yours. . . . Evil and sorrow to thee and thine!"

"Tell me this thing. What is the rune that is said for the throwing into the sea of the sins of the dead? See here, Maisie Mac-donald. There is no money of that man that I would carry a mile with me. Here it is. It is yours, if you will tell me that rune."

Maisie took the money hesitatingly. Then, stooping, she said slowly the few lines of the old, old rune.

"Will you be remembering that?"

"It is not forgetting it I will be, Maisie."

"Wait a moment. There is some warm milk here."

With that she went, and then, from within, beckoned to him to enter.

"There is no one here, Neil Ross. Drink the milk."

He drank; and while he did so she drew a leather pouch from some hidden place in her dress.

"And now I have this to give you."

She counted out ten pennies and two farthings.

"It is all the coppers I have. You are welcome to them. Take them, friend of my friend. They will give you the food you need, and the ferry across the Sound."

"I will do that, Maisie Macdonald, and thanks to you. It is not forgetting it I will be, nor you, good woman. And now, tell me, is it safe that I am? He called me a 'scapegoat'; he, Andrew Blair! Can evil touch me between this and the sea?"

"You must go to the place where the evil was done to you and yours and that, I know, is on the west side of Iona. Go, and God preserve you. But here, too, is a *sian* that will be for the safety."

Thereupon, with swift mutterings she said this charm: an old, familiar Sian against Sudden Harm:

"*Sian a chuir Moire air Mac ort,*
Sian ro' marbhadh, sian ro' lot ort,
Sian eadar a chlioch 's a' ghlun,*
Sian nan Tri ann an aon ort,
O mhullach do chinn gu bonn do chois ort :
Sian seachd eadar a h-aon ort,
Sian seachd eadar a dha ort,
Sian seachd eadar a tri ort,

98

Sian seachd eadar a ceithir ort,

Sian seachd eadar a coig ort

Sian seachd eadar a sia ort,

Sian seachd paidir nan seach paidir dol deiseil ri diugh narach ort, ga do ghleidheadh

   bho bheud 's bho mhi-thapadh!"

Scarcely had she finished before she heard heavy steps approaching.

"Away with you," she whispered, repeating in a loud, angry tone, "Away with you! *Seachad! Seachad!*"

And with that Neil Ross slipped from the milk-shed and crossed the yard, and was behind the byres before Andrew Blair, with sullen mien and swift, wild eyes, strode from the house. It was with a grim smile on his face that Neil tramped down the wet heather till he reached the high road, and fared thence as through a marsh because of the rains there had been.

For the first mile he thought of the angry mind of the dead man, bitter at paying of the silver. For the second mile he thought of the evil that had been wrought for him and his. For the third mile he pondered over all that he had heard and done and taken upon him that day.

Then he sat down upon a broken granite heap by the way, and brooded deep till one hour went, and then another, and the third was upon him. A man driving two calves came towards him out of the west. He did not hear or see. The man stopped: spoke again. Neil gave no answer. The drover shrugged his shoulders, hesitated, and walked slowly on, often looking back.

An hour later a shepherd came by the way he himself had tramped. He was a tall, gaunt man with a squint. The small, pale-blue eyes glittered out of a mass of red hair that almost covered his face. He stood still, opposite Neil, and leaned on his *cromak*.

"*Latha math leaf*" he said at last: "I wish you good day."

Neil glanced at him, but did not speak.

"What is your name, for I seem to know you?"

But Neil had already forgotten him. The shepherd took out his snuff-mull, helped himself, and handed the mull to the lonely wayfarer. Neil mechanically helped himself.

"*Am bheil thu 'dol do Fhionphort?*" tried the shepherd again: "Are you going to Fionnaphort?"

"*Tha mise 'dot a dti I - challum - chille?*" Neil answered, in a low, weary voice, and as a man in a dream: " I am on my way to Iona."

"I am thinking I know now who you are. You are the man Macallum."

Neil looked, but did not speak. His eyes dreamed against what the other could not see or know. The shepherd called angrily to his dogs to keep the sheep from straying; then, with a resentful air, turned to his victim.

"You are a silent man for sure, you are. I'm hoping it is not the curse upon you already."

"What curse?"

"Ah, *that* has brought the wind against the mist! I was thinking so!"

"What curse?"

"You are the man that was the Sin-Eater over there?"

"Ay."

"The man Macallum?"

"Ay."

"Strange it is, but three days ago I saw you in Tobermory, and heard you give your name as Neil Ross to an Iona man that was there."

"Well?"

"Oh, sure, it is nothing to me. But they say the Sin-Eater should not be a man with a hidden lump in his pack."

"Why?"

"For the dead know, and are content. There is no shaking off any sins, then for that man."

"It is a lie."

"Maybe ay and maybe no."

"Well, have you more to be saying to me? I am obliged to you for your company, but it is not needing it I am, though no offence."

FIONNA MACLEOD ❖ THE SIN EATER

"Och, man, there's no offence between you and me. Sure, there's Iona in me, too; for the father of my father married a woman that was the granddaughter of Tomais Macdonald, who was a fisherman there. No, no; it is rather warning you I would be."

"And for what?"

"Well, well, just because of that laugh I heard about."

"What laugh?"

"The laugh of Adam Blair that is dead."

Neil Ross stared, his eyes large and wild. He leaned a little forward. No word came from him. The look that was on his face was the question.

"Yes: it was this way. Sure, the telling of it is just as I heard it. After you ate the sins of Adam Blair, the people there brought out the coffin. When they were putting him into it, he was as stiff as a sheep dead in the snow and just like that, too, with his eyes wide open. Hell, someone saw you trampling the heather down the slope that is in front of the house, and said, 'It is the Sin-Eater!' With that, Andrew Blair sneered, and said 'Ay, 'tis the scapegoat he is!' Then, after a while, he went on: 'The Sin-Eater they call him: ay, just so: and a bitter good bargain it is, too, if all's true that's thought true!' And with that he laughed, and then his wife that was behind him laughed, and then . . ."

"Well, what then?"

"Well, 'tis Himself that hears and knows if it is true! But this is the thing I was told: After that laughing there was a stillness and a dread. For all there saw that the corpse had turned its head and was looking after you as you went down the heather. Then, Neil Ross, if that be your true name, Adam Blair that was dead put up his white face against the sky, and laughed."

At this, Ross sprang to his feet with a gasping sob.

"It is a lie, that thing!" he cried, shaking his fist at the shepherd. "It is a lie!"

"It is no lie. And by the same token, Andrew Blair shrank back white and shaking, and his woman had the swoon upon her, and who knows but the corpse might have come to life again had it not been for Maisie Macdonald, the deid-watcher, who clapped a handful of salt on his eyes, and tilted the coffin so that the bottom

101

of it slid forward, and so let the whole fall flat on the ground, with Adam Blair in it sideways, and as likely as not cursing and groaning, as his wont was, for the hurt both to his old bones and his old ancient dignity."

Ross glared at the man as though the madness was upon him. Fear and horror and fierce rage swung him now this way and now that.

"What will the name of you be, shepherd?" he stuttered huskily.

"It is Eachainn Gilleasbuig I am to ourselves; and the English of that for those who have no Gaelic is Hector Gillespie; and I am Eachainn mac Ian mac Alasdair of Strath-sheean that is where Sutherland lies against Ross."

"Then take this thing and that is, the curse of the Sin-Eater! And a bitter bad thing may it be upon you and yours."

And with that Neil the Sin-Eater flung his hand up into the air, and then leaped past the shepherd, and a minute later was running through the frightened sheep, with his head low, and a white foam on his lips, and his eyes red with blood as a seal's that has the death-wound on it.

On the third day of the seventh month from that day, Aulay Macneill, coming into Balliemore of Iona from the west side of the island, said to old Ronald MacCormick, that was the father of his wife, that he had seen Neil Ross again, and that he was "absent" for though he had spoken to him, Neil would not answer, but only gloomed at him from the wet weedy rock where he sat.

The going back of the man had loosed every tongue that was in Iona. When, too, it was known that he was wrought in some terrible way, if not actually mad, the islanders whispered that it was because of the sins of Adam Blair. Seldom or never now did they speak of him by his name, but simply as "The Sin-Eater." The thing was not so rare as to cause this strangeness, nor did many (and perhaps none did) think that the sins of the dead ever might or could abide with the living who had merely done a good Christian charitable thing. But there was a reason.

Not long after Neil Ross had come again to Iona, and had settled down in the ruined roofless house on the croft of Ballyrona, just like a fox or a wild-cat, as the saying was, he was given fishing-work to do by Aulay Macneill, who lived at Ard-an-teine, at the rocky north end of the *Machar* or plain that is on the west Atlantic coast of the island.

One moonlit night, either the seventh or the ninth after the earthing of Adam Blair at his own place in the Ross, Aulay Macneill saw Neil Ross steal out of the shadow of Ballyrona and make for the sea. Macneill was there by the rocks, mending a lobster-creel. He had gone there because of the sadness. Well, when he saw the Sin-Eater, he watched.

Neil crept from rock to rock till he reached the last fang that churns the sea into yeast when the tide sucks the land just opposite. Then he called out something that Aulay Macneill could not catch. With that he springs up, and throws his arms above him.

"Then," says Aulay when he tells the tale, "it was like a ghost he was. The moonshine was on his face like the curl o' a wave. White! there is no whiteness like that of the human face. It was whiter than the foam about the skerry it was; whiter than the moon shining; whiter than well, as white as the painted letters on the black boards of the fishing-cobles. There he stood, for all that the sea was about him, the slip-slop waves leapin' wild, and the tide making, too, at that. He was shaking like a sail two points off the wind. It was then that, all of a sudden, he called in a womany, screamin' voice ⁓ 'I am throwing the sins of Adam Blair into the midst of ye, white dogs o' the sea! Drown them, tear them, drag them away out into the black deeps! Ay, ay, ay, ye dancin' wild waves, this is the third time I am doing it, and now there is none left; no, not a sin, not a sin!

"'O-hi, O-ri, dark tide o' the sea,
I am giving the sins of a dead man to thee!
By the Stones, by the Wind, by the Fire, by the Tree,
From the dead man's sins set me free, set me free!
Adam mhic Anndra mhic Adam and me,
Set us free! Set us free!'"

"Ay, sure, the Sin-Eater sang that over and over; and after the third singing he swung his arms and screamed:

"'And listen to me, black waters an' running tide,

That rune is the good rune told me by Maisie the wise,
And I am Neil the son of Silis Macallum
By the black-hearted evil man Murtagh Ross,
That was the friend of Adam mac Anndra, God against him!'"

And with that he scrambled and fell into the sea. But, as I am Aulay mac Luais and no other, he was up in a moment, an' swimmin' like a seal, and then over the rocks again, an' away back to that lonely roofless place once more, laughing wild at times, an' muttering an' whispering."

It was this tale of Aulay Macneill's that stood between Neil Ross and the isle-folk. There was something behind all that, they whispered one to another.

So it was always the Sin-Eater he was called at last. None sought him. The few children who came upon him now and again fled at his approach, or at the very sight of him. Only Aulay Macneill saw him at times, and had word of him.

After a month had gone by, all knew that the Sin-Eater was wrought to madness because of this awful thing: the burden of Adam Blair's sins would not go from him! Night and day he could hear them laughing low, it was said.

But it was the quiet madness. He went to and fro like a shadow in the grass, and almost as soundless as that, and as voiceless. More and more the name of him grew as a terror. There were few folk on that wild west coast of Iona, and these few avoided him when the word ran that he had knowledge of strange things, and converse, too, with the secrets of the sea.

One day Aulay Macneill, in his boat, but dumb with amaze and terror for him, saw him at high tide swimming on a long rolling wave right into the hollow of the Spouting Cave. In the memory of man, no one had done this and escaped one of three things: a snatching away into oblivion, a strangled death, or madness. The islanders know that there swims into the cave, at full tide, a Mar-Tarbh, a dreadful creature of the sea that some call a kelpie; only it is not a kelpie, which is like a woman, but rather is a sea-bull, offspring of the cattle that are never seen. Ill indeed for any sheep or goat, ay, or even dog or child, if any happens to be leaning over the edge of the Spouting Cave when the Mar-tarv roars: for, of a surety, it will fall in and straightway be devoured. With awe and trembling Aulay listened for the screaming of the doomed man. It was full tide, and the sea-beast would be there.

The minutes passed, and no sign. Only the hollow booming of the sea, as it moved like a baffled blind giant round the cavern-bases: only the rush and spray of the water flung up the narrow shaft high into the windy air above the cliff it penetrates.

At last he saw what looked like a mass of seaweed swirled out on the surge. It was the Sin-Eater. With a leap, Aulay was at his oars. The boat swung through the sea. Just before Neil Ross was about to sink for the second time, he caught him and dragged him into the boat.

But then, as ever after, nothing was to be got out of the Sin-Eater save a single saying: *Tha e lamhan fuar: Tha e lamhan fuar!* ~ "It has a cold, cold hand!"

The telling of this and other tales left none free upon the island to look upon the "scapegoat" save as one accursed. It was in the third month that a new phase of his madness came upon Neil Ross.

The horror of the sea and the passion for the sea came over him at the same happening. Oftentimes he would race along the shore, screaming wild names to it, now hot with hate and loathing, now as the pleading of a man with the woman of his love. And strange chants to it, too, were upon his lips. Old, old lines of forgotten runes were overheard by Aulay Macneill, and not Aulay only: lines wherein the ancient sea-name of the island, *Ioua*, that was given to it long before it was called Iona, or any other of the nine names that are said to belong to it, occurred again and again.

The flowing tide it was that wrought him thus. At the ebb he would wander across the weedy slabs or among the rocks: silent, and more like a lost duinshee than a man.

Then again after three months a change in his madness came. None knew what it was, though Aulay said that the man moaned and moaned because of the awful burden he bore. No drowning seas for the sins that could not be washed away, no grave for the live sins that would be quick till the day of the Judgment!

For weeks thereafter he disappeared. As to where he was, it is not for the knowing.

Then at last came that third day of the seventh month when, as I have said, Aulay Macneill told old Ronald MacCormick that he had seen the Sin-Eater again.

It was only a half-truth that he told, though. For, after he had seen Neil Ross upon the rock, he had followed him when he rose, and wandered back to the roofless place which he haunted now as of yore. Less wretched a shelter now it was, because of the summer that was come, though a cold, wet summer at that.

"Is that you, Neil Ross?" he had asked, as he peered into the shadows among the ruins of the house.

"That's not my name," said the Sin-Eater; and he seemed as strange then and there, as though he were a castaway from a foreign ship.

"And what will it be, then, you that are my friend, and sure knowing me as Aulay mac Luais Aulay Macneill that never grudges you bit or sup?"

"I am Judas."

"And at that word," says Aulay Macneill, when he tells the tale, "at that word the pulse in my heart was like a bat in a shut room. But after a bit I took up the talk.

"'*Indeed" I said; 'and I was not for knowing that. May I be so bold as to ask whose son, and of what place?'

"But all he said to me was,*I am Judas!"

"Well," I said, to comfort him, 'Sure, it's not such a bad name in itself, though I am knowing some which have a more home-like sound.' But no, it was no good.

"'I am Judas. And because I sold the Son of God for five pieces of silver . . .'

"But here I interrupted him and said, 'Sure, now, Neil I mean, Judas it was eight times five.' Yet the simpleness of his sorrow prevailed, and I listened with the wet in my eyes.

"'I am Judas. And because I sold the Son of God for five silver shillings, He laid upon me all the nameless black sins of the world. And that is why I am bearing them till the Day of Days.'"

And this was the end of the Sin-Eater; for I will not tell the long story of Aulay Macneill, that gets longer and longer every winter: but only the unchanging close of it. I will tell it in the words of Aulay.

"A bitter, wild day it was, that day I saw him to see him no more. It was late. The sea was red with the flamin' light that burned up the air betwixt Iona and all that is west of West. I was on the shore, looking at the sea. The big green waves came in like the chariots in the Holy Book. Well, it was on the black shoulder of one of them, just short of the ton o' foam that swept above it, that I saw a spar surgin' by.

"'What is that?' I said to myself. And the reason of my wondering was this: I saw that a smaller spar was swung across it. And while I was watching that thing another great billow came in with a roar, and hurled the double spar back, and not so far from me but I might have gripped it. But who would have gripped that thing if he were for seeing what I saw?

"It is Himself knows that what I say is a true thing.

"On that spar was Neil Ross, the Sin-Eater. Naked he was as the day he was born. And he was lashed, too, ay, sure, he was lashed to it by ropes round and round his legs and his waist and his left arm. It was the Cross he was on. I saw that thing with the fear upon me. Ah, poor drifting wreck that he was! Judas on the Cross: It was his eric!

"But even as I watched, shaking in my limbs, I saw that there was life in him still. The lips were moving, and his right arm was ever for swinging this way and that. 'Twas like an oar, working him off a lee shore: ay, that was what I thought.

"Then, all at once, he caught sight of me. Well he knew me, poor man, that has his share of heaven now, I am thinking!

"He waved, and called, but the hearing could not be, because of a big surge o' water that came tumbling down upon him. In the stroke of an oar he was swept close by the rocks where I was standing. In that flounderin', seethin' whirlpool I saw the white face of him for a moment, an' as he went out on the re-surge like a hauled net, I heard these words fallin' against my ears, '*An eirig wtanama* ... In ransom for my soul! ' "And with that I saw the double-spar turn over and slide down the back-sweep of a drowning big wave. Ay, sure, it went out to the deep sea swift enough then. It was in the big eddy that rushes between Skerry-Mor and Skerry-Beag. I did not see it again no, not for the quarter of an hour, I am thinking. Then I sawjust the whirling top of it rising out of the flying yeast of a great, black-blustering wave, that was rushing northward before the current that is called the Black-Eddy. With that you have the end of Neil Ross ay, sure, him that was called the Sin-Eater. And that is a true thing; and may God save us the sorrow of sorrows.

"And that is all."

THE UNBROKEN CHAIN

IRVIN S. COBB

WE KNOW LOVECRAFT WAS FAMILIAR with the work of popular writer Irvin S. Cobb. The latter's "Fishhead" was manifestly an influence upon HPL's "The Shadow over Innsmouth." Another rare tale of Cobb's is "The Unbroken Chain" (*Cosmopolitan*, September, 1923). It came into my hands through the strenuous detective work of Cobb specialist Remington Guy (whom I hereby thank with a great thanksgiving!). This one seems to have caught Lovecraft's three-lobed burning eye, too, and it is not hard to see the story's similarity to Lovecraftian tales including "The Facts in the Case of the Late Arthur Jermyn and his Family" and "Medusa's Coil." In the latter, the terrible revelation, explaining all the rest of the eldritch horrors, is the mere fact of Marceline's African ancestry! The same punch-line, in a manner reminiscent of the allegorical miscegenation of Innsmouth, meets us in "Arthur Jermyn" transformed into actual *prehuman* African ancestry. Naturally, for Lovecraft, an old-time racist "gentleman," being an African Negro and a prehuman were the same thing. Lovecraft had written "Arthur Jermyn" three years before "The Unbroken Chain" was published, and we may speculate that Cobb's story attracted HPL's attention because of the similarity to his own, slightly earlier, tale.

S.T. Joshi has suggested that Cobb's "The Unbroken Chain" contributed thematic content to Lovecraft's "The Rats in the Walls," too, since it features a recluse cut off from his Southern (Dixie) roots, having been reared and educated in the North among family business interests (like Lovecraft's Delapore). More importantly, Cobb's Mr. Brissot, who bears a trace of the African racial "contagion," reveals it by reverting to type in a moment of stress, even as de la Poer does in "The Rats in the Walls." I am willing to accept Joshi's judgment. It does look like one of many instances where Lovecraft incorporated somewone else's minor point or theme as one ingredient in the mulligan stew of a more complex story. For me, what clinches the theory is that Cobb early on describes the relevant Africans as having filed their teeth to a point, implying they are *cannibals*—just like the ancestors of the Delapores!

On a very different note, no reader will fail to derive an indignant chuckle at the understated irony of Cobb's descripton of his pious Christian slave-shipper,

Captain Hosea Plummer, victim of oblivious hypocrisy. Lest anyone dismiss this as unfair caricature, I include an excerpt from a book of sermons (*New Testament Holiness*) by Weslyan evangelist Thomas Cook:

> The Rev. John Newton, the author of some of the most valuable hymns in the English language, was once, as is well-known, a slave-trader on the coast of Africa. After his conversion his moral stupor was such that he saw no necessity for abandoning his diabolical trade. On his last voyage to the African coast for cargo, he said, he 'experienced sweeter and more frequent hours of Divine communion than he had ever known before.' He wrote again of his infamous occupation: 'No other employment affords greater advantages for promoting the life of God in the soul, especially to one who has command of a ship.' This is the testimony of a slave-dealer. Yet the piety of John Newton at the time was scarcely less questionable than that of St. Paul. His moral sense had not been educated to see the exceptional depravity of the course he was pursuing.
>
> The Bible itself speaks of conscience as being seared, blunted, and blinded... In Newton's case it was drugged, so as to give out delirious judgment. He had written several hymns for Christian worship which the Church sings today before he found out the depth of the moral abyss in which his moral nature was rotting. But when the awakening did come, he vaulted from the extreme of moral stupor to the extreme of moral hysteria. (pp. 147-148)

§)(ℛ

IN THE YEAR 1819 a string of twenty-one black slaves was passing along an African game trail bound for Mombassa. In this connection the word *string* advisedly is used. These twenty-one blacks were hitched in a tether, one after another, like a mess of fish on a stringer. Only, in the case of the fish the cord would have been threaded through the gills; this lot were yoked together.

They were chained, neck by neck. Each one of them wore an iron collar, clamped on. A four-foot length of iron chain, springing from this collar in front, teamed him with the fellow going before him; a similar chain joined him fast to the slave following next in order. This left his legs free for the march and his hands for carrying a burden – if one were given him to carry – or for scratching himself or for beating himself on the breast in lamentation for his captivity; yet in all respects held him well secured.

If there were any places of favor, they belonged to the pair who traveled at the far ends of the leash. The file leader had no chain dragging under his chin but only a chain at his back. The one at the extreme rear likewise had to support just half the burden of metal which each of the nineteen intermediates bore.

The gang lived and ate and slept in their chain. At nighttime they lay down in a ring, their feet pointing to a common focus where a fire burned to keep off the leopards and the lions. By day they moved along to the accompaniment of a constant grating and clanking, each using his free hand, if he had one, to ease the pressure of the neck ring upon the base of his throat or where its rivets irked the top joinings of his chain behind. They were naked excepting for monkey skin breech clouts.

They were all adult males and therefore, in the eyes of their present proprietors, rather more to be prized than the run of a mixed assortment would have been. They were members of a tribe living well back in the country, in the foothills of the mountains; their tribal mark was the filing of their upper front teeth to sharp points. They had been taken in a night raid of the valorous Massai. Formerly they would have been massacred on the spot by the light of the blazing huts or reserved for sacrificial torture on the return of the victors to their village. But lately the Massai had found a more profitable if less congenial way of disposing of all able-bodied prisoners.

Now they bound them and brought them out to a place called Kilwa and lodged them in a barracoon. To this place the Arabs came up from the sea – and once in a while the Portuguese – and these exporters bargained with the Massai for their human spoils and carried them away. On this side of Africa the trade had not attained the proportions which made the trade on the Guinea Coast so enormously profitable. Indeed, on the Indian Ocean the traffic never amounted to a fifth of what it did where the Congo ran down to the Atlantic; but at this time it was growing fast – thanks to a steadily rising market and a steady demand for prime and prize offerings in a certain part of the world, notably Persia and Turkey in the East, and Cuba, Brazil and the more southerly states of the new North American republic on the other side of the world.

This especial group of slaves was in herd to six Arabs who bore weapons for defense and heavy hippo-pelt whips for disciplining their purchases. If the subchief who strode on ahead to set the pace wished to halt the procession, he cut backward at the nearest pair of bare legs; if his squad thought to stimulate the troop to brisker speed, they made general play with their lashes on the limbs and bodies most convenient to them. Thus it was that without words the commands and desires of the owners were made manifest to – and obeyed by – the newly bought. In any tongue, or lacking any, a rawhide speaks a parable which the dullest wit may comprehend.

On a morning when the Arabs and their yoked commodities still were ten days from salt water, an adventure and a disaster befell the little caravan. On this day they were moving east by south across a high plateau. We who have never been there are accustomed to think of interior Africa as one great jungle, dark, miasmic, knotted with poisonous tropic growths. But here stretched a vast upland plain lying some thousands of feet above sea level. It was clothed with a rich pasturage through which game trails crossed and crisscrossed like the wrinkles in the palm of a washwoman's hand. It was packed with fine trees in an effect of studied and ordained landscaping. It was fairly well watered, and it literally rippled with game both great and small. Wild animals – and not so very wild, either, some of them – abounded in a plentitude which those of us who know only the temperate zones are accustomed to associate with our idea of insect life in midsummer, but not with four-legged or with two-legged creatures. Where the antelope and zebra fed they filled the scope of the eye, multiplying themselves by thousands and uncountable thousands. When, taking panic from some real or fancied dangers they fled to other grazing grounds, they streaked away interminably in a suggestion of driven rain slanting across the earth; and the noise of their hoofs made suitable thunder for the living storm-burst that they were.

At a point where the herbage grew rank and high a bull rhino charged the travelers. There were no elephants in this part; here the rhino was the largest of all the brutes as, indeed, next only to the

112

elephant, he is the largest quadruped to be found anywhere in the world and, for his bulk and his swiftness and his malignant disposition, almost the most dreaded and the most dreadful. He may stand six feet and more at the shoulder, may, in the instance of a full-grown male specimen, weigh up to six thousand pounds – the strength of a three ton truck, the sheathing of an enormous tank, the power and speed of a runaway switch engine; and with all this, the snout of a unicorn, the eyes of a mole, the brain of a very stupid boar pig, but a scent and a hearing as keen as any and keener than most, and as quick on his feet, to check and to pivot, as a toe dancer.

The rhino which assailed the passing file was as big as they grew and as mean natured. Probably the sound made by the convoy as it drew near him – the *pat-pat* of naked feet padding upon the hard trodden path, the clangor of all that jouncing metal ware, perhaps the crack of a well aimed whiplash as the agonized screech of its mark as his flesh flinched and wealed under the stroke – was an irritation to him. From Cummings and Speke on down to this present time the game hunters have told us that about the sulky bull rhino you can never be sure. He may take it into his horned and leathery head to run away from a single stalker, or in a sudden fit of purblind rage may elect to attack a whole *safari*. But whatsoever he takes it into his head to do, that he does, bulging straight ahead at a gait which is incredibly fast for a thing so lumbersome and, while at rest, apparently so awkward. Forward on he rushes, an irresistible, crushing, ripping, rending projectile; vicious, fearless, devilish; seeming more a machine than a mammal, more the spectacle of a monstrous wound-up mechanism than an affair of blood and bones.

It was so with this particular rhino which on this particular bygone time charged down upon the slave squad. He heaved himself up into sight from a trampled wallow some two hundred yards distant, at the left-hand side of the trail, just as these invaders on the privacy of his bedchamber were abreast of him. He squealed once or twice, sniffed at the taint in the air, and then, lowering his front until the slobbery lower lip almost touched the earth, he came at right angles thundering down upon the travelers, uttering sharp, furious snorts that were like the blasts of a steam whistle as he came.

For the Arabs the tooted danger signal was ample. They scattered, leaping spraddle-legged into the high grass and making for some trees which rose near-by. From personal experience and from hearsay they knew that, once they cleared out of the direct way of the brute, he probably would not swerve to pursue a single fugitive unless possibly the wind, blowing from one of them to him, informed his nose of what his poor eyes could not tell him. Even so, they veered off frantically toward the trees with intent to climb them.

Brief as the time was, the slaves likewise had full warning of what was upon them. All in a frenzied half-minute or so they did many futile, purposeless things. They gibbered and shrieked, they fought against their fetters, they dragged the line out to its full length, trying all of them, to flee from the point of greatest peril; they huddled in together next, tangling themselves in the chains, then once more swung away from the common center, so that for an instant there presented this tragic grotesquerie – it was like a figment from a nightmare - of ten joined black shapes straining to move in one direction and ten more striving to move in the opposite direction; but each batch by its own crazed efforts, defeating the intent of the other; and in between, as the connecting link for this foolish and antic tug-of-war, a dancing and dangling puppet figure of a black man, his head half twisted off his shoulders, his distorted body writhing and shrinking, his toes lifted bodily off the earth, his eyes bulging from his skull as he glared full-faced upon the misshapen deadly mass which bore him down.

The rhino struck this fairest of all possible targets a perfect bulls-eye, impaling it on the longer of his two horns. For an instant the Arabs, looking back from among the tree trunks, beheld an even more fantastical japery than the one of a moment before. In the middle space of their vision they saw the armed prow of the beast, with the spitted wretch held high up on the great head which now was upraised; and from this clumped apex there stretched out to right and left a slanted, rigid, V-formation – a prong forty feet long from tip to tip, formed on either plane of naked forms, ten this side and ten that regularly spaced apart, the necks lengthened inordinately, the heads aiming all the same way, the poised, taut

114

bodies pulled straight out behind, the arms set and trailing aft, the legs drawn back horizontally and kept so by the might which had lifted and now carried them forward – for all the world like a flock of black geese in ordered geometric flight along the banks of a swift craft that had shoved her bow into their alignment.

For the briefest of timable spaces this triangled phenomenon endured. Then the hurtling wedge lost shape, flapped down, folded in on itself and collapsed in the grass when the rhino, freeing his head of that which cumbered it, whirled about to slash and trample the confused litter underfoot and then was gone from sight, puffing out the last of his vented spleen as he vanished.

Cautiously the dispersed Arabs tracked back to the trail. The damage to them in property values was greater than they feared it would be. Indeed, the loss well-nigh was a total loss. The middle slave practically was in bits; his breast was little more than a great hole, and where the gross brute, turning back, had side-swiped at him, the flesh was sheared away from his ribs like fillets from a dressed cod; some such casualty as this they had expected, naturally. But from this chief victim's chainmates they found the life gone, also. No hangman's noose ever had cracked a single spine more expeditiously than those iron necklets under that terrific jolt had cracked the spines of the hapless bondsmen. Broken-necked, they lay in the coil of their own heaped bodies.

At first look it seemed the entire twenty-one were jarred dead. But as it turned out there was an item for possible reclamation. A slave whose station had been at the extreme rear of the string was found to be breathing. His chest was battered and his chin torn and his shoulders were all roweled by the tough grass blades through which he had been ploughed and dragged; but his neck lay straight in his collar band, not twisted about as were the necks of the twenty; and soon he groaned and moved and threshed with his body.

His escape from the common fate might easily be accounted for. By virtue of his having been at the tail end of the tether, the colliding jerk that had killed the rest had come to him from one way only – from in front; also, in the instant following the impact, there had been no pendant weight of dragged forms behind to help snap his vertebrae for him. Moreover, just before the rhino struck, he

115

either had the wit to seize the chain in his two hands and hold it fast, with a few precious inches of slack between him and his grip, or else involuntarily he had done this. At any rate, it had been his salvation; his fingers still were cramped in the links. Under prodding, he presently sat up.

He hardly seemed worth saving, though. He was idiotic from fright. He continued to tug at his coupling, trying to drag himself farther from the dead pile which anchored him. In his blubbering, bubbly speech repeatedly he shrieked out words which the Arabs took to be his name for a bull rhinoceros. Nonetheless, they elected to take him along with them; better a scrap of salvage from the calamity than none at all.

By a species of butcher's work which need not here be described, but it was done with knives and spear blades, they redeemed their hampered ironmongery and they lashed the jarred imbecile to his feet and resumed the interrupted trek, going now seven all told where before there had been twenty-seven. Since they traveled light they also traveled fast. That night they overtook at its camping place a larger convoy under command of their sheik and accompanied by a Portuguese factor. Having told their story they incorporated their remaining chattel with the main stock and drove him on down to Mombasa. There a dhow took him and his new companions aboard and carried them to an appointed rendezvous off-shore. Being young and able-bodied and in good case, save for his abiding fright, he was bartered at current rates to a lanky Yankee skipper who, at home in Maine, was a church deacon and a citizen walking in most mindful ways. Chained now at wrist and ankle instead of neckwise, the solitary survivor of the rhino's pettishness was stowed, with sundry hundreds of his kind, in the 'tween decks of a smart, fast, American-built clipper ship. This being done, Captain Hosea Plummer and his crew of good men and true had up the mudhook and headed away for a far distant place of entry on the soil of their own, their native land of freedom.

The Middle Voyage, as they called it then, was without mishap and with no more than the average percentage of mortality among the live freightage. Having successfully eluded the British and the American men-of-war which popularly were supposed to keep watch for such as he, the master in due time dropped anchor in a certain estuary well sheltered behind a certain island lying between Charleston and Savannah. Here he smuggled to shore his cargo – or what part of it had lived out the trip – and then, having dealt for cash with his consignees and with a fine jag of money in his pockets, went up the coast to the godly Down-East town of Portland for a period of vacation and sober thanksgiving.

For, mind you, Captain Hosea Plummer not only was a pious soul but he was a grateful one.

In the year 1920 a Mr. G. Claybourne Brissot was living the life of a gentleman in retirement near Smithtown, Long Island. He was known to be by birth a Southerner, but he spoke with scarcely a trace of a Southern accent. Judging by his speaking voice, you would have said he came from some cultured New England stock; only when he spoke rapidly or under stress did there slur into his tone a suggestion ∕ a trace, as a chemist might say – of the softening of the consonant r and the slovenly treatment of the final g. This, though, might easily be accounted for. It would appear that in his early youth he had been sent North to be educated. Up here he had been tutored; later he went through Harvard and thereafter remained in the North, living first for a while in New York City and now on this estate which he owned north of Smithtown village, on a site half a mile back from the Sound.

He seemed to have no ties in the section where he had been born. He never visited the South although his wealth, which was considerable, had been created there; and he rarely spoke of it. Nor did he make mention, ever, of any kinspeople, living or dead, that he might have down there. He did not belong to the Southern Society in New York or to any of the state societies. It was almost inevitable that as a child he must have had black playfellows or, at the least, a black nurse; but in his household staff there were no negroes whatsoever; a rather unusual thing when you remember that most transplanted Southerners like to have colored domestics around them. His valet was a Frenchman, his cook an Armenian – Mr. Brissot favored his foods spiced and well oiled – his chauffeur a second generation Italian, his head gardener a Scot, and his maidservants were usually Irish girls or Swedish.

He lived very much to himself; really, you might call him a recluse. When he traveled he traveled alone excepting that he took his valet and occasionally his chauffeur. I mean to say he had no traveling companion of his own sort. He knew Europe thoroughly and especially Southern Europe, where he had motored extensively, but of his own country all he saw was a narrow strip along the Eastern seaboard.

As a young man he had married, but it would appear that within a year or two after his marriage he and his wife, who since was dead, had separated and had thereafter lived apart. There had been one child and, according to a more or less vague hearsay, the child still lived, although the father was not known ever to have spoken of it. By one report, the child had been born with a deformity on it or a blemish of some sort and had been sent away elsewhere by the father. This was only gossip; proofs to back it were lacking.

Mr. Brissot was not a member of any club. Apparently he had no intimate, no confidante whatsoever, unless his lawyer in New York, Mr. Cyrus H. Tyree, might be termed such. The acquaintance he had with his neighbors on Long Island, many of them persons of refinement and property, was no more than a bowing acquaintance. Not one, speaking with truth, could say he was a friend to this reserved and secluded gentleman. For such associates as he had he mainly preferred foreigners, and notably Frenchmen. Once in a while he had some visiting foreigner for his guest. Otherwise he did no entertaining; accepting very few invitations and extending practically none at all. Perhaps the typical educated Frenchman's tolerance, his special freedom from so many of the prejudices which bind so many of us – perhaps these appealed to him. Or perhaps his preference might be explained on the ground – since he had a French name and presumably was, on one side at least, of Latin descent – that some handed-down sentiment in his nature inclined him to seek the company of men of a Latin strain.

He loved music, being himself a fair pianist and better than a fair singer. In his singing and in his playing invariably he favored French and German and Italian music. For our native folk songs and for our more ambitious work he seemed not to care at all. As for the rest, he was a plump man of middle age and medium height, with straight, dark hair, rather sensitive features, brooding brown eyes and an aloof, almost a shrinking manner. It was as though, having a distinct personality of his own, he nevertheless strove to subdue it to hide it away from people as he hid himself away. Always he wore plain, dark, well cut garb, but always, too, he wore a bright colored necktie and on his fingers heavy jeweled rings; and these stipplings of florid color, taken with his otherwise somber garments and his tan, seemed oddly out of place.

Naturally, Mr. Brissot was an object of interest to his neighbors. People discussed him in the terms of a mild and restrained curiosity; they wondered about him; some probably built up mythical and more or less fantastic theories of their own to account for him and his ways. So there was a distinct stir of polite surprise one afternoon when he came to an amateur race meet on a private half-mile track at the Blackburn estate, which adjoined his own.

Staying at the Blackburn place at this time was Judge Martin Sylvester, who before his elevation to the Federal bench had been a member of the lower house of Congress and before that lieutenant-governor of one of the South Atlantic states. That same night, meaning by that the night following the racing, Mr. George Blackburn sat with his distinguished visitor on the terrace of the house overlooking the Sound. It was after midnight; the other members of the household had gone off to bed. The two men, both of them elderly, were having the last of a last smoke before they turned in. There befell between them one of those small silences which come sometimes when a pair of men in excellent accord with each other and reasonably well content smoke good cigars together. It was the guest who broke the spell of it.

"Blackburn," he said, "what's the greatest tragedy, almost, that our American civilization has to offer?" Without pausing, he went on, answering his own question. "I'm going to tell you what I think it is. I think that about the cruelest tragedy we've got in this country today is the man with a tincture of negro blood in his veins – the infinitesimal trace which according to our laws of consanguinity nevertheless brands him a negro – and who still has education, good taste, refinement, even may have in him sometimes the seed of genius which makes him an artist or a creator. But in our national scheme of things, North or South, there's no place for him at all.

"Life must be hell for such a man - it's bound to be. Think of it - he goes through his days despising his enforced contact with the run of his own race - the race to which we arbitrarily and, as I hold, properly, assign him - and yet denied association on equal terms with white people of his own cultural rating. Oh, yes, yes, I know you Northerners sometimes make a pretense of according him companionship of a sort, but it's only a pretense - a shadow and not the substance of the social equality for which he must crave, world without end. Mind you, I'm not arguing in favor of any other convention for treating him. I have the orthodox convictions of an orthodox Southerner - prejudices you'd call 'em, some of 'em, - but even so I can't help from seeing the pitiable side of it.

"And the most pitiable part of it is that there's nothing he can do or you and I can do, or would do, to better things for him. We've got to keep our own stock clean and undefiled if we can - got to sacrifice the exceptionable individual for the sake of ourselves and our race. One drop of black ink in a pint of clear water discolors the whole cupful - the stain goes all the way through from top to bottom. That's true in chemistry; it's true in biology; true of all creation and all procreation. And you can't get away from it. You can't buck against the everlasting laws. You're only a fool and a criminal if you try. But that don't keep you from being sorry sometimes, does it?

"I can think of just one other tragedy to equal it - a kindred tragedy, this is, and maybe it's a greater one. And that's the case of a man who, let us say, has in him only a sixteenth or a thirty-second or even a sixty-fourth degree of the negroid admixture, a man who passes for a pure Caucasian, who goes unsuspected and yet must go always with a curse hanging over him - the curse of the fear that some day, somehow, somewhere, some word from him, some involuntary spasmodic act of his, some throw-back manifestation of motive or thought that's been hiding in his breed for generation after generation, will betray his secret and utterly undo him. Call it by whatever scientific jargon or popular term you please - hereditary instinct, reversion to type, transmitted impulse, dormant primitiveness, elemental recurrence - still the haunting dread of it must be walking with him in every waking minute. It must be there always, poisoning his thoughts and warping his nature. *Ugh!*"

"Say Judge," asked Blackburn, "conceded that all you say is true – and I guess it is, every word – what on earth set you off at that unhappy tangent upon such a night as this?"

"Oh I don't know," said the Southerner. He laughed a cryptic little laugh. "The moonlight, I reckon. It's the sort of moon which Private John Allen of Mississippi liked to say we used to have down South before the War. It's set me to thinking of things I've seen and heard down in my country – distressing things mainly. Now, I remember once–" He broke off, considering his shriveled peak of cigar ash as though this were a thing immensely important.

Presently he spoke again, making his tone casual. "Blackburn, this next door neighbor of yours, this Mr. Brissot who was over here this afternoon for a little while – he interested me."

"He must have – judging by the questions you've been asking about him ever since he left. Well, there's not much I can tell you that I haven't already told you, and that's precious little; Brissot is by way of being our one small neighborhood mystery. He's a puzzle to you, I take it. Well, I'm not surprised at that – he's been a puzzle to us these last four or five years since he moved in."

"Yes," said the Judge, "he is a puzzle. Or, at any rate, I'd say he was a rarity. I only saw him for a few minutes – only talked with him a few minutes, I mean – but I've had him on my mind ever since. There were certain things about the man –" Again he left a sentence unfinished before it was well begun. For his next words he lowered his voice and before uttering them glanced behind him as though to make sure no servant was within hearing.

"Blackburn, I might as well get it off my chest. But remember what I'm going to say is said in the strictest confidence – on the square." He stressed the last word with a special intonation.

"I get you," said his host, putting the same ritualistic emphasis into his answer. "We're in Lodge; the door's locked and the Tyler on guard. But why all this secrecy?"

"Because, lacking proof, I commit an indiscretion when I even hint at what's been working inside my brain. It's the sort of thing that a man down my way doesn't dare whisper unless he's prepared, in case of a show-down, to back up his insinuation with sworn evidence or a gun or both. Even then compassion might make him hesitate. But that's enough for a preamble. I reckon we understand each other.

"Now, this Mr. Brissot – while we were being introduced I felt sort of drawn to him. Some way, in all that big crowd of fine, clever, kindly people, he seemed so terribly alone. And when you happened to mention that he also was from the South, I decided right off that at least we'd have one congenial topic to talk over together – one thing in common. But, as it turned out, we didn't. Because when I spoke of families and said I had a sister-in-law whose mother had been a Claybourne – you remember you called him by his full name in introducing us – he shied away from the subject like a galled colt that's been flicked on a raw place. And he didn't have any state pride about him, either – not a particle – and that's a blamed peculiar thing, too, in a Southerner born.

"To have been born in certain states of this union is an incident. But to have been born in certain others is, to the man who was born there, a profession. Take a man, let's say, from Ohio. Unless he happens to be a Republican candidate for President he makes no capital out of the circumstances that his parents chose to set up housekeeping in Ohio instead of Illinois or Iowa or Michigan. Ask him where he was born and he says, 'Ohio,' like that, and lets it go at that. But it's apt to be different with a man who hailed originally from Indiana or with one from California - being a Native Son is a thing for him to advertise – and to a degree the same thing applies up here in the North, to a Massachusetts man, if he came from Boston, or to a Philadelphian or to one of your old Knickerbocker line in New York.

"As for the South – well, go anywhere below Mason and Dixon's Line and see what happens. Especially you take a Virginian or a Marylander or a Kentuckian or a Louisiana man, or a Carolinian – above all, a South Carolinian. He may be modest enough in most regards but just mention his home state and he'll start bragging as though a special virtue resided in it and a special virtue in him for having had the forethought and the good taste to have been born there. He never forgets it and he's not likely to let you forget it, either. Ninety-nine times out of a hundred, family means a lot to him. Probably he had a Confederate daddy or a Revolutionary great-granddaddy that he's proud of. Or maybe an ambassador for a cousin or somebody for a great-uncle who was in Buchanan's cabinet.

"I know how it is because I'm a victim of the habit myself. I come from a stock that boasts the loudest. One of my grandfathers came from Richmond and my mother was a Charleston woman – born in one of those old houses down by the Battery, a house that has been in her family for more than a hundred years. See there – I'm beginning to take credit to myself for my forebears even while I'm describing how the other fellow behaves. It's in us – we just naturally can't get away from it.

"But your hermit friend over here next door – why, he actually flinched when I tried to talk family with him. And yet, if his name counts for anything, he's of that old Huguenot stock down there in the tidewater country who're vainer than Lucifer of their breed – vainer even, as a rule, than the rest of us are. Funny – very funny! It's as though he had something to conceal, as if – well, what would you say about it yourself?"

"But surely just because of that you wouldn't suspect the – the other thing?" said Blackburn. "The man is sallow, I admit – dark-skinned, in fact, but –"

"That has nothing to do with it," said Judge Sylvester. "In my time I've known a hundred men of the so-called Nordic strain – clean-bred Anglo-Saxon or straight Celtic – who were darker by ten shades than he is. I'm right smart of a brunette myself, if it comes to that, or anyhow I used to be before my hair turned white. And his fingernails would pass muster – I looked closely at them, and the little half-moons at their bases as yours are or mine – no suggestion there of the tell-tale dark blush that's like a bruise. Nor any chalk, as we say, in his eye-balls; they had the right bluish-white cast. But as he turned away from me – I was studying him closely – I don't know why but I was – there suddenly came into his face as I saw it in profile a sort of – well, I won't say a cast; I don't know how to put it in words – but a something or other as if another face under the skin were fitting itself into the contour of his face, a face that – oh, thunder, I can't express it and yet I sensed it, I felt it, recognized it intuitively! I don't want to be morbid but just to satisfy my own curiosity I'd certainly like to have a look at the man stripped."

"Why stripped, of all things in the world?"

"I'll tell you why – it's the final test for the negroid smudge. Or at least that's what the people down in my country all firmly believe. I don't know what ethnologists would say about it, but we believe that if a human being has in him the smallest possible tincture of African blood it will reveal itself in a sort of stain or streak or smear right down the middle of his back. The eyes, the nails, the arches of the insteps – they may all be above suspicion; the features may be as Caucasian as George Washington's were, or Lord Byron's – but along the line of the spine, thicker and darker at the base of the column and growing fainter and lighter as the vertebrae grow smaller at the top, where the nape is, will run that faint unmistakable smear that's like the stroke of a tar brush. Like the stroke of the Tar Brush – to put it brutally!

"I repeat – I don't want to be morbid, Blackburn, but I surely would like to have at your neighbor's spine. Mind you, though, no living soul is ever to know what I've just said. Maybe I'm wrong – the Lord knows I hope I am."

But of course Judge Sylvester never had his curious wish. Two days later he finished out his visit and went back to his home near Augusta, and two weeks later, to the day, Mr. Brussot was dead at a grade-crossing of the Long Island railroad after an electric locomotive ran into his automobile.

He instantly was killed and so was his chauffer. The third occupant of the car was the famous explorer and big game hunter, Colonel Bate-Farnaro, who had licked the desert and bested the jungle, only by this ironic trick of destiny, to be smashed up while riding on a paved avenue through a modern real estate development in a suburban addition to one of Greater New York's outlying suburbs.

This noted man, who was English by birth and of mixed English and Italian ancestry, had been staying a couple of days with his friend, Mr. Brissot. The two men had known each other abroad, and when the Colonel came over here to lecture, Mr. Brissot invited him down to his place for a quiet week-end in the country before the beginning of the tour. On a Monday morning they started back for town in Brissot's closed car, bringing with them the visitor's luggage. Being mainly British, the Colonel might travel across Thibet with a tooth brush for equipment – if he had to – but by that same token could not bring himself to go Friday-to-Mondaying without taking along at least one very large, very English looking kit bag and a suitcase or so.

Where the collision occurred, one of the electrified branches of the railway bisected the highroad at acute angles. The junction for the moment was untended; the watchman was absent from his post. It was a bad time for him, as it proved, to be absent. For a high-powered locomotive was moving west at high speed, carrying a single flat with an emergency crew aboard and bound for the scene of a small freight derailment farther down the line. The engineer of the wrecker had orders to make time, and he was making it – giving his motor all the juice she would take.

Two hundred yards distant the locomotive tore out of a shallow cut into view of the crossing just as the Brissot car came up a slight elevation. The engineer did what he could, which was mighty little, seeing he could not materially check his gait in so short a distance. He sounded his whistle in warning and he shut off his power and braked down hard.

The chauffer did his best, too, but it would seem the trouble with him – a fatal trouble, as it turned out – was that in the imminent and impending face of the whizzing menace which so suddenly had come upon him, he altogether lost his head. Subsequent inquiry tended to develop the fact – or rather the theory – that first he tried to get over the track before the onrushing locomotive and then that he tried to halt his car on the nearer side and that the upshot was that he stalled his motor. Be that as it may, the outstanding circumstance was this: The automobile, at a dead stop, stood squarely straddling the rails for an appreciable period of time before the squatty locomotive, bleating in sharp staccato blasts, struck it broadside and flung it sixty feet in a scrapheap of crumpled metal and broken parts.

Mr. Brissot and Luigi, his chauffer, were both of them dead when they were picked up. The latter terribly was mutilated; he was scrodded like a fish where he had been hurled through his windshield. By some freak of physics or of fate, Colonel Bate-Farnaro had been spared his life. He had a broken leg, though, and several of his ribs were caved in. He was carried, unconscious, to a hospital in Jamaica. At first it was feared his skull might be fractured. As it proved, he was suffering from a considerable concussion of the brain; that, mainly, was what kept him unconscious so long. It was two days later when he came to his senses and a day after that before he was allowed to see visitors.

The first to see him was the late Mr. Brissot's lawyer. Mr. Cyrus Tyree came hurrying from town immediately on hearing of the lamentable thing that had happened; he had been waiting, ever since, for this opportunity to get from the injured Englishman his version of the affair. Mr. Tyree anticipated, since Colonel Bate-Farnaro was accustomed to quick danger, that the latter had kept his head and should be able to give a reasonably coherent account of what passed in those few dreadful seconds between the appearance of the wrecker and its collision with the automobile. Nor was the lawyer disappointed in this hope. But almost the first extended remark by the bandaged-up Englishman seemed profoundly to disturb the caller.

"Ever since I got my wits back I've been lying here puzzling over a most extraordinary circumstance connected with this distressing occurrence," said the invalid. "In the midst of my regret for the shocking death of my host and my reflections on my own close squeak, I've not been able to put it out of my mind. Poor dear Brissot, God rest him, always struck me as being a remarkably closed-mouthed person – not in the least given to idle talk about this and that. But why he should have been so secretive regarding his African experiences – I mean to say, why to me of all persons, he should have been so secretive – well..."

"Pardon me," interrupted Mr. Tyree in a suddenly concerned way, "did you say his African experiences?"

"Yes, yes. He had knowledge, naturally, of the years I'd spent in interior Africa. If only he'd chosen to tell me that he'd been there too we'd have had something in common, something that would have been most confoundedly interesting for both of us to talk about."

"But Mr. Brissot was never in Africa," said Mr. Tyree, still in that strained tone; "I can positively assure you of that."

"My dear sir, I can't possibly be mistaken." The Colonel spoke emphatically.

"I can only repeat that you must be mistaken," stated Mr. Tyree gravely. "My late client had traveled extensively, as you probably know. But he never visited Africa. There were reasons why of all the places in the world, he would never have gone..." He broke off and started afresh: "I give you my word of honor, Colonel, that Claybourne Brissot never in all his life set foot on African soil."

"Your pardon again, my dear fellow, but surely you are the one who is wrong. We practically are strangers; even so, I assume that as Brissot's solicitor and presumably as his friend, you enjoyed his confidence?"

"I did to a greater extent than any living being did."

"Well then, in that case, there was a chapter in his life he could not have told you of. I may be a bit knocked about but, in view of past experiences I myself have had, there are certain matters regarding which I could not possibly be deceived. Why, from my recollection of that horrid disaster on Monday there stands out above all the rest of the details a certain phase of it which absolutely convinced me of this: Brissot, at some time or another, must have had intimate acquaintance with African wildlife - with the language of a certain very remote tribe - with matters that one could learn only at first hand, on the spot."

Mr. Tyree bent forward. There was a curious intent look, almost a startled look, on his face.

"Colonel," he said, "would you please tell me in detail exactly what happened - with particular reference to these - these disclosures which, you say, aroused your - *hum* - suspicion?"

"There isn't much to tell. There we were, and yonder was that cursed engine coming down upon us. Here I sat, penned up in that confounded coop of a car, and alongside me was Brissot, and there, just directly in front of us, was the chauffer, who at once seemed to have gone quite mad from fright and was screaming out most horribly. You see, we all three had sufficient time for apprehending what was about to happen. In a time like that things may pass in a flash - but you see them all, and if you live through it you remember them afterwards.

"We even had opportunity for making a move to get out of the car. I don't say we could have succeeded, any of us, but at least there was an appreciable time for trying.

"No use, though! The chauffeur seemed to be entangled all in his steering wheel. And the car door on my side of the car was caught. We'd noticed that morning before we left Brissot's place that the lock was jammed and wouldn't work. On the running board upon the other side - the side from which the locomotive was coming - my luggage had been piled up and tied on after we got in. So there we were, you see, all three of us practically prisoners and quite helpless.

"Poor Brissot did his best. He seized the door handle on his side and he turned it and tried to shove his way out. But his head was all he succeeded in getting entirely out. I figure my larger kit bag - it was quite heavy, really - must have slumped down or slipped forward in some way just at that instant - possibly his sudden push at the door shifted it - for the door was forced directly back again, pinching Brissot by the throat so that he stuck fast, as though his neck were locked in a vise; and there he stayed, poor chap, like one set in a pillory, unable to move either way and directly facing his doom till the blow came.

"I recall the entire thing very clearly, even though it all happened in much less time than I require now to tell you of it. It was as though I had one eye for Brissot's hideous plight and one for the chauffeur's state and an extra one for watching that engine approach and for calculating, by its speed, how long it would be before we were struck. Somehow my interest in myself was semi-detached, as you might say - I'd made up my mind already that I, for one, had no earthly chance to escape. I've noticed the same thing before in emergencies that might be called comparable to this one.

"And it was just then, at that precise moment, while poor Brissot's head was held so tightly, that he cried out the words which made me know he had been where, in my time, I have been – away up theinterior, well on toward the Uganda district. As he uttered them I too, in spite of all else, was struck by the same paralleling fact which, through some abnormal, spasmodic trick of memory, must have driven itself then and there right into his brain. It was a curious freak; probably one of these psychological sharps could explain it. I can't. I only know that I also was impressed, even in the one brief instant and under these circumstances, by the graphic resemblance which that locomotive, rushing straight at us, snorting and grinding and tooting, bore to a bull rhino charging as the brute always does, with its head down and its belly hugging the earth."

"Do you actually mean to say he called out the word *rhinoceros?*"

"Yes and no; the thing was more remarkable even than if he had used the English word. What he exclaimed – shrieked, rather – was a phrase of two native words. The very looks of that approaching monster must vividly have brought these words back to him now years and years perhaps after he first heard them used, no doubt under somewhat similar conditions.

"He cried out – not once but three times – *'Niama tumba! Niamba tumba!'* just so. And that is from the language of the Mbama, a tribe now almost extinct, who live beyond the country of the Masai on the inner side of our British Protectorate in what was formerly Portuguese East Africa. There are only a few of them left – the slave trade first and the white man's diseases afterwards, long ago decimated them. The words, literally translated, mean 'great animal' – and that's the Mbamas' only name for the bull rhino. Extraordinary coincidence, I call it – if one may speak in such a sense of such a thing's being coincidence."

Mr. Tyree made no answer. For a bit he sat like a man stunned by an incredible tale of an incredible manifestation.

THE RATS IN THE WALLS

H.P. LOVECRAFT

LOVECRAFT DEEMED TWO OF POE'S TALES, "Ligeia" and "The Fall of the House of Usher," as his predecessor's best. And it happens that "The Rats in the Walls," one of Lovecraft's own best (though Algernon Blackwood did not much care for it, thinking it too gory) is based on both these stories. As Lovecraft astutely observes in his *Supernatural Horror in Literature*, "The Fall of the House of Usher" "displays a linked trinity of entities at the end of a long and isolated family history - a brother, his twin sister, and their incredibly ancient house all sharing a single soul and meeting one common dissolution at the same moment." The same scenario occurs in "The Rats in the Walls," though instead of a twin sister we have Captain Norrys, who functions clearly as a substitute son for the narrator, whose boy served alongside Norrys and was lost in the war. Captain Norrys actually functions at once as surrogate son and surrogate father for the narrator, since it is Norrys who fills him in on much of the terrible lore contained in the envelope that had been passed down from father to son till it was lost. As for the identity of the house (Exham Priory), and the past it represents, with de la *Poer* and Norrys, this is made absolutely clear in the parallel between the descent of the two men into deeper and ever deeper levels of the Priory, on the one hand, and de la Poer's final descent through successively deeper levels of ancestral memory, on the other ("Anchester," of course, equals "ancestor"). Barton Levi St. Armand, in his ground-breaking *The Roots of Horror in the Fiction of H.P. Lovecraft* draws attention to a dream of Carl Jung's that parallels de la Poer's descent in astonishing detail:

"I dreamed I was in 'my home,' apparently on the first floor, in a cosy, pleasant sitting room furnished in the manner of the 18th century. I was astonished that I had never seen this room before, and began to wonder what the ground floor was like. I went downstairs and found the place was rather dark, with paneled walls and heavy furniture dating from the 16th century or even earlier. My surprise and curiosity increased. I wanted to see more of the whole structure of this house. So I went down to the cellar, where I found a door opening onto a flight of stone steps that led to a large vaulted room. The floor consisted of large slabs of stone and the walls seemed very ancient. I examined the mortar and found it was mixed with splinters of brick. Obviously the walls were of Roman origin. I became increasingly excited. In one corner, I saw an

130

iron ring on a stone slab. I pulled up the slab and saw yet another narrow flight of steps leading to a kind of cave, which seemed to be a prehistoric tomb, containing two skulls, some bones, and broken shards of pottery. Then I woke up" (*Man and his Symbols*, 56, cited in St. Armand, 15).

Here Jung had his first glimpse of the multi-leveled human psyche, conscious ("inhabited") levels giving way to subconscious and finally unconscious, collective layers, shared with the race. As St. Armand shows, Lovecraft's strikingly similar descent sequence is a perfect commentary on Jung's interpretation, as well as a perfect dramatization of it. De la Poer descends into, and past, his own selfhood. The very convergence of images between Jung's dream and Lovecraft's story corroborates Jung's belief that on the deepest level of human consciousness dwell a set of archetypes that resurface throughout the race, spontaneously, again and again.

ଔ)ଔ

On 16 July 1923, I moved into Exham Priory after the last workman had finished his labours. The restoration had been a stupendous task, for little had remained of the deserted pile but a shell-like ruin; yet because it had been the seat of my ancestors, I let no expense deter me. The place had not been inhabited since the reign of James the First, when a tragedy of intensely hideous, though largely unexplained, nature had struck down the master, five of his children, and several servants; and driven forth under a cloud of suspicion and terror the third son, my lineal progenitor and the only survivor of the abhorred line.

With this sole heir denounced as a murderer, the estate had reverted to the crown, nor had the accused man made any attempt to exculpate himself or regain his property. Shaken by some horror greater than that of conscience or the law, and expressing only a frantic wish to exclude the ancient edifice from his sight and memory, Walter de la Poer, eleventh Baron Exham, fled to Virginia and there founded the family which by the next century had become known as Delapore.

Exham Priory had remained untenanted, though later allotted to the estates of the Norrys family and much studied because of its peculiarly composite architecture; an architecture involving Gothic towers resting on a Saxon or Romanesque substructure, whose foundation in turn was of a still earlier order or blend of orders ~ Roman, and even Druidic or native Cymric, if legends speak truly. This foundation was a very singular thing, being merged on one side with the solid limestone of the precipice from whose brink the priory overlooked a desolate valley three miles west of the village of Anchester.

Architects and antiquarians loved to examine this strange relic of forgotten centuries, but the country folk hated it. They had hated it hundreds of years before, when my ancestors lived there, and they hated it now, with the moss and mould of abandonment on it. I had not been a day in Anchester before I knew I came of an accursed house. And this week workmen have blown up Exham Priory, and are busy obliterating the traces of its foundations. The bare statistics of my ancestry I had always known, together with the fact that my first American forebear had come to the colonies under a strange cloud. Of details, however, I had been kept wholly ignorant through the policy of reticence always maintained by the Delapores. Unlike our planter neighbours, we seldom boasted of crusading ancestors or other mediaeval and Renaissance heroes; nor was any kind of tradition handed down except what may have been recorded in the sealed envelope left before the Civil War by every squire to his eldest son for posthumous opening. The glories we cherished were those achieved since the migration; the glories of a proud and honourable, if somewhat reserved and unsocial Virginia line.

During the war our fortunes were extinguished and our whole existence changed by the burning of Carfax, our home on the banks of the James. My grandfather, advanced in years, had perished in that incendiary outrage, and with him the envelope that had bound us all to the past. I can recall that fire today as I saw it then at the age of seven, with the federal soldiers shouting, the women screaming, and the negroes howling and praying. My father was in the army, defending Richmond, and after many formalities my mother and I were passed through the lines to join him.

When the war ended we all moved north, whence my mother had come; and I grew to manhood, middle age, and ultimate wealth as a stolid Yankee. Neither my father nor I ever knew what our hereditary envelope had contained, and as I merged into the greyness of Massachusetts business life I lost all interest in the mysteries which evidently lurked far back in my family tree. Had I suspected their nature, how gladly I would have left Exham Priory to its moss, bats and cobwebs!

My father died in 1904, but without any message to leave to me, or to my only child, Alfred, a motherless boy of ten. It was this boy who reversed the order of family information, for although I could give him only jesting conjectures about the past, he wrote me of some very interesting ancestral legends when the late war took him to England in 1917 as an aviation officer. Apparently the Delapores had a colourful and perhaps sinister history, for a friend of my son's, Capt. Edward Norrys of the Royal Flying Corps, dwelt near the family seat at Anchester and related some peasant superstitions which few novelists could equal for wildness and incredibility. Norrys himself, of course, did not take them so seriously; but they amused my son and made good material for his letters to me. It was this legendry which definitely turned my attention to my transatlantic heritage, and made me resolve to purchase and restore the family seat which Norrys showed to Alfred in its picturesque desertion, and offered to get for him at a surprisingly reasonable figure, since his own uncle was the present owner.

I bought Exham Priory in 1918, but was almost immediately distracted from my plans of restoration by the return of my son as a maimed invalid. During the two years that he lived I thought of nothing but his care, having even placed my business under the direction of partners.

In 1921, as I found myself bereaved and aimless, a retired manufacturer no longer young, I resolved to divert my remaining years with my new possession. Visiting Anchester in December, I was entertained by Capt. Norrys, a plump, amiable young man who had thought much of my son, and secured his assistance in gathering plans and anecdotes to guide in the coming restoration. Exham Priory itself I saw without emotion, a jumble of tottering mediaeval ruins covered with lichens and honeycombed with rooks' nests, perched perilously upon a precipice, and denuded of floors or other interior features save the stone walls of the separate towers.

As I gradually recovered the image of the edifice as it had been when my ancestors left it over three centuries before, I began to hire workmen for the reconstruction. In every case I was forced to go outside the immediate locality, for the Anchester villagers had an almost unbelievable fear and hatred of the place. The sentiment was so great that it was sometimes communicated to the outside labourers, causing numerous desertions; whilst its scope appeared to include both the priory and its ancient family.

My son had told me that he was somewhat avoided during his visits because he was a de la Poer, and I now found myself subtly ostracized for a like reason until I convinced the peasants how little I knew of my heritage. Even then they sullenly disliked me, so that I had to collect most of the village traditions through the mediation of Norrys. What the people could not forgive, perhaps, was that I had come to restore a symbol so abhorrent to them; for, rationally or not, they viewed Exham Priory as nothing less than a haunt of fiends and werewolves.

Piecing together the tales which Norrys collected for me, and supplementing them with the accounts of several savants who had studied the ruins, I deduced that Exham Priory stood on the site of a prehistoric temple; a Druidical or ante-Druidical thing which must have been contemporary with Stonehenge. That indescribable rites had been celebrated there, few doubted, and there were unpleasant tales of the transference of these rites into the Cybele worship which the Romans had introduced.

Inscriptions still visible in the sub-cellar bore such unmistakable letters as 'DIV... OPS ... MAGNA. MAT...', signs of the Magna Mater whose dark worship was once vainly forbidden to Roman citizens. Anchester had been the camp of the third Augustan legion, as many remains attest, and it was said that the temple of Cybele was splendid and thronged with worshippers who performed nameless ceremonies at the bidding of a Phrygian priest. Tales added that the fall of the old religion did not end the orgies at the temple, but that the priests lived on in the new faith without real change. Likewise was it said that the rites did not vanish with the Roman power, and that certain among the Saxons added to what remained of the temple, and gave it the essential outline it subsequently preserved, making it the centre of a cult feared through half the heptarchy. About 1000 A.D. the place is mentioned in a chronicle as being a substantial stone priory housing a strange and powerful monastic order and surrounded by extensive gardens which needed no walls to exclude a frightened populace. It was never destroyed by the Danes, though after the Norman Conquest it must have declined tremendously, since there was no impediment when Henry the Third granted the site to my ancestor, Gilbert de la Poer, First Baron Exham, in 1261.

Of my family before this date there is no evil report, but something strange must have happened then. In one chronicle there is a reference to a de la Poer as "cursed of God" in 1307, whilst village legendry had nothing but evil and frantic fear to tell of the castle that went up on the foundations of the old temple and priory. The fireside tales were of the most grisly description, all the ghastlier because of their frightened reticence and cloudy evasiveness. They represented my ancestors as a race of hereditary daemons beside whom Gilles de Retz and the Marquis de Sade would seem the veriest tyros, and hinted whisperingly at their responsibility for the occasional disappearances of villagers through several generations.

The worst characters, apparently, were the barons and their direct heirs; at least, most was whispered about these. If of healthier inclinations, it was said, an heir would early and mysteriously die to make way for another more typical scion. There seemed to be an inner cult in the family, presided over by the head of the house, and sometimes closed except to a few members. Temperament rather than ancestry was evidently the basis of this cult, for it was entered by several who married into the family. Lady Margaret Trevor from Cornwall, wife of Godfrey, the second son of the fifth baron, became a favourite bane of children all over the countryside, and the daemon heroine of a particularly horrible old ballad not yet extinct near the Welsh border. Preserved in balladry, too, though not illustrating the same point, is the hideous tale of Lady Mary de la Poer, who shortly after her marriage to the Earl of Shrewsfield was killed by him and his mother, both of the slayers being absolved and blessed by the priest to whom they confessed what they dared not repeat to the world.

These myths and ballads, typical as they were of crude superstition, repelled me greatly. Their persistence, and their application to so long a line of my ancestors, were especially annoying; whilst the imputations of monstrous habits proved unpleasantly reminiscent of the one known scandal of my immediate forebears ~ the case of my cousin, young Randolph Delapore of Carfax who went among the negroes and became a voodoo priest after he returned from the Mexican War.

I was much less disturbed by the vaguer tales of wails and howlings in the barren, windswept valley beneath the limestone cliff; of the graveyard stenches after the spring rains; of the floundering, squealing white thing on which Sir John Clave's horse had trod one night in a lonely field; and of the servant who had gone mad at what he saw in the priory in the full light of day. These things were hackneyed spectral lore, and I was at that time a pronounced sceptic. The accounts of vanished peasants were less to be dismissed, though not especially significant in view of mediaeval custom.

Prying curiosity meant death, and more than one severed head had been publicly shown on the bastions ~ now effaced ~ around Exham Priory.

A few of the tales were exceedingly picturesque, and made me wish I had learnt more of the comparative mythology in my youth. There was, for instance, the belief that a legion of bat-winged devils kept witches' sabbath each night at the priory ~ a legion whose sustenance might explain the disproportionate abundance of coarse vegetables harvested in the vast gardens. And, most vivid of all, there was the dramatic epic of the rats ~ the scampering army of obscene vermin which had burst forth from the castle three months after the tragedy that doomed it to desertion ~ the lean, filthy, ravenous army which had swept all before it and devoured fowl, cats, dogs, hogs, sheep, and even two hapless human beings before its fury was spent. Around that unforgettable rodent army a whole separate cycle of myths revolves, for it scattered among the village homes and brought curses and horrors in its train.

Such was the lore that assailed me as I pushed to completion, with an elderly obstinacy, the work of restoring my ancestral home. It must not be imagined for a moment that these tales formed my principal psychological environinent. On the other hand, I was constantly praised and encouraged by Capt. Norrys and the antiquarians who surrounded and aided me. When the task was done, over two years after its commencement, I viewed the great rooms, wainscoted walls, vaulted ceilings, mullioned windows, and broad staircases with a pride which fully compensated for the prodigious expense of the restoration.

Every attribute of the Middle Ages was cunningly reproduced and the new parts blended perfectly with the original walls and foundations. The seat of my fathers was complete, and I looked forward to redeeming at last the local fame of the line which ended in me. I could reside here permanently, and prove that a de la Poer (for I had adopted again the original spelling of the name) need not be a fiend. My comfort was perhaps augmented by the fact that, although Exham Priory was mediaevally fitted, its interior was in truth wholly new and free from old vermin and old ghosts alike.

As I have said, I moved in on 16 July 1923. My household consisted of seven servants and nine cats, of which latter species I am particularly fond. My eldest cat, "Nigger-Man", was seven years old and had come with me from my home in Bolton, Massachusetts; the others I had accumulated whilst living with Capt. Norrys' family during the restoration of the priory.

For five days our routine proceeded with the utmost placidity, my time being spent mostly in the codification of old family data. I had now obtained some very circumstantial accounts of the final tragedy and flight of Walter de la Poer, which I conceived to be the probable contents of the hereditary paper lost in the fire at Carfax. It appeared that my ancestor was accused with much reason of having killed all the other members of his household, except four servant confederates, in their sleep, about two weeks after a shocking discovery which changed his whole demeanour, but which, except by implication, he disclosed to no one save perhaps the servants who assisted him and afterwards fled beyond reach.

This deliberate slaughter, which included a father, three brothers, and two sisters, was largely condoned by the villagers, and so slackly treated by the law that its perpetrator escaped honoured, unharmed, and undisguised to Virginia; the general whispered sentiment being that he had purged the land of an immemorial curse. What discovery had prompted an act so terrible, I could scarcely even conjecture. Walter de la Poer must have known for years the sinister tales about his family, so that this material could have given him no fresh impulse. Had he, then, witnessed some appalling ancient rite, or stumbled upon some frightful and revealing symbol in the priory or its vicinity? He was reputed to have been a shy, gentle youth in England. In Virginia he seemed not so much hard or bitter as harassed and apprehensive. He was spoken of in the diary of another gentleman adventurer, Francis Harley of Bellview, as a man of unexampled justice, honour, and delicacy.

On 22 July occurred the first incident which, though lightly dismissed at the time, takes on a preternatural significance in relation to later events. It was so simple as to be almost negligible, and could not possibly have been noticed under the circumstances; for it must be recalled that since I was in a building practically fresh and new except for the walls, and surrounded by a well-balanced staff of servitors, apprehension would have been absurd despite the locality.

What I afterward remembered is merely this ~ that my old black cat, whose moods I know so well, was undoubtedly alert and anxious to an extent wholly out of keeping with his natural character. He roved from room to room, restless and disturbed, and sniffed constantly about the walls which formed part of the Gothic structure. I realize how trite this sounds ~ like the inevitable dog in the ghost story, which always growls before his master sees the sheeted figure ~ yet I cannot consistently suppress it.

The following day a servant complained of restlessness among all the cats in the house. He came to me in my study, a lofty west room on the second storey, with groined arches, black oak panelling, and a triple Gothic window overlooking the limestone cliff and desolate valley; and even as he spoke I saw the jetty form of Nigger-Man creeping along the west wall and scratching at the new panels which overlaid the ancient stone.

I told the man that there must be a singular odour or emanation from the old stonework, imperceptible to human senses, but affecting the delicate organs of cats even through the new woodwork. This I truly believed, and when the fellow suggested the presence of mice or rats, I mentioned that there had been no rats there for three hundred years, and that even the field mice of the surrounding country could hardly be found in these high walls, where they had never been known to stray. That afternoon I called on Capt. Norrys, and he assured me that it would be quite incredible for field mice to infest the priory in such a sudden and unprecedented fashion.

That night, dispensing as usual with a valet, I retired in the west tower chamber which I had chosen as my own, reached from the study by a stone staircase and short gallery ~ the former partly ancient, the latter entirely restored. This room was circular, very high, and without wainscoting, being hung with arras which I had myself chosen in London.

Seeing that Nigger-Man was with me, I shut the heavy Gothic door and retired by the light of the electric bulbs which so cleverly counterfeited candles, finally switching off the light and sinking on the carved and canopied four-poster, with the venerable cat in his accustomed place across my feet. I did not draw the curtains, but gazed out at the narrow window which I faced. There was a suspicion of aurora in the sky, and the delicate traceries of the window were pleasantly silhouetted.

At some time I must have fallen quietly asleep, for I recall a distinct sense of leaving strange dreams, when the cat started violently from his placid position. I saw him in the faint auroral glow, head strained forward, fore feet on my ankles, and hind feet stretched behind. He was looking intensely at a point on the wall somewhat west of the window, a point which to my eye had nothing to mark it, but toward which all my attention was now directed.

And as I watched, I knew that Nigger-Man was not vainly excited. Whether the arras actually moved I cannot say. I think it did, very slightly. But what I can swear to is that behind it I heard a low, distinct scurrying as of rats or mice. In a moment the cat had jumped bodily on the screening tapestry, bringing the affected section to the floor with his weight, and exposing a damp, ancient wall of stone; patched here and there by the restorers, and devoid of any trace of rodent prowlers.

Nigger-Man raced up and down the floor by this part of the wall, clawing the fallen arras and seemingly trying at times to insert a paw between the wall and the oaken floor. He found nothing, and after a time returned wearily to his place across my feet. I had not moved, but I did not sleep again that night.

140

In the morning I questioned all the servants, and found that none of them had noticed anything unusual, save that the cook remembered the actions of a cat which had rested on her windowsill. This cat had howled at some unknown hour of the night, awaking the cook in time for her to see him dart purposefully out of the open door down the stairs. I drowsed away the noontime, and in the afternoon called again on Capt. Norrys, who became exceedingly interested in what I told him. The odd incidents ～ so slight yet so curious ～ appealed to his sense of the picturesque and elicited from him a number of reminiscenses of local ghostly lore. We were genuinely perplexed at the presence of rats, and Norrys lent me some traps and Paris green, which I had the servants place in strategic localities when I returned.

I retired early, being very sleepy, but was harassed by dreams of the most horrible sort. I seemed to be looking down from an immense height upon a twilit grotto, knee-deep with filth, where a white-bearded daemon swineherd drove about with his staff a flock of fungous, flabby beasts whose appearance filled me with unutterable loathing. Then, as the swineherd paused and nodded over his task, a mighty swarm of rats rained down on the stinking abyss and fell to devouring beasts and man alike.

From this terrific vision I was abruptly awakened by the motions of Nigger-Man, who had been sleeping as usual across my feet. This time I did not have to question the source of his snarls and hisses, and of the fear which made him sink his claws into my ankle, unconscious of their effect; for on every side of the chamber the walls were alive with nauseous sound ～ the veminous slithering of ravenous, gigantic rats. There was now no aurora to show the state of the arras ～ the fallen section of which had been replaced - but I was not too frightened to switch on the light.

As the bulbs leapt into radiance I saw a hideous shaking all over the tapestry, causing the somewhat peculiar designs to execute a singular dance of death. This motion disappeared almost at once, and the sound with it. Springing out of bed, I poked at the arras with the long handle of a warming-pan that rested near, and lifted one section to see what lay beneath. There was nothing but the patched stone wall, and even the cat had lost his tense realization of abnormal presences. When I examined the circular trap that had been placed in the room, I found all of the openings sprung, though no trace remained of what had been caught and had escaped.

Further sleep was out of the question, so lighting a candle, I opened the door and went out in the gallery towards the stairs to my study, Nigger-Man following at my heels. Before we had reached the stone steps, however, the cat darted ahead of me and vanished down the ancient flight. As I descended the stairs myself, I became suddenly aware of sounds in the great room below; sounds of a nature which could not be mistaken.

The oak-panelled walls were alive with rats, scampering and milling whilst Nigger-Man was racing about with the fury of a baffled hunter. Reaching the bottom, I switched on the light, which did not this time cause the noise to subside. The rats continued their riot, stampeding with such force and distinctness that I could finally assign to their motions a definite direction. These creatures, in numbers apparently inexhaustible, were engaged in one stupendous migration from inconceivable heights to some depth conceivably or inconceivably below.

I now heard steps in the corridor, and in another moment two servants pushed open the massive door. They were searching the house for some unknown source of disturbance which had thrown all the cats into a snarling panic and caused them to plunge precipitately down several flights of stairs and squat, yowling, before the closed door to the sub-cellar. I asked them if they had heard the rats, but they replied in the negative. And when I turned to call their attention to the sounds in the panels, I realized that the noise had ceased.

With the two men, I went down to the door of the sub-cellar, but found the cats already dispersed. Later I resolved to explore the crypt below, but for the present I merely made a round of the traps.

All were sprung, yet all were tenantless. Satisfying myself that no one had heard the rats save the felines and me, I sat in my study till morning, thinking profoundly and recalling every scrap of legend I had unearthed concerning the building I inhabited. I slept some in the forenoon, leaning back in the one comfortable library chair which my mediaeval plan of furnishing could not banish. Later I telephoned to Capt. Norrys, who came over and helped me explore the sub-cellar.

Absolutely nothing untoward was found, although we could not repress a thrill at the knowledge that this vault was built by Roman hands. Every low arch and massive pillar was Roman ~ not the debased Romanesque of the bungling Saxons, but the severe and harmonious classicism of the age of the Caesars; indeed, the walls abounded with inscriptions familiar to the antiquarians who had repeatedly explored the place ~ things like "P. GETAE. PROP... TEMP... DONA..." and "L. PRAEG... VS... PONTIFI... ATYS..."

The reference to Atys made me shiver, for I had read Catullus and knew something of the hideous rites of the Eastern god, whose worship was so mixed with that of Cybele. Norrys and I, by the light of lanterns, tried to interpret the odd and nearly effaced designs on certain irregularly rectangular blocks of stone generally held to be altars, but could make nothing of them. We remembered that one pattern, a sort of rayed sun, was held by students to imply a non-Roman origin suggesting that these altars had merely been adopted by the Roman priests from some older and perhaps aboriginal temple on the same site. On one of these blocks were some brown stains which made me wonder. The largest, in the centre of the room, had certain features on the upper surface which indicated its connection with fire ~ probably burnt offerings.

Such were the sights in that crypt before whose door the cats howled, and where Norrys and I now determined to pass the night. Couches were brought down by the servants, who were told not to mind any nocturnal actions of the cats, and Nigger-Man was admitted as much for help as for companionship. We decided to

143

keep the great oak door ~ a modern replica with slits for ventilation ~ tightly closed; and, with this attended to, we retired with lanterns still burning to await whatever might occur.

The vault was very deep in the foundations of the priory, and undoubtedly far down on the face of the beetling limestone cliff overlooking the waste valley. That it had been the goal of the scuffling and unexplainable rats I could not doubt, though why, I could not tell. As we lay there expectantly, I found my vigil occasionally mixed with half-formed dreams from which the uneasy motions of the cat across my feet would rouse me.

These dreams were not wholesome, but horribly like the one I had had the night before. I saw again the twilit grotto, and the swineherd with his unmentionable fungous beasts wallowing in filth, and as I looked at these things they seemed nearer and more distinct ~ so distinct that I could almost observe their features. Then I did observe the flabby features of one of them ~ and awakened with such a scream that Nigger-Man started up, whilst Capt. Norrys, who had not slept, laughed considerably. Norrys might have laughed more ~ or perhaps less ~ had he known what it was that made me scream. But I did not remember myself till later. Ultimate horror often paralyses memory in a merciful way.

Norrys waked me when the phenomena began. Out of the same frightful dream I was called by his gentle shaking and his urging to listen to the cats. Indeed, there was much to listen to, for beyond the closed door at the head of the stone steps was a veritable nightmare of feline yelling and clawing, whilst Nigger-Man, unmindful of his kindred outside, was running excitedly round the bare stone walls, in which I heard the same babel of scurrying rats that had troubled me the night before.

An acute terror now rose within me, for here were anomalies which nothing normal could well explain. These rats, if not the creatures of a madness which I shared with the cats alone, must be burrowing and sliding in Roman walls I had thought to be solid limestone blocks ... unless perhaps the action of water through more than seventeen centuries had eaten winding tunnels which rodent bodies had worn clear and ample ... But even so, the spectral horror was no less; for if these were living vermin why did not Norrys hear their disgusting commotion? Why did he urge me to watch Nigger-Man and listen to the cats outside, and why did he guess wildly and vaguely at what could have aroused them?

By the time I had managed to tell him, as rationally as I could, what I thought I was hearing, my ears gave me the last fading impression of scurrying; which had retreated still downward, far underneath this deepest of sub-cellars till it seemed as if the whole cliff below were riddled with questing rats. Norrys was not as sceptical as I had anticipated, but instead seemed profoundly moved. He motioned to me to notice that the cats at the door had ceased their clamour, as if giving up the rats for lost; whilst Nigger-Man had a burst of renewed restlessness, and was clawing frantically around the bottom of the large stone altar in the centre of the room, which was nearer Norrys' couch than mine.

My fear of the unknown was at this point very great. Something astounding had occurred, and I saw that Capt. Norrys, a younger, stouter, and presumably more naturally materialistic man, was affected fully as much as myself ~ perhaps because of his lifelong and intimate familiarity with local legend. We could for the moment do nothing but watch the old black cat as he pawed with decreasing fervour at the base of the altar, occasionally looking up and mewing to me in that persuasive manner which he used when he wished me to perform some favour for him.

Norrys now took a lantern close to the altar and examined the place where Nigger-Man was pawing; silently kneeling and scraping away the lichens of the centuries which joined the massive pre-Roman block to the tessellated floor. He did not find anything, and was about to abandon his efforts when I noticed a trivial circumstance which made me shudder, even though it implied nothing more than I had already imagined.

145

I told him of it, and we both looked at its almost imperceptible manifestation with the fixedness of fascinated discovery and acknowledgment. It was only this – that the flame of the lantern set down near the altar was slightly but certainly flickering from a draught of air which it had not before received, and which came indubitably from the crevice between floor and altar where Norrys was scraping away the lichens.

We spent the rest of the night in the brilliantly-lighted study, nervously discussing what we should do next. The discovery that some vault deeper than the deepest known masonry of the Romans underlay this accursed pile, some vault unsuspected by the curious antiquarians of three centuries, would have been sufficient to excite us without any background of the sinister. As it was, the fascination became two-fold; and we paused in doubt whether to abandon our search and quit the priory forever in superstitious caution, or to gratify our sense of adventure and brave whatever horrors might await us in the unknown depths.

By morning we had compromised, and decided to go to London to gather a group of archaeologists and scientific men fit to cope with the mystery. It should be mentioned that before leaving the sub-cellar we had vainly tried to move the central altar which we now recognized as the gate to a new pit of nameless fear. What secret would open the gate, wiser men than we would have to find.

During many days in London Capt. Norrys and I presented our facts, conjectures, and legendary anecdotes to five eminent authorities, all men who could be trusted to respect any family disclosures which future explorations might develop. We found most of them little disposed to scoff but, instead, intensely interested and sincerely sympathetic. It is hardly necessary to name them all, but I may say that they included Sir William Brinton, whose excavations in the Troad excited most of the world in their day. As we all took the train for Anchester I felt myself poised on the brink of frightful revelations, a sensation symbolized by the air

146

of mourning among the many Americans at the unexpected death of the President on the other side of the world.

On the evening of 7 August we reached Exham Priory, where the servants assured me that nothing unusual had occurred. The cats, even old Nigger-Man, had been perfectly placid, and not a trap in the house had been sprung. We were to begin exploring on the following day, awaiting which I assigned well-appointed rooms to all my guests.

I myself retired in my own tower chamber, with Nigger-Man across my feet. Sleep came quickly, but hideous dreams assailed me. There was a vision of a Roman feast like that of Trimalchio, with a horror in a covered platter. Then came that damnable, recurrent thing about the swineherd and his filthy drove in the twilit grotto. Yet when I awoke it was full daylight, with normal sounds in the house below. The rats, living or spectral, had not troubled me; and Nigger-Man was still quietly asleep. On going down, I found that the same tranquillity had prevailed elsewhere; a condition which one of the assembled savants ~ a fellow named Thornton, devoted to the psychic ~ rather absurdly laid to the fact that I had now been shown the thing which certain forces had wished to show me.

All was now ready, and at 11 A.M. our entire group of seven men, bearing powerful electric searchlights and implements of excavation, went down to the sub-cellar and bolted the door behind us. Nigger-Man was with us, for the investigators found no occasion to depise his excitability, and were indeed anxious that he be present in case of obscure rodent manifestations. We noted the Roman inscriptions and unknown altar designs only briefly, for three of the savants had already seen them, and all knew their characteristics. Prime attention was paid to the momentous central altar, and within an hour Sir William Brinton had caused it to tilt backward, balanced by some unknown species of counterweight.

There now lay revealed such a horror as would have overwhelmed us had we not been prepared. Through a nearly square opening in the tiled floor, sprawling on a flight of stone steps so prodigiously worn that it was little more than an inclined plane at the centre, was a ghastly array of human or semi-human bones. Those which retained their collocation as skeletons showed attitudes of panic fear, and over all were the marks of rodent gnawing. The skulls denoted nothing short of utter idiocy, cretinism, or primitive semi-apedom.

Above the hellishly littered steps arched a descending passage seemingly chiselled from the solid rock, and conducting a current of air. This current was not a sudden and noxious rush as from a closed vault, but a cool breeze with something of freshness in it. We did not pause long, but shiveringly began to clear a passage down the steps. It was then that Sir William, examining the hewn walls, made the odd observation that the passage, according to the direction of the strokes, must have been chiselled from beneath.

I must be very deliberate now, and choose my words. After ploughing down a few steps amidst the gnawled bones we saw that there was light ahead; not any mystic phosphorescence, but a filtered daylight which could not come except from unknown fissures in the cliff that over-looked the waste valley. That such fissures had escaped notice from outside was hardly remarkable, for not only is the valley wholly uninhabited, but the cliff is so high and beetling that only an aeronaut could study its face in detail. A few steps more, and our breaths were literally snatched from us by what we saw; so literally that Thornton, the psychic investigator, actually fainted in the arms of the dazed men who stood behind him. Norrys, his plump face utterly white and flabby, simply cried out inarticulately; whilst I think that what I did was to gasp or hiss, and cover my eyes.

The man behind me ~ the only one of the party older than I ~ croaked the hackneyed "My God!" in the most cracked voice I ever heard. Of seven cultivated men, only Sir William Brinton retained his composure, a thing the more to his credit because he led the party and must have seen the sight first.

It was a twilit grotto of enormous height, stretching away farther than any eye could see; a subterraneous world of limitless mystery and horrible suggestion. There were buildings and other architectural remains ~ in one terrified glance I saw a weird pattern of tumuli, a savage circle of monoliths, a low-domed Roman ruin, a sprawling Saxon pile, and an early English edifice of wood ~ but all these were dwarfed by the ghoulish spectacle presented by the general surface of the ground. For yards about the steps extended an insane tangle of human bones, or bones at least as human as those on the steps. Like a foamy sea they stretched, some fallen apart, but others wholly or partly articulated as skeletons; these latter invariably in postures of daemoniac frenzy, either fighting off some menace or clutching other forms with cannibal intent.

When Dr Trask, the anthropologist, stopped to classify the skulls, he found a degraded mixture which utterly baffled him. They were mostly lower than the Piltdown man in the scale of evolution, but in every case definitely human. Many were of higher grade, and a very few were the skulls of supremely and sensitively developed types. All the bones were gnawed, mostly by rats, but somewhat by others of the half-human drove. Mixed with them were many tiny bones of rats ~ fallen members of the lethal army which closed the ancient epic.

I wonder that any man among us lived and kept his sanity through that hideous day of discovery. Not Hoffmann nor Huysmans could conceive a scene more wildly incredible, more frenetically repellent, or more Gothically grotesque than the twilit grotto through which we seven staggered; each stumbling on revelation after revelation, and trying to keep for the nonce from thinking of the events which must have taken place there three hundred, or a thousand, or two thousand or ten thousand years ago. It was the antechamber of hell, and poor Thornton fainted again when Trask told him that some of the skeleton things must have descended as quadrupeds through the last twenty or more generations.

149

Horror piled on horror as we began to interpret the architectural remains. The quadruped things ~ with their occasional recruits from the biped class ~ had been kept in stone pens, out of which they must have broken in their last delirium of hunger or rat-fear. There had been great herds of them, evidently fattened on the coarse vegetables whose remains could be found as a sort of poisonous ensilage at the bottom of the huge stone bins older than Rome. I knew now why my ancestors had had such excessive gardens ~ would to heaven I could forget! The purpose of the herds I did not have to ask.

Sir William, standing with his searchlight in the Roman ruin, translated aloud the most shocking ritual I have ever known; and told of the diet of the antediluvian cult which the priests of Cybele found and mingled with their own. Norrys, used as he was to the trenches, could not walk straight when he came out of the English building. It was a butcher shop and kitchen ~ he had expected that ~ but it was too much to see familiar English implements in such a place, and to read familiar English graffiti there, some as recent as 1610. I could not go in that building ~ that building whose daemon activities were stopped only by the dagger of my ancestor Walter de la Poer.

What I did venture to enter was the low Saxon building whose oaken door had fallen, and there I found a terrible row of ten stone cells with rusty bars. Three had tenants, all skeletons of high grade, and on the bony forefinger of one I found a seal ring with my own coat-of-arms. Sir William found a vault with far older cells below the Roman chapel, but these cells were empty. Below them was a low crypt with cases of formally arranged bones, some of them bearing terrible parallel inscriptions carved in Latin, Greek, and the tongue of Phyrgia.

Meanwhile, Dr Trask had opened one of the prehistoric tumuli, and brought to light skulls which were slightly more human than a gorilla's, and which bore indescribably ideographic carvings. Through all this horror my cat stalked unperturbed. Once I saw him monstrously perched atop a mountain of bones, and wondered at the secrets that might lie behind his yellow eyes.

Having grasped to some slight degree the frightful revelations of this twilit area ~ an area so hideously foreshadowed by my recurrent dream ~ we turned to that apparently boundless depth of midnight cavern where no ray of light from the cliff could penetrate. We shall never know what sightless Stygian worlds yawn beyond the little distance we went, for it was decided that such secrets are not good for mankind. But there was plenty to engross us close at hand, for we had not gone far before the searchlights showed that accursed infinity of pits in which the rats had feasted, and whose sudden lack of replenishment had driven the ravenous rodent army first to turn on the living herds of starving things, and then to burst forth from the priory in that historic orgy of devastation which the peasants will never forget.

God! those carrion black pits of sawed, picked bones and opened skulls! Those nightmare chasms choked with the pithecanthropoid, Celtic, Roman, and English bones of countless unhallowed centuries! Some of them were full, and none can say how deep they had once been. Others were still bottomless to our searchlights, and peopled by unnamable fancies. What, I thought, of the hapless rats that stumbled into such traps amidst the blackness of their quests in this grisly Tartarus?

Once my foot slipped near a horribly yawning brink, and I had a moment of ecstatic fear. I must have been musing a long time, for I could not see any of the party but plump Capt. Norrys. Then there came a sound from that inky, boundless, farther distance that I thought I knew; and I saw my old black cat dart past me like a winged Egyptian god, straight into the illimitable gulf of the unknown. But I was not far behind, for there was no doubt after another second. It was the eldritch scurrying of those fiend-born rats, always questing for new horrors, and determined to lead me on even unto those grinning caverns of earth's centre where

151

Nyarlathotep, the mad faceless god, howls blindly in the darkness to the piping of two amorphous idiot flute-players.

My searchlight expired, but still I ran. I heard voices, and yowls, and echoes, but above all there gently rose that impious, insidious scurrying; gently rising, rising, as a stiff bloated corpse gently rises above an oily river that flows under the endless onyx bridges to a black, putrid sea.

Something bumped into me ~ something soft and plump. It must have been the rats; the viscous, gelatinous, ravenous army that feast on the dead and the living ... Why shouldn't rats eat a de la Poer as a de la Poer eats forbidden things? ... The war ate my boy, damn them all ... and the Yanks ate Carfax with flames and burnt Grandsire Delapore and the secret ... No, no, I tell you, I am not that daemon swineherd in the twilit grotto! It was not Edward Norrys' fat face on that flabby fungous thing! Who says I am a de la Poer? He lived, but my boy died! ... Shall a Norrys hold the land of a de la Poer? ... It's voodoo, I tell you ... that spotted snake ... Curse you, Thornton, I'll teach you to faint at what my family do! ... 'Sblood, thou stinkard, I'll learn ye how to gust ... wolde ye swynke me thilke wys?... Magna Mater! Magna Mater!... Atys... Dia ad aghaidh's ad aodaun... agus bas dunarch ort! Dhonas's dholas ort, agus leat-sa!... Ungl unl... rrlh ... chchch...

This is what they say I said when they found me in the blackness after three hours; found me crouching in the blackness over the plump, half-eaten body of Capt. Norrys, with my own cat leaping and tearing at my throat. Now they have blown up Exham Priory, taken my Nigger-Man away from me, and shut me into this barred room at Hanwell with fearful whispers about my heredity and experience. Thornton is in the next room, but they prevent me from talking to him. They are trying, too, to suppress most of the facts concerning the priory. When I speak of poor Norrys they accuse me of this hideous thing, but they must know that I did not do it. They must know it was the rats; the slithering scurrying rats whose scampering will never let me sleep; the daemon rats that race behind the padding in this room and beckon me down to greater horrors than I have ever known; the rats they can never hear; the rats, the rats in the walls.

SOME VERY ODD HAPPENINGS AT KIBBLESHAM MANOR HOUSE

MICHAEL HARRISON

JUST AS, AT THE LAST, ALBERT WILMARTH FOUND he had been tricked and was no longer talking with Henry Akeley, only a clever and nefarious substitution, even so one is destined to discover there is no Michael Harrison. 'Tis but the pen name of Maurice Desmond Rohan (1907-1991). This distinguished Englishman had written no fewer than seventeen novels in the two decades between 1934 and 1954. Then he began writing detective fiction, including faithful pastiches of both Sherlock Holmes and Chevalier Auguste Dupin. One reads this and thinks, "Surely he would have done a good job dipping into the Lovecraftian genre!" And he did!

One can (almost *must*) imagine Harrison reading through "The Rats in the Walls," getting to the part about the Roman-era Attis and Cybele worship, and then flipping the page back to see if he's missed something. How could Lovecraft breeze through the degraded fanaticism of the Magna Mater without more ado? Why waste it as a mere bit of atmosphere? Harrison must have reflected, "Someone ought to write a new version, pausing to linger upon the Attis cult surviving in English ruins. And it might as well be me!" The result was "Some Very Odd Happenings at Kibblesham Manor House" (which first appeared in the dimension-spanning pages of *Fantasy and Science Fiction*, April 1969).

I WAS standing at the bar of the new Marine Hotel, looking through the plate-glass picture windows at the promenade and the sea, when I saw a little old man, shriveled of face and tottery of legs, come into view. His eyes were sunk in the enormous hollows of his skeletal face, and this death's-head was framed in wispy grey hair – for he wore a long beard. Yet, for all the shocking difference in his appearance, I could not hesitate a moment in recognizing Andy, the

very Compleat Sportsman of pre-war years, and my intimate friend
for a decade or so before the coming of Hitler had disrupted so
many of our lives. I had gone into the Army; Andy into the Navy,
that "Senior Service" in which his dashing style as one of Britain's
most spectacular yachtsmen soon earned him speedy and impressive
promotion. And now, as I stared at him through the plate-glass
window of the Marine Hotel's bar, I saw a shriveled old man who,
once his startled gaze had met mine through the glass, was evidently
intent on avoiding me.

I felt, I confess, that I was taking rather an unfair advantage of my
old friend when I realized that only his inability to quicken his pace
prevented his making a determined effort to disappear before I had
time to leave the bar and catch him up in the street.

But I did catch him up in the street, and when I said, "Andy! How
wonderful seeing you again!" - like that - and put out my hand, he
returned the clasp, for all that his grin was a bit rueful. As much, I
couldn't help thinking, because he hadn't been able to escape me, as
because he knew how his appearance had shocked me.

As Englishmen of our upbringing do, we began tentatively to
probe the situation from behind our traditional defenses of banal
remarks: "What a marvelous day it is, isn't it?" "You living down
here now, Andy?" "Let's have a drink... unless you prefer some other
place?" "No... I quite like the Marine. I go there every now and
then." And so on.

But, at any rate, I got him to turn back, and to join me at a table
in a corner of the big bar, out of the direct heat of the sun. When
the waiter had brought our drinks, Andy anticipated all my
questions by saying,

"You knew that my parents died, did you? Yes, you'd have seen
that. And Verena's dead, too...."

"No," I said, pretending to see something on a table, so that I
should not have to meet his eyes. "No, I didn't know that. She... she
never got any better?"

"No," said Andy. "There's that dreadful old phrase about 'a
merciful relief.' Well, in this case - in Verena's case - it was true
enough. You could well call it a merciful relief. You could, indeed."

And, quite shockingly, he began to laugh. I looked up, and he saw what I was thinking. "No... you don't understand. When I said it was a merciful relief, I wasn't referring to Verena, poor darling. I was referring to us – to what was left of the Johnstones. Poor old Father, Mother. Me. And now there's nothing left of the Johnstones but me. And, as you see, there's precious little left of me."

"When did they die?" I asked, to show that I could take this sort of matey outspokenness, that I hadn't developed weak nerves in the years since the war. "Your people, I mean..."

"Father died just after the war, as you know. They said it was cancer. Mother died about a year later. They didn't have to think anything up. She just died. But, as you knew that already, you meant, when you said, 'When did your people die?' – 'When did Verena die?' She died when they pulled Kibblesham down. I'd got her into a very special home.... I may tell you about it, later. I may not, I don't know." He passed a shaking hand across his skeletal face, and shivered, as though with ague. "And then I sold Kibblesham."

"I'm very sorry about Verena," I said. "I would like to have seen her again."

Andy stared at me, and then – again, and even more frighteningly this time – he began to laugh.

"My God, Tim, you don't know your luck! Thank everything you pray to that you can't even *imagine* what it was you missed!"

Old friends – especially old friends of the same sex – should be able to ask questions, to ask the other to explain exactly what is meant by a half-understood remark. But I couldn't. I hadn't the courage. I didn't know what it was that I feared to know. But I was certain that, in this, as in so many other things of past days, Andy was right. Better that I should not even begin to guess what it was which had taken Verena upstairs to her bedroom – suddenly and (for all the outer world knew) inexplicably – never to leave it, save to go to what Andy had called 'a very special home.'

I remembered then the curious atmosphere surrounding the fact of Verena's illness. Juliet had gone down to Kibblesham – it was still the countryside thirty miles from London then – to meet me; we

were to join Andy and Verena, and to go to one of those Hunt Club
hops without which, so they used to say, Christmas , my dear fellow,
wouldn't be complete.

But when I got down to Kibblesham by the 6 P.M. train from
Paddington, I found that we were to go to the dance one short.
Verena was in her room, had been confined to her room for several
days past, and wouldn't, on any account, let either of us up to wish
her a Happy Christmas and say how sorry we were that she would
have to miss the dance. Verena, a tall, horsy blonde, would almost
certainly have been the one to borrow the hunter from the stable,
and ride him through the dance.

"Sends you both her salaams," said Andy, briefly, "but she'd just
as soon you saw her when she's a bit better." 'Just as soon,' in our
idiom, meant, 'positively forbids you to.' We didn't see Verena that
night. We never saw Verena again.

I said, to bring the conversation back to normality,

"Who bought Kibblesham in the end?"

"A local order of nuns. Thy wanted the site for a new school."

"Oh, so some bright boy didn't get the chance of developing – as
you should have done!"

"Well, the nuns did. They put up flats and shops, and have let
them all. They built their school where the Five-acre Meadow used
to be. They've shown a good deal of business sense. Mother, as you
may remember, always used to support their convent. So, when they
approached me, I let them have it."

"You must have lost a good bit on the deal."

"If you mean by that, that I could have got more in another
market, I suppose so. But... but there were reasons why I wanted to
get rid of Kibblesham... no, not because the family had died; there
were other things, things you don't know about... and I let them
have it. Funnily, the better offer came from the Rector. His Bishop
apparently wanted to build a school, too ~ London won't be long
before it gobbles up Kibblesham, and all these far-seeing characters
buy for the eventual property rise."

"Why didn't you let the Rector have it?"

"I was going to. I was baptized and confirmed in his church, and

157

much as I admire the nuns, I'm not an R.C. In fact," said Andy, absently, frowning down on the rings he was making on the tabletop with the bottom of his glass, "I had nearly said yes, when suddenly the significance of his church's name struck me."

"St. Theobald's...? Why, what's the significance of *that?*"

"It's not Theo-balds," said Andy, impatiently. "The local pronunciation is 'Tibbles – St. *Tibbles.*"

"Well...?"

"Well," he said, sullenly and shiftily, "'Tibbles' is the same as 'Kibbles' – and 'Kibblesham' means 'the Village of Kibble.' Or 'of Tibble.' It's the same thing. You don't know what 'Kibble' means, you say?" he asked anxiously.

"Nor of 'Tibble,' if it comes down to that," I said, facetiously.

"It's nothing to laugh at," said Andy. "Waiter! Bring us another drink."

"Do you remember what Kibblesham looked like before all that rebuilding changed the look of everything?"

"Andy, I've never been back. So far as I am concerned, it's the same."

"Oh well. Then you remember how everything was. The Manor House, the Parish Church, the row of shops, the tied cottages... that sort of thing. You remember across the road from the Manor House, there was a big field ~ it was under barley, the last time I saw it – with a windbreak of enormous elms in the top left-hand corner? Yes, I know you do. And do you remember my telling you that the ploughman – it was farmer Richards' land—used to plough up colored *tesserae*... bits of a Roman tessellated pavement, and that I suggested that you and I should excavate for the Roman villa which *must* lie under Richard's land, under the road which cuts between... *cut* between... his land and ours, and supposedly, under the Manor House itself?"

"I remember. I've seen the Ordnance Survey Map of Roman Britain, since then. It's all Roman-settled country round Kibblesham. It's quite likely that there *was* a Roman villa under the Manor House. It's even possible that the Manor House is the direct descendant of the villa itself."

"Kibblesham is Roman," said Andy. "But it wasn't a villa... it was a temple. That's why I'm glad it was the nuns who bought it... to pull it down. If anyone can make the break between Kibblesham's past and Kibblesham's present, they can. I wish to God... but what's the good? Kibblesham's gone; the others have gone, and I won't be long. It's what I'm... it's what I *might* be going to be... which scares the daylights out of me. Do you really want to know what happened to Verena...?" The waiter brought the drinks. I paid, and when the man had gone, Andy said, "Look, we'll finish this up, and you can come to my place. I've got furnished rooms at the back of this place, and there's something I'd like to show you. If *I* know, there's no reason why you shouldn't." He picked up his glass and drained it in one swallow –just like the Andy of the old days. I felt my heart lift at this evidence, slender as it was, that all of my old friend had not vanished in these strange changes which had overtaken him. "Know what a *gallus* is?"

"Isn't it an old-fashioned word for what the Americans call 'suspenders,' and we call 'braces'?"

"It's a certain kind of priest," said Andy. "'Gallus.' Come on, let's go back to my place. I'm sorry I tried to avoid you. I should have known you wouldn't take the brush-off. Anyway, you're old enough a friend to hear what happened to us all at Kibblesham Manor House.

"I know you remember everything of Kibblesham. We didn't, as you know, keep up a big establishment, but I want to emphasize that there were fourteen or fifteen people coming or going about the house – I mean, beside ourselves and our guests – and never once did we have a single complaint that the house was haunted."

"*Was* it haunted?"

"Yes," said Andy. "Very haunted. Haunted in the worst possible way."

I was on extremely dangerous ground – my common sense told me that. But my curiosity, at that moment, was stronger. I simply couldn't resist asking, "What's the worst possible way in which the dead can haunt a house?"

"When they're still alive," said Andy.

Outside, an ice-cream van chimed its way along the quiet street. All the inhabitants of Worthing, on this sunny day, were by the sea. Except for the noise of the ice-cream man's chimes, dying away to a distant, elfin tinkling, a Sunday silence had fallen on the seaside town.

But inside the room, there was not only quiet, there was chill as well. I said, "We never got around to digging for that Roman villa."

"But Verena did," said Andy.

"Did she really!"

"And she found something. She thought they were a pair of Roman nutcrackers, and in a way," Andy said, with a wry, tortured grin, "that might have been one way of describing them. She cleaned them up with metal polish, and she got quite a polish on them, but in spite of that, Mother wouldn't ever touch them because 'you don't know where such things have been,' and Father because, though he'd faced practically every savage tribe in the world one way and another, he firmly believed that anything dug out of the earth which wasn't a vegetable was alive with what he called 'tetanus germs.' You couldn't have got the Governor to touch that object with a stack of five-pound notes."

"And you...?"

"I never touched them because Verena got a bit miffed that my people weren't more impressed with what she'd found, and in a huff she took them up to her room and put them in an old tea caddy in which she kept needles and cotton and that sort of thing. I was away at the time. Had I been at home, why, yes, I almost certainly would have handled them. Why not? But I didn't. Verena put them away, and not until... until later... did I see them and realize what they were."

"What were they...?"

"I'll tell you in a minute. What do you know of Cybele, the Great Mother?"

"Not much. Exotic religion, imported into Rome when – was it Hannibal? – threatened, and the oracle advised the Senate to have a word with the Idaean Mother. Doesn't Livy tell the story? The priests – here! Yes, I *do* remember! The Galloi: Gauls, because no

Roman was permitted to demean himself by becoming a priest of so outlandish a religion... screaming through the streets of Rome, gashing themselves, and dressed in women's clothing, and..."

And then I remembered why the ritual of Cybele, the Great Mother, used 'nutcrackers,' and what it was that they crushed.

"She put them into her workbox," said Andy, staring vacantly through the window, "and that night she heard the piping. You hear all sorts of noises in what they call 'the quiet of the countryside,' and all sound damned odd at night, and not a few sound damned frightening as well. But Vee was a level-headed girl, and she didn't pay too much attention to the piping, except that it kept her awake wondering what on earth it could be. She only thought she heard voices, chanting, that night – she wasn't sure, but what startled her was the dream which followed when she fell asleep at last.

"She was dancing down a street that she knew, in her dream, wasn't in Rome, but in London. The architecture was vaguely classical, but it had a homey sort of look, as though everything had been done on a fairly tight budget. It was definitely provincial, but quite grand, nevertheless. The streets were lined with dense crowds, and she was dancing with a lot of other men, all dressed as women. Only Vee wasn't dressed as a woman; she was still dressed as a man...."

"Why the change? Men dressed as women, women dressed as men...."

"Oh," said Andy, as though I'd missed a simple point. "Vee was dressed as a man because she *was* a man. *Still* a man, I mean. She was gashing her arms like the others and screaming out, 'Io! Io! Magne Mater! Mater Omnium! Mater Omnium Deorum!' – and in some odd fashion, she seemed to be something special in the procession. People looked at her differently, and some made signs as she came near. She felt she was someone – something – special, but what that was, she didn't know. So she went on slashing herself, and flinging the blood over herself and over the people standing by. She remembered that she had been at some special ceremony and was bound for another. The procession came to London Bridge and went into a temple alongside the northern entrance to the bridge. The rest was a bit shadowy, but she remembered being led down some steps to a boat, rowed by sailors, but with a single sail. There was a procession of boats up the River, until they all came to a place that she thinks must have been about where Maidenhead is now. Then there were more celebrations, and another walk, and then they were all taken in creaking bullock-carts to Kibblesham – the Settlement of Cybele. And there," said Andy, "her initiation should have ended."

"*Should* have ended...?"

"Well, poor Vee couldn't quite remember that bit... it was all in a dream, you understand...and some details were sharp and clear, and others were dim and a bit shadowy. But she got the sense that if she did something that she had to do – some tremendous obligation, a test, a ritual – something terrific would happen to her. And then, she told me, she had an overwhelming sense of having failed someone – failed that someone and failed herself. You know how fond she used to be of Tennyson? Well, she said she felt as Sir Bedivere must have felt when he found that he had failed in his duty. Like that."

"What had she failed to do...?"

"The next night," said Andy, as though I hadn't spoken, "she heard the piping again. But this time, she heard clearly the voices – the chanting she had thought she'd heard on the previous night. The words were the same as those that she'd heard in her dream. They were calling on the Great Mother... and they sounded near. Very near, indeed. It was at that point," said Andy, staring down at his great freckled hands, "that she began to change.

"Every night," he continued, "she dreamt of the *Galloi* – the priests of Cybele. Every night she expected to become one of them – and every damned night she failed to do something or other, which prevented her actually joining them. She remembered a lot – in her dream, of course – of what had happened to her earlier. She had seen other people undergo the *taurobolium* – where they used to stand under a grating, whilst a bull was killed above: a baptism of blood. She saw the crushers being used, and learned, she said, how to weave the screams into the melody that she was jangling out with her *sistrum*. But though, in her dream, she was a man, no one used the crushers on her – nor would they, she told me, until she had passed the Final Test. She couldn't tell me then what it was... and I'd no idea. Have you?"

"No. What did you mean, Andy, when you said just now that she began to change? I heard a funny story... could it possibly have come from the servants? I heard that Verena had changed her sex."

Andy shook his head. "If it had been only that!"

"Then what did change?"

"She herself."

"I don't quite understand you. She was Verena... the Verena who we both knew and liked. What did she become?"

"She became what the Chosen Ones become... she became the Great Mother Herself...."

I stared at my old friend in horror. He had talked of the 'very special home' to which Verena had gone to die – but for what 'very special home' did this lunacy to which I was now listening qualify *him*?

He stared at me, and reached down into the 'poacher's pocket' of his tweed hacking jacket.

"Know what these are?" he said, casually. He reached over, and before I knew what I had done, I had unthinkingly accepted a pair of rust-stained forceps, the arms of which were set with tiny heads, amongst which I recognized those of some Roman gods. "They're forceps used for the ritual castration – when the novice, having passed his tests, made the final renunciation of his manhood to the Great Mother. Henceforward, having lost his manhood, having sacrificed the severed parts to Cybele, he would no longer be a man. He would dress as a woman; speak as a woman; use the places reserved for women. On the Day of the Great Mother, he would come out into Rome, and all the other cities of the Empire where the Great Mother was worshiped, and down the streets he'd run and dance, gashing himself, scourging himself...."

"Why?" I wondered. "Why on earth did they do it?"

"Eh?" said Andy, as though I had asked a question whose answer was obvious. "Why, *for the rewards*, of course."

I gulped. How much of all this wild stuff that Andy was talking had a basis in fact?

Andy was mumbling now – and I had to strain my ears to catch the words.

"Great rewards, though," he muttered, "don't come to one except for having done great acts. Only a few could ever find the strength to go through with a... with the trials, I mean... and the tests... and the final renunciations...."

"The greater renunciations...?"

"Why, yes," he turned towards me, faintly astonished that I should have cared to reveal my ignorance. "Castration, transvestism, squeaky voice, self-wounding and so on... these are merely *physical* renunciations. The Great Mother, in return for the rewards that She alone could give, demanded renunciations far more important than these. Dehumanization called for a complete break with all one's past, with all one's *mores*, with all social traditions and obligations. Particularly it called for the complete severance of family ties."

"Well, yes," I said, desperately striving to introduce even the semblance of normality into our conversation, "but don't all religions call for the break with one's family?"

The Great Mother wanted something more than that the Chosen Ones should say goodbye to their family ties. She wanted something a great deal more positive. A great deal more final. Something which would *prove* the neophyte's sincerity. Something so *horrible* – so against nature – that the very act of doing it would not only prove the neophyte's sincerity, but would cut him off forever from humankind. Only then could he enter into the Goddess – become one with her. Become Her, indeed."

"Something so horrible..." I whispered. "What could be so horrible that that one would dehumanize oneself in the very act of doing it? What sin against the Holy Ghost could it be which would prevent one's ever becoming human again?"

"There's a moral in that story of Arthur's taking the sword out of the stone. The sword was for him – for him only. Yet, the moment that he got the sword, he was the King. The forceps... the forceps have the same sort of power..."

"What do you mean?" I asked, my blood running cold in panic, fear of I knew not what.

"They are the instruments of the priest, but they are, in a fashion I don't quite understand, the controller of the priest. *No one can handle them and ever be the same again.*"

I stared down in horror at the rusty object in my hands, and cast it violently from me.

"It doesn't matter now," said Andy, in a tired voice. "What you and I want doesn't matter. We are the slayers and the slain. We are the priests and the victims. We are the sacrifice and the Goddess herself. I don't know... but when I heard Father scream like that... scream, scream, *scream*... I knew that he was the very special sacrifice, and that, in using the forceps on Father, Verena was proving that she could perform the act which would cut her off from all humanity.

"I don't know whether Father ever realized what had happened. He wasn't a young man, but he was physically very strong. He said nothing... after that terrible scream. Mother was in her own room, and Father - God knows how he did it - said that he'd had a terrible nightmare when Mother came in to see what the noise was all about.

"He saw Dr. Lawrence - and you know that country doctors aren't like the modern city boys: the country doctors *still* don't talk. They fixed up a crack plastic surgeon, and repaired the damage to Father. Then, a few months later, behind a door on which the locks had been changed, Father committed suicide, without fuss, without scandal."

"How on earth did he do that?"

"He was a diabetic... I don't suppose you knew that? Well, he was. So all that he had to do was to 'forget' to take his Insulin, fall into the diabetic coma, and die. He left it to me to see that Verena was dealt with suitably... poor old Governor! What an end! To be castrated by one's own daughter... no wonder he was glad to die!"

I was swamped with the horror of the tale, whether or not it were true. If true, it passed the bounds of decent terror; if untrue, it marked the depths to which Andy's madness had plunged. But suppose that it *were* true...?

Still striving to get this insanity back on to a rational basis, if such a thing sound not too absurd, I managed to choke out: "But Verena wasn't a man. She was a woman. I thought the *Galloi* were all men...?"

"Not all," said Andy. "There were exceptions. Verena was Chosen. It didn't matter what she had been at the beginning, and in the end her original sex mattered not a bit. After she'd ceased to be human, she became what the Great Mother changed her to. That's what killed Mother. I forgot to keep Verena's door locked, and Mother walked in. I'd told her that Verena wanted no one to see her but me, but... well, you know what Mother was. She walked in, saw what was lying in Verena's bed, and collapsed. Dr. Lawrence shot her full of sedatives, and – fortunately for poor Mother – she died. That's when I decided to get Verena off to a very special home. Dr. Lawrence arranged that, too. Verena hasn't long. She might as well be where people are paid a great deal of money to have nerves of steel... it isn't every nurse who can face the sight of the Great Mother and stay even half sane. I know," he added, "because I've seen Her...

"You are trying to ask me where I stand in all this," said Andy, with a wan smile. "I'm not a Chosen One. I'm just a simple priest... a *Gallos*."

And then, for all the horror that I had known, came the most terrible experience of all.

"I must get out of these clothes," Andy said. "*She* isn't served best in this kind of clothing." And, opening a drawer, he began to take out filmy, lace-trimmed garments of silk...

That was six weeks ago. I got out of Andy's rooms somehow, and stumbled down the stairs into the blessed dust and sunlight of the Worthing back street.

The horror persisted, but, like all other human emotions, even horror dims a bit with time. After a fortnight or so, I found that I could think, without shuddering, on all that Andy had told me. I began to feel a strong impulse to revisit Kibblesham and see how

total had been the changes wrought by the nuns who had bought
the property.

There were changes. Indeed! Not merely in the land on which
Kibblesham Manor House had once stood, but in the village – now
the town – of Kibblesham itself. Kibblesham had become as faceless,
as characterless, as any other London suburb.

Where Kibblesham Manor House had stood, with its meadows
and paddocks and stabling and ponds and kitchen gardens and rose-
walks, now rose an eight-story block of flats above a four story strip
of shops with flats above.

The new convent, of mixed glass and shining concrete, stood
isolated in the midst of its asphalted playgrounds, and the noise of
children's voices came loud and clear across the open space. The
children filed into their classrooms, and I heard one nun call to
another, "Oh, Sister Francis Xavier, will you be taking the French
class this afternoon?" – and the younger nun answered, "Yes,
Mother."

Mother... but in what a different context was the word used here!
Bright, clean, airy buildings, even though designed without
imagination, were better raised where an ancient evil had once had
possession – and the nuns' innocence would keep that evil forever
at bay. The multiple stores were filled with shoppers, all making
their small and ordinary purchases. Andy's horrors... and the touch
of the rusted forceps... seemed curiously remote. I felt the terror of
the night slipping from me, as though I had been suddenly released
from the bondage of a nightmare not of this world.

The silence of a suburban lunchtime descended upon the new
Kibblesham. The shops closed, the children went in to their midday
'dinner.' Even the dogs retired for either a meal or a sleep.

I got into the car, and was about to start up, when I heard it.

I sat, frozen, trying to tell myself that what I had heard was
nothing – the wind in a television antenna (except that there was no
wind on that still day), that an errand boy was whistling (save that
there was no errand boy), that it was the song of a bird (save that,
now, there were no more trees, and no more birds to sing at
Kibblesham). I waited, remembering what Andy had said

aboutthose who even touched the forceps of the Great Mother.

I did not have to wait long. This place was consecrated to a force from which a little modern rebuilding could hardly drive it – both Andy and I had been foolish to believe that the Ancient Mysteries may be expelled from their Ancient Places.

I did not start the car. I sat in the noonday silence of Kibbleshamand waited.

The piping had begun....

CATS, RATS, AND BERTIE WOOSTER

PETER H. CANNON

PETER CANNON IS WELL KNOWN TO LOVECRAFTIANS for his wide-ranging and invariably fascinating critical articles and books on the Old Gent's work. He is a fictioneer in his own right, too. Almost all of his Lovecraftian fiction features a satirical edge, beginning with his classic "The Madness out of Time" (see my collection *The New Lovecraft Circle*) and continuing, a laugh a minute, through the stories in two collections of his tales, *Forever Azathoth* and *Scream for Jeeves*, the last being a trilogy of Lovecraftian tales starring the aristocratic twit Bertie, borrowed from P.G. Wodehouse. What is so frightening about this uncanny hybridization is the naturalness of it! How little must be changed! How close they already are to one another! The present tale, "Cats, Rats, and Bertie Wooster," comes from this collection, though it first appeared (under what is now the title of the whole trilogy) in *Dagon* # 27, 1990.

"**I** AM AFRAID, Jeeves, that we shall have to go," I said, as I nipped into the eggs and b. late one bright summer morning.

"Go, sir? Pray may I ask where to, sir?"

"To Anchester—to Exham Priory."

The telegram that Jeeves had delivered with the breakfast tray had been a lulu, a *cri de coeur* from my old friend Captain Edward "Tubby" Norrys:

I say Bertie old man help! I am stuck here in this newly restored medieval monstrosity trying to buck up this gloomy old American

169

bird progenitor of my late comrade at arms Alf Melmoth Delapore. Pop Delapore or de la Poer as he now styles himself you know how these Americans like to affect ancestral spellings Bertie has been having dreams of the queerest sort. All the cats have been acting rum as well. Come here at once and bring Jeeves. Jeeves is the only one who can get to the bottom of this mystery Bertie.—TUBBY

"What do you make of it, Jeeves?"

"Most sinister, sir."

"I know, Jeeves. Americans with sackfuls of the greenstuff to roll in tend to the eccentric. Throw in a few over-excited cats and you've got a recipe for disaster." As a rule I'm fond of the feline tribe, but in the aftermath of a certain luncheon engagement—of which more later—cats were for the moment low on my list.

"I would advocate the utmost caution in any effort to assist Captain Norrys, sir."

"But dash it all, Jeeves. Tubby and I were at school together. I suppose there's nothing for it. Telegraph the chump we're on our way, then crank up the two-seater. We leave in half-an-hour."

"Very good, sir."

I don't know if you've travelled much in the remoter reaches of the Welsh border, but that is where Jeeves and I found ourselves at dusk that evening. First the deserted streets of a forgotten village, where Jeeves spoke of the Augustan legion and the clash of arms, and all the tremendous pomp that followed the eagles; then the broad river swimming to full tide, the wide meadows, the cornfields whitening, and the deep lane winding on the slope between the hills and the water. At last we began to ascend and could see the half-shaped outlines of the hills beyond, and in the distance the glare of the furnace fire on the precipice from whose brink Exham Priory overlooked a desolate valley three miles west of the village of Anchester.

"A lonely and curious country, Jeeves," I said, casting the eye at the great and ancient wood on either side of the road. It was not a sight to put one in the mood to pull over for a loaf of bread and a jug of wine, if you know what I mean.

"In the words of Machen, sir, 'A territory all strange and unvisited, and more unknown to Englishmen than the very heart of Africa.'"

170

"Machen?"

"Arthur Machen, sir."

The name was new to me. "Pal of yours?"

"Indeed, sir, the distinguished Welsh mystic and *fantasiste* was a frequent visitor to my Aunt Purefoy's house in Caerleon-on-Usk."

A short time later we turned into a drive and the towers of the priory, formerly part of the estate of the Norrys family, hove into view. The light was dim but I could not help thinking of that morbid American poet—the chappie who went about sozzled with a raven on his shoulder, don't you know, the one who penned those immortal lines:

Tum tum tum-tum tum tum tum-tum
  By good angels tum-tum-tum
Tum tum tum tum stately palace–
  Tum-tum-tum palace–reared its head.

"Quite the stately palace, er stately home, Jeeves, what?"

"Exham Priory is known for its peculiarly composite architecture, sir. Gothic towers rest on a Saxon or Romanesque substructure, whose foundation in turn is of a still earlier order or blend of orders—Roman, and even Druidic or native Cymric, if legends speak truly. Furthermore, sir, the priory stands on the site of a prehistoric temple; a Druidical or ante-Druidical thing which must have been contemporary with Stonehenge."

"Thank you, Jeeves." It beats me where Jeeves picks up this stuff, but the man is forever improving the mind by reading books of the highest brow.

We were greeted in the front hall by Tubby, who as he waddled across the marble more than ever resembled one of those Japanese Sumo wrestlers after an especially satisfying twelve-course meal—except in this case, of course, dinner had been held up pending our arrival.

"I'm so glad you and Jeeves are finally here, Bertie. I'm afraid Pop de la Poer has been suffering from increasingly severe delusions."

"Off his onion, is he?"

"You must jolly along the old boy as best you can, Bertie. Humour him in his every whim, until Jeeves can figure out what the devil is going on."

"You can count on Bertram to rally round and display the cheerful countenance," I assured the amiable fathead, who shook in gratitude like a jelly—or more precisely a pantry full of jellies.

A servant showed me to my room, a circular chamber in the east tower, where by the light of electric bulbs which rather clumsily counterfeited candles, I changed into evening clothes. Jeeves shimmered in as invisibly as the sheeted figure of ghostly lore and, as usual, assisted with the knotting of the tie.

"Mr. de la Poer's valet has just informed me of restlessness among all the cats in the house last night, sir."

"*All* the cats? Tell me, Jeeves, just how many of the bally creatures do you suppose infest this infernal shack?"

"Nine, sir. They were seen to rove from room to room, restless and disturbed, and to sniff constantly about the walls which form part of the old Gothic structure."

The subject of cats reminded me of the recent occasion on which Sir Roderick Glossup, the nerve specialist, came to lunch at my flat. Jeeves had fixed it so that the young master had appeared an absolute loony, one of his fruitier wheezes having been to stick an overripe salmon in the bedroom by an open window. No sooner had Sir Roderick and I slipped on the nose-bags than a frightful shindy started from the next room, sounding as though all the cats in London, assisted by delegates from outlying suburbs, had got together to settle their differences once and for all. You can see why the prospect of a chorus of cats at Exham Priory did not appeal.

"When he reported the incident to his master, sir," continued Jeeves, "the man suggested that there must be some singular odour or emanation from the old stonework, imperceptible to human senses, but affecting the delicate organs of cats even through the new woodwork."

"Something smells fishy here, Jeeves," I said, still quaking from the memory of the remains I had found on the bedroom carpet after about a hundred-and-fifteen cats had finished their picnic.

"I suspect the source of this odour or emanation is a bird of an altogether feather, sir, if you will pardon my saying so. In my estimation, the evidence indicates intramural murine activity."

"Rats in the walls, eh? Well, I'll give you odds on, Jeeves, that nine cats will make short work of any vermin that dares poke its whiskers into the cheese *chez* de la Poer."

"I would not wish to hazard a wager on the outcome, sir, until we have ascertained the exact nature of this rodent manifestation."

"Speaking of the Stilton, Jeeves, it's time I legged it for the trough."

"A *bon chat, bon rat*, sir."

I went down to the dining room, where seated at the head of the table was a cove of about sixty-five, an austere New England type about whom there still seemed to cling the greyness of Massachusetts business life.

"What ho, what ho, what ho!" I said, trying to strike the genial note.

My host, who had been sipping at the soup like some small animal, suspended the spoon just long enough to murmur a reply, as if to say the arrival of a Wooster at the watering-hole was to him a matter of little concern. As I took my place at his elbow, I surmised that the old buzzard was going to prove about as garrulous as "Silent" Cal Coolidge, soon to become the American president after that other bloke would so unexpectedly cash in the poker chips. Tubby was clearly too busy shovelling the feed down the pit to hold up his end of the bright and sparkling. So, after a few crisp remarks on the weather, I turned the conversation round to ancestors. You know how Americans like to burble on about their ancestors, especially when they have any worth the price of eggs, and Pop de la Poer did not disappoint.

"Do you realise, Mr. Wooster, that the fireside tales represent the de la Poers as a race of hereditary daemons besides whom Gilles de Retz and the Marquis de Sade would seem the veriest tyros?"

"Retz and Sade," I replied with a knowing nod of the lemon. "Weren't they those two French johnnies who went sixteen rounds with no decision in '03?"

"Some of the worst characters married into the family. Lady Margaret Trevor from Cornwall, wife of Godfrey, the second son of the fifth baron, became a favourite bane of children all over the countryside, and the heroine of a particularly horrible old ballad not yet extinct near the Welsh border."

"A ballad? Not the one by chance that starts, 'There was a young lady from Dorset / Who couldn't unfasten her corset'? I forget the middle part, but it ends something like 'Whatever you do, my good man, don't force it.'"

"Preserved in balladry, too, though not illustrating the same point is the hideous tale of Mary de la Poer, who shortly after her marriage to the Earl of Shrewsfield was killed by him and his mother, both of the slayers being absolved and blessed by the priest to whom they confessed what they dared not repeat to the world."

"Frightful dragon, was she? Sounds a bit like my Aunt Agatha."

When the geezer had exhausted the subject of his ancestors—and a rum lot they were too, all cultists and murderers and health-food fanatics, if you could credit the old legends—he filled me in on present family circs.

"Mr. Wooster, I am a retired manufacturer no longer young. Three years ago I lost my only son, Alfred, my motherless boy."

"But surely your son must have had aunts?"

"When he returned from the Great War a maimed invalid, I thought of nothing but his care, even placing my business under the direction of partners."

"Great War? Cavaliers and Roundheads, what?"

He went on to describe the restoration of the priory—it had been a stupendous task, for the deserted pile had rather resembled the ruins of one's breakfast egg—until finally, after wiping the remnants of an indifferent pear *soufflé* from the chin, the last of the de la Poers announced that he was sleepy and we packed it in for the night.

I wish I could report that the chat over the breakfast table the next morning was all sunshine and mirth, but it was not.

"I trust you slept well, Mr. Wooster," said my host, as he pushed the kippers about the plate in a morose, devil-take-the-hindmost sort of way.

"Like a top, old sport. Like a top."

"I was harassed by dreams of the most horrible sort. First there was a vision of a Roman feast like that of Trimalchio, with a horror in a covered platter."

"Could it have been something you ate?" I said, sounding the solicitious note. I didn't want to hurt the old fellow's feelings, of course, so I refrained from saying that the fish sauce the night before had been somewhat below par. In truth, the cook at Exham Priory was not even in the running with Anatole, my Aunt Dahlia's French chef and God's gift to the gastric juices.

"Next I seemed to be looking down from an immense height upon a twilit grotto, knee-deep in filth, where a white-bearded demon swineherd drove about with his staff a flock of fungous, flabby beasts whose appearance filled me with unutterable loathing."

"Could it have been something you read before retiring? 'Mary Had a Little Lamb' perhaps? Mind you, that one's about a shepherdess, not a swineherd, but it's the same sort of thing, don't you know."

"Then, as the swineherd paused and nodded over his task, a mighty swarm of rats rained down on the stinking abyss and fell to devouring beasts and man alike."

"Rats! By Jove, this is getting a bit thick. My man Jeeves thinks rats may have been the party to blame for your cats carrying on the other day like they had broken into the catnip."

Well, this emulsion of cats and rats would soon get even thicker. Tubby and I spent an uneventful afternoon messing about the priory's extensive gardens, filled with coarse vegetables, which were to turn up at the evening meal as a sodden *mélange*. That night the pumpkin had barely hit the pillow of the four-poster before there arose a veritable nightmare of feline yelling and clawing from somewhere below. I put on the dressing gown and went out to investigate, finding a pyjama-clad Pop de la Poer in the midst of an army of cats running excitedly around the oak-panelled walls of the study.

"The walls are alive with nauseous sound—the verminous slithering of ravenous, gigantic rats!" exclaimed the master of the manse.

"You don't say. As a child I think I read something about a giant rat of Sumatra—or at any rate, a passing reference."

"You imbecile, can't you hear them stampeding in the walls?"

Before I could reply in the negative, the entire four-footed crew plunged precipitously out the door, down several flights of stairs, beating us in the biped class by several lengths to the closed door of the sub-cellar. There the gang proceeded to squat, yowling. Shortly we were joined at the portal by Tubby, Jeeves, and a host of household servants, and after some floor debate the committee resolved to explore the sub-cellar while the trail was still hot, so to speak. As we descended, lantern in hand and the cats in the vanguard, we could not repress a thrill at the knowledge that the vault was built by Roman mittens.

"Every low arch and massive pillar is Roman, sir," observed Jeeves. "Not the debased Romanesque of the bungling Saxons, but the severe and harmonious classicism of the age of the Caesars."

"I say, Jeeves, take a gander at these inscriptions: P. GETAE... TEMP... L. PRAEC... VS... PONTIFI... ATYS... Atys? Isn't he one of those chaps one reads in third-year Latin?"

"Atys is not an author, sir, but I have read Catullus and know something of the hideous rites of the Eastern god, whose worship was so mixed with that of Cybele."

"Catullus." The name had an ominous ring. "No connection with cats, I hope?"

"None, sir."

"Ah, that's a relief."

The dumb chums, if that's the term I want, had in fact ceased their howls and were licking their fur and otherwise behaving in a peaceful, law-abiding manner near a group of brown-stained blocks—or altars, according to Jeeves—except for one alabaster old gentleman, who was pawing frantically around the bottom of the large stone altar in the centre of the room.

"Hullo, what is it, Snow-Man?" asked Tubby. Like the proverbial mountain that toddled off to Mahomet, my friend rolled over to the altar in question and set down the lantern the better to scrape among the lichens clustered at the base. He did not find anything, and was about to abandon his efforts, when Jeeves coughed in that unobtrusive way of his, like a sheep clearing its throat in the mist.

"Pardon me, sir, but I think the company should note that the lantern is slightly but certainly flickering from a draught of air which it had not before received, and which comes indubitably from the crevice between floor and altar where Captain Norrys was scraping away the lichens."

"How right you are, Jeeves." We Woosters are renowned for our fighting ancestors—the grand old Sieur de Wocestre displayed a great deal of vim at the Battle of Agincourt—but there are times when it is prudent to blow the horn of alarm and execute a tactical withdrawal.

We spent the rest of the night in the brilliantly lighted study, wagging the chin over what we should do next. The discovery that some vault deeper than the deepest known masonry of the Romans underlay the sub-cellar had given us a nasty jar. Should we try to move the altar stone and risk landing in the soup below—or throw in the towel and wash our hands of it for good?

"Well, Jeeves," I said at last, after the rest of us had exercised the brain cells to no avail. "Do you have any ideas?"

"I would recommend that you compromise, sir, and return to London to gather a group of archaeologists and scientific men fit to cope with the mystery."

"I say, that's a capital idea!" exclaimed Tubby. Even de la Poer *père* grumbled his assent, and everyone agreed that this was a masterly course of action, one that Napoleon would have been proud to hit upon in his prime.

"You stand alone, Jeeves," I said.

"I endeavour to give satisfaction, sir."

"Er... any chance you might like to have a go at braving the unknown depths by yourself, Jeeves?"

"I would prefer not to, sir. *Nolle prosequi.*"

"As you please, Jeeves."

"Thank you, sir."

Less than a fortnight later I was still congratulating myself upon my narrow escape from Castle de la Poer and its pestilential pets—I had begged off the subsequent recruitment drive and been lying low ever since—when Jeeves floated in and accounced a visitor on the doorstep.

"Captain Norrys to see you, sir."

"Tubby, eh? Did he say what he wanted, Jeeves?"

"He did not confide his mission to me, sir."

"Very well, Jeeves," I said, hoping against hope that the poor sap wished to see me on some neutral affair, like our going partners in the forthcoming annual Drones Darts Tournament. "Show him in."

For a moment I thought a gelatin dessert of a size to gag an elephant had come to pay its respects—and spoil the sitting-room rug with its viscous trail—but it was, of course, only my roly-poly pal.

"Bertie, how are you?"

"Couldn't be better—now that I've returned to the metrop." I meant to sound cool and distant, but it did no good. The human pudding continued to wax enthusiastic.

"Bertie, you must come back to Exham Priory to explore the sub-sub-cellar with us. It'll be such a lark."

"Tubby, I'd sooner saunter down the aisle with Honoria Glossup than go back to that dungeon." In case I didn't mention it, la Glossup is Sir R.'s daughter, a dreadful girl who forced me to read Nietzsche during the brief period of our engagement. Or am I confusing her with Florence Craye, another horror who once viewed Betram as ripe for reform through matrimony?

"Please, Bertie. We've rounded up some prize scientific chaps, five real corkers, including Sir William Brinton."

"Sir William who?"

"As I recall, sir," said Jeeves from the sideboard, "Sir William's excavations in the Troad excited most of the world in their day."

"Thank you, Jeeves, but this egghead's credentials are not—what's the word I want, Jeeves?"

"Germane, sir?"

"Yes—they are not germane to the issue. For another thing, I have the distinct feeling I've worn out the welcome mat in this de la Poer's baleful eyes. For all my lending of the sympathetic ear and shoulder, ours was hardly a teary farewell."

"I'm not asking much, Bertie."

"What would you have me do next, Tubby, pinch the old blister's favourite cat?"

Well, what could I do? In the final appeal a Wooster always rallies round his old schoolmates. One must obey the Code.

"All right then, I'll go."

"Stout fellow, Bertie. Oh, and be sure you bring Jeeves. While these scientific chappies may be brainy enough in their own fields, no one beats Jeeves in the overall grey-matter department."

It may in fact have been a sign of his high intelligence that Jeeves was not particularly keen on the idea of a return engagement at Exham Priory, but in the end he dutifully accompanied the young master for an encore performance. All was tranquil late that August morning when we gathered in the sub-cellar. The cast included nine members of the human species and one of the feline, for the investigators were anxious that Snow-Man be present in case any rats, living or spectral, tried to give us the raspberry. While Sir William Brinton, discreetly assisted by Jeeves, directed the raising of the central altar stone, I chatted with one of the assembled savants, a fellow named Thornton, devoted to the psychic.

"Any notions what might lie in store below?" I asked, thinking he might have more insight than those with a more materialist bent.

"Matter is as really awful and unknown as spirit," the man explained in a tone that suggested it all should be perfectly plain to a child. "Science itself but dallies on the threshold, scarcely gaining more than a glimpse of the wonders of the inner place."

"Yes, quite. I see what you mean," I replied, though frankly I didn't.

Within an hour the altar stone was tilting backwards, counterbalanced by Tubby, and there lay revealed— But how shall I describe it? I don't know if you've ridden much through the tunnel-of-horrors featured at the better amusement parks, but the scene before us reminded me strongly of same. Through a nearly square opening in the tiled floor, sprawling on a flight of stone steps, was a ghastly array of human or semi-human bones. Not a pretty sight, you understand, but at least there was a cool breeze with something of freshness in it blowing up the arched passage. I mean to say, it could have been a noxious rush as from a closed vault. We did not pause long, but shiveringly began to cut a swath through the ancestral debris down the steps. It was then that Jeeves noticed something odd.

"You will observe, sir, that the hewn walls of the passage, according to the direction of the strokes, must have been chiselled from beneath."

"*From beneath*, you say, Jeeves?"

179

"Yes, sir."

"But in that case—"

"For the sake of your sanity, sir, I would advise you not to ruminate on the implications."

I wonder that any man among us wasn't sticking straws in his hair ere long, for at the foot of the steps we stumbled into a twilit grotto of enormous height that in atmosphere rivalled the scalier London nightclubs in the wee hours.

"Great Scott!" I cried.

"My God!" croaked another throat.

Tubby in his inarticulate way merely gargled, while Jeeves raised his left eyebrow a quarter of an inch, a sure sign of emotional distress.

There were low buildings that I imagine even Noah would have considered shabby with age—and bones heaped about everywhere, as if someone intent on emptying the closet of the family skeleton had instead uprooted the entire family tree. After recovering from the initial shock, the others set about examining the dump, a fascinating process if you were an anthropologist or an architect—but not so to Bertram, whose nerve endings by this time were standing an inch out from the skin. I had just lit up a calming gasper, when that fiend Snow-Man, taking offence perhaps at the sudden flare of the match, pounced out of the shadows toward the trouser leg. My nerves shot out another inch, and for the nonce panic overthrew sweet reason in the old bean. I fled headlong into the midnight cavern, with the hell-cat in hot pursuit.

I gave the blasted animal the slip in the dark, but dash it, I eventually realised I'd lost the human herd.

"I say there, Tubby, where are you?" I hollered. "Jeeves, I say, hall-o, hall-o, hall-o!"

Well, I kept wandering about and calling, don't you know, and thinking how tiresome it was to play blind-man's-bluff for one. Then something bumped into me—something hard and lean. I knew it wasn't rats—though in a manner of speaking, I imagine you could say it was one big rat. I instantly recognised the American accent: "Shall a Wooster hold the hand of a de la Poer? ... He's cuckoo, I tell you ... that spineless worm ... Curse you, Wooster, I'll teach you

180

to goggle at what my family do!" Further aspersions on the Wooster name followed, some in Latin, a language I rather enjoy hearing, especially from Jeeves, but not in present circs. When the blighter began to growl like a pagan lion in search of its next Christian, I decided it was high time to hoof it. It wasn't a graceful exit. I scampered off and was cruising at about forty m.p.h. when I rammed the coco-nut against an object even harder on Mohs' scale than Pop de la Poer—or so it felt in that final moment before everything went black.

After what seemed like aeons, I awoke to find myself home in bed, the melon throbbing. I was just about to ring for Jeeves, when the faithful servitor drifted in with the tissue-restorer on the salver.

"Good Lord! Was it Boat-Race Night last night?" Then I quaffed the soothing brew, and our underground adventure all came back to me like a pulp thriller.

"What happened, Jeeves?" I groaned.

"After three hours we discovered you in the blackness, sir. It appears that you collided with a low-hanging rock. You will be relieved to learn that the physicians anticipate a full recovery."

"Venture far into that grisly Tartarus, did you?"

"We shall never know what sightless Stygian worlds yawn beyond the little distance we went, sir, for it was decided that such secrets are not good for mankind."

"Quite the wisest course, Jeeves, if you ask me. Man has done jolly well to date without shining the spotlight at the dirt under the carpet at Exham Priory, and I daresay if he keeps a lid on it for the future he'll be all right."

"*Dulce est ignorantia*, sir."

Despite his assurances, however, I could see by a faint twitching of the lip that Jeeves was troubled.

"Do you have something unpleasant to tell me, Jeeves?"

"Yes, sir. Unfortunately, I have some extremely disturbing news to impart."

"Out with it then, my man. Don't brood."

"I regret that it is my mournful duty to inform you, sir, that certain members of our subterranean expedition suffered grave harm." The lip again wavered. "Mr. de la Poer..." "Gone totally potty, has he?" "It is my understanding of his case that his aberration has grown from a mere eccentricity to a dark mania, involving a profound and peculiar personality change. Reversion to type, I believe, is the term employed by the professional psychologists. Mr. de la Poer is presently ensconced at Hanwell Hospital, under the direct supervision of Sir Roderick Glossup."

"Takes a loony to cure a loony, I always say."

"As for Captain Norrys, sir..." Jeeves coughed, like a sheep choking on a haggis. "An accident befell him that resulted in massive and irreversible physical trauma."

"You mean to say, Jeeves, he's handed in the dinner-pail?"

"Yes, sir. If I may say so, the manner of his passing was exceedingly gruesome."

"Spare me the details, Jeeves." I laughed. One of those short bitter ones.

"It would seem that Providence doesn't always look after the chumps of this world," I said, after some sober reflection.

"Indeed not, sir."

"And now I'm faced with having to scare up a new partner for the Drones Darts Tournament, what?"

"Yes, sir."

"Any ideas?"

"As the matter does not require immediate attention, sir, I suggest you devote yourself to gaining further repose."

"Right then, Jeeves. I'll catch a spot more of the dreamless."

"Most sensible, sir. So soon after your ordeal you should take care to avoid passing beyond the Gate of Deeper Slumber into dreamland."

EXHAM PRIORY

ROBERT M. PRICE

I HEREBY APOLOGIZE TO THOSE WHO BELIEVE editorial etiquette ought to forbid an editor including one of his own stories in an anthology. I see your point, but my thinking is this: if I were reading a collection of tales where the whole idea is to gather all the stories related to "The Rats in the Walls," and the editor had written one but humbly declined to include it simply because he had written it, I would feel cheated by the technicality. Pretend somebody else wrote it if you want. If you like it, hell, pretend *you* wrote it, I don't care. My sequel to Lovecraft's "The Rats in the Walls" first appeared in *Crypt of Cthulhu* # 72, 1990. Robert A. W. ("Doc") Lowndes declared it "absolutely the best pastiche of Lovecraft ever done." So maybe it's worth inclusion. In any case, what I present here is a significantly longer version. Looking back over it, I felt I had skimped in a couple of places, taken short-cuts, and I felt this would be my chance to rectify that.

From the Papers of Sir William Brinton

On August 15, 1923, Thomas Delapore, or de la Poer, to use the older form of his family name he had affected in late months, was incarcerated in a barred and padded cell in the asylum for the mad at Hanwell. De la Poer, an expatriate Englishman and last scion of an ancient if not venerable baronial line, had only recently arrived from America to take up residence in the newly reappointed seat of the de la Poers, Exham Priory. He had resolved, all other worldly interests spent, to live out his remaining days in the centuried halls of his forbears. Yet a fate decreed beforehand by his tainted bloodline, an hereditary madness lurking latent only to be nudged to full wakefulness with the proper surroundings as catalyst, assigned him rather different lodgings in which to spend what days remained to him. Padding replaced the black oak panelling and polished wainscotting on the walls around him, though I am told by Dr. Pettijohn that at the last poor de la Poer no longer knew the difference, having sought refuge in the delusion that he dwelt after all in an unsullied Exham about which hovered legends that were no more than legends and could be easily dismissed. His ghostly rats had left him, or rather they had driven his mind into a retreat in which their spectral echoes could no longer be heard. Thus one paranoiac fancy replaced another, and at length he died in peace, two years ago, I believe.

His strange case, however, would not be put to rest as easily. For none of the survivors of the party of seven who had accompanied him on his descent into the Stygian recesses below the Priory could easily forget what we had seen, nor yet the beguiling yet maddening suggestions of what we had *not* seen: those lightless caverns and abysses that yawned below. All of us sought as best we could to retreat into the numbing comfort of mundane pursuits and wholesome scholarly activities. I now think that de la Poer in his flight into madness had chosen the wiser course, as his delusion shielded him from a reality far more insane, a reality the rest of us would seek to face again.

We had not sought to stay in contact after the affair of Exham Priory, indeed had sought not to, as if never again to discuss it would lend it the aspect of unreality. One cannot easily dismiss as nightmare what several acquaintances recall in common. All of us were specialists representing different fields, each chosen by de la Poer and his ill-fated companion Norrys based on our reputations. No two of us had natural professional acquaintance, so it was easy, by unspoken agreement, to part company and keep quiet.

So things remained until we all received copies of a letter from Dr. Randolf Holmes Pettijohn, one of the original party and an alienist recruited for the adventure by de la Poer whose recent dreams and apparent auditory hallucinations had led him to suspect his own sanity, rightly as I once thought. After the tragedy, the murder of Norrys, Pettijohn had immediately taken charge of de la Poer and had arranged his committal to Hanwell. The case was so spectacular, from a clinical as well as a journalistic standpoint, that Pettijohn had made it his business to delve into de la Poer's family origins as fully and deeply as time allowed. None of the rest of us knew even this much until the arrival of his letter so informed us. He had at last, he said, made a discovery that shed unexpected light not only upon de la Poer's case but on our common subterranean adventure as well. Pettijohn was urgent in his insistence that the exploration party regather to hear his findings. After some deliberation, I replied in the affirmative though my reluctance and foreboding colored every sentence of my reply.

On the appointed day we gathered in the London rooms of Dr. Pettijohn; besides myself and the alienist there was, to my surprise, only one other present, the anthropologist Francis Abelard Trask. My initial surprise was mitigated as soon as I recalled that, of the original seven, Norrys and de la Poer were both now dead, and the unstable psychic Thornton had accompanied de la Poer to Hanwell, never to emerge. To tell the truth, I could no longer recall the seventh member, a man I had only met briefly on that occasion. I now assumed he had judged sleeping dogs better left to lie and had declined to appear. This was not the meaning attached to the man's absence by Dr. Pettijohn, however, who had for purposes of his inquest secured and maintained information on each of the seven. The absent man was Andrew Powys Thayer, a folklorist expert in the local Anchester legendry concerning Exham Priory. De la Poer had often consulted Thayer as to local folk belief attached to his family seat and had felt the man's detailed knowledge of the Priory and its history might prove invaluable in the exploration of its catacombs.

Professor Thayer had indeed been sent the identical letter that had summoned Trask and myself, but as Pettijohn expected, it had gone unanswered. Thayer, a recluse since his retirement from teaching, was often unavailable or unresponsive, but Pettijohn had recently had to conclude that more than this was involved. Upon revisiting Anchester to interview some of the local workmen and townspeople in connection with the de la Poer case, Pettijohn had learned that he was not the first to return there. Thayer, too, had been on the scene with unwelcome inquiries, once even asking after hidden entrances to the Priory's interior through unseen crevices of the cliff-face.

For indeed Exham Priory still stood. Pettijohn had thought it best to deceive de la Poer on the matter, informing him of its supposed demolition and hoping that with the focus of his delusions thus removed, the poor madman might give up his dangerous ancestral fixations. I have said that he did not, de la Poer finally rebuilding his Priory again in his own mind and living there happily. But very soon the ancient pile would be destroyed in truth, and at the frenzied petitionings of the people of Anchester.

Pettijohn's alarm came from his conviction, unprovable to the authorities, that the eccentric Thayer lurked somewhere, perhaps injured, within the walls of Exham Priory. If indeed he were trapped there, there would be no better search party than the three of us who had shared his experience and were familiar with the lay of the land. With this Trask and I had to concur. Besides, the only concrete physical danger faced on our previous descent was that from the mad de la Poer himself.

But what, I asked, of this discovery that so excited Pettijohn? Here his demeanor changed: the severity of concern he felt for the missing Thayer fell away as the gleam of professional, scholarly discovery lit his face. He told us how, judging from the confession of poor de la Poer, much of his self-appointed task of reclaiming his ancestral manor was in truth an unconscious quest to cure himself of a kind of family amnesia, knowledge of his line that had been lost in the burning of Carfax Plantation during the War Between the States. Until then some great secret had been passed in a sealed envelope in the spidery hand of ancestor Walter de la Poer from each father on his deathbed to his eldest son. This rite of full manhood included not merely the inheritance of the burden of family responsibility, but a burden of self-knowledge, too; some secret without knowledge of which one could never know what it was to be a de la Poer. Shameful or frightful though the secret might be, ignorance of it might seem worse to a curious mind forever tantalized by its irretrievable absence. De la Poer, in the alienist Pettijohn's professional judgment, had been in all his efforts trying to regain that lost knowledge. Apparently he had succeeded, or thought he had, his fevered mind supplying a mad revelation perhaps much worse than any the lost envelope might have contained.

Of course the very existence of the bone-choked Tartarus we seven had stumbled upon beneath Exham Priory lent an undeniable element of the fantastic to de la Poer's family history. But who could say if old Walter de la Poer, who fled England for American shores, had known of the caverns? Only the flame-obliterated record once sealed in that mysterious envelope might answer that question.

Pettijohn's news was that the envelope *had in fact come to light*! Following the most improbable of hunches, Pettijohn had gambled upon the notorious rapacious tendencies of Federal soldiers during the War. Seldom did they fire a plantation home without sacking it first. Suppose Carfax had been thus ransacked by the Yankees before they torched it? And suppose they had discovered a lockbox they were unable to open? Might not a determined and greedy man have borne his stubborn prize away for further attention later? And, minus money and valuables, might not the personal effects, including the sealed letter, have made their way into some closet where, with the passage of decades, they would accumulate a certain antiquarian interest? And might they not have passed thence into the hands of one of the many dealers in such artifacts?

It was all improbable to say the least, absurdly improbable really, but it would cost the determined researcher little in either money or time to set in motion the necessary inquiries. The trail led at length to a historian on the faculty of one of the Border State universities. Astonishingly, the Delapore papers had actually come to rest in the University archives. Pettijohn lost no time in acquiring photostatic copies of the relevant material. It was, as rumored, the confession of Walter de la Poer, he who, fleeing his ancestral England, transplanted his ancient line in the soil of the New World. It was an ill-fated lineage; he could not after all extricate himself and his heirs from its predestined shadows, as the experiences of our late friend had demonstrated. Here is the text, slightly updated as to style.

It was to have been a great day for me, a rite of passage of some undisclosed sort, unknown to and unsanctioned by the Church, to which our family had always professed formal allegiance, as any lordly house must. I knew that the de la Poers had long celebrated certain rituals, held fast to certain beliefs, scarcely common to the run of Englishmen of whatever class, but I never troubled my incurious young head as to their nature or origin. On the single occasion I had asked an aged nursemaid, she had drawn a comparison which I little understood to the marriages of King Solomon to the princesses of a hundred heathen kingdoms by way of making peace with them. That satisfied me, if only by way of convincing me I should never understand a matter so obscure and therefore dull. I thought not of it again till my twentieth birthday came round, when I was informed with an air of whispered gravity that I should now learn what all de la Poer men, and even women, learned when they came of age. Hitherto the secrets of our immemorial house should be my property as well as my burden to protect and to maintain. This announcement sounded fully as mystifying as the answer I had received some years previous, but at least it implied I was now to be trusted with the privileges, albeit of unknown character, attaching to maturity. And this must mean other pleasures and rights that my young mind could understand should be mine as well. It was only some years later, with my growing acquaintance with the ways of a wider world outside Exham Priory, that I understood how late such a rite of maturity had been delayed, occurring some seven or eight years earlier in most societies, or so our travellers inform us.

I found myself gently shaken awake one midnight by masked servants. I knew their heights and gaits, and thus more than suspected their identities, but I said nothing, feeling vaguely fearful to break their peculiar silence. Once I had relieved myself with the chamber pot and splashed my face to some degree of wakefulness, I returned to my bedside where the two servants had laid out a yellow silken robe for me, much like theirs, though of a discernibly finer material. Once I had donned it, I felt I had stepped onto a stage and was already performing, along with these other actors, in a play whose script I had never laid eyes on. What should my role be? I could only accompany them and wait.

The light in my room had come from a pair of torches which my visitors had brought with them, passing them back and forth as each required free hands to help or guide me. The shrouded figures now held them aloft as we paced solemnly down familiar halls and through secret doors cleverly set into walls in such a manner that no seam or crack suggested, much less betrayed, their presence. My curiosity now blazing more brightly than our torch flames, I followed in a mood of adventurous expectancy. One has perhaps entertained dreams of stumbling upon a hitherto unknown chamber in one's house. I now experienced such a dream in very truth. True, I had never mentally traced out the probable contours of the vast pile in which my family resided, but long familiarity with our capacious quarters had banished any curiosity about what I might not have seen. Now I was seeing it, and the further our miniature procession wended its way through labyrinthine corridors, forever downward, the greater my sense of wonder grew, and forsooth I questioned more than once whether I was caught in a dream, my physical body yet reclining asleep in its warm bed. But it would prove all too real—unless even to this hour I sleep and pitch amid unending nightmare.

I noticed in the flickering light how the plaster-coated walls along which we passed were covered with murals of a decadent Roman type. I mean their artistic style, but their subject, too, deserved the epithet. There were scenes of bloody flagellation, apparently of masters and mistresses by servants, offerings of infants to ancient deities or demons on altars shaped like gaping maws. Most disturbingly, the persons depicted were dressed not in ancient togas but in the familiar clothing of our own day. There were, too, more familiar scenes of great hunting parties, then also of butcher shops, not an accustomed subject for artistic representation. Still other scenes involved forms plainly human and animal, but others also, and the peculiar relative positions of all the painted forms suggested the repugnant.

We descended endless spirals of stairs, beaten smooth with the treading of centuries, until the sounds of chanting reached my ears. When we reached our destination, what I expected would be an initiation chamber, the place was cold, damp, and hollow, though the barrenness was broken by the hanging of great black and purple drapes of velvet. Banqueting tables formed a great square at whose center there lay a feather mattress, also of black velvet. Sewn into the nightish surface was the armigerous crest of the de la Poers. Patches of discoloration were not difficult to pick out even in the wavering illumination of the bracketed candles. All other chairs were occupied but one. My guides led me silently to my chair, and, as I sat down, I scanned the rows of guests, hoping for some sign of recognition. While I assumed most or all would be familiar to me unmasked and in proper daylight, I could guess at the identity of none of them. There were rather too many for all of them to represent the resident menfolk of the de la Poer clan, and this suggested the possibility of honored guests from outside our family home, though certainly no locals could be here. At second glance I took note both that the robes, all shining golden in the torchlight, were yet of different shades, some tending more toward red, others toward the palest yellow. Were they significant of rank within what was now plainly some esoteric order cherished by my ancient line? Or was the choice of colors entirely gratuitous? Perhaps these and other details awaited a catechism that should ensue upon completion of whatever ceremony awaited me. But was it not proper order for instruction to precede initiation rather than follow it? Unless of course the idea were for the initiate to get in too deep, become *implicated*, and be unable henceforward to turn back. In many ways I was as naïve as I was young, but the reader will know that no de la Poer can long remain without a necessary degree of craft and guile.

The banquet began and continued in absolute silence, and yet the movements and gestures of all appeared convivial, even festive, as if one were to observe a raucous surfeit through a screen that muffled all sound. It was unearthly in effect. Nor did the momentary uplifting of silken veils furnish much of a glimpse of the identity beneath. Once a diner rose to his feet, as if to read from an unrolled scroll. But when, in his pantomime, he made a quarter turn, I could see that the vellum surface was entirely as blank as his hooded visage. And somehow it was only then that it occurred to my marveling senses that many of the guests' hoods had no visible eye holes! In such a state of dreamlike confusion I finally turned my attention to the plate before me, only to wonder again at what lay thereupon. Meat of more than one variety totally unfamiliar to me was passed me from circulating platters or by the attentive hands of costumed servants. Much of this repast fairly swam in blood, ordinarily no affront to me. But occasional strands of human hair amid the meaty chunks extinguished my appetite.

The voiceless reading of the invisible text was, it turned out, the beginning of the ceremonies of the night. Events succeeded one another rapidly from here on in. Once the plates were taken away, replaced by flagons of familiar wine and ale, the after dinner entertainment commenced. Armed guardsmen, their faces but crudely masked with wound up rags and kerchiefs, brought in a series of girls and young women, villagers from the looks of them, some seemingly not fed for many days, and half-led, half-dragged each one in turn through a gap at the corner where the banquet tables had been drawn to an incomplete square. All were naked, none masked, and the bruises of ill-treatment during captivity were plainly to be seen. I knew that, even in our advanced century, the nobility, if the name be used of such men, abused their baronial privileges much as our tyrannical ancestors had. Such things were less tolerated now, but the common peasantry still suffered much. How much, I was about to learn. What measure of threatening or bribery had it taken to persuade local fathers to sell their nubile daughters to the servants of their de la Poer masters? And could the girls have been allowed to know what fates they were about to suffer?

For next I saw the use of the stained mattress, as, one after the other, the robed dignitaries on the side of the table square opposite mine began to cast aside their garments, all but their facial coverings, revealing themselves in a disgusting state of animal arousal. They lost no time in positioning themselves astride the firmly bound, vainly struggling forms of the village girls beneath them, the latter screaming through muffling gags. I felt not only disgust but self-loathing as well, as I knew it was my kind, my caste, my kin, who perpetrated these outrages and thought nothing of it, any more than a hunter bringing down game birds for idle target practice. Strangely, I did not yet think of intervening. I cannot account for my paralysis of will, save that I felt I must be locked in nightmare's grasp when, following on each lewd predation, the perpetrator received from the attendant guardsman a long knife with which he proceeded to slit the throat of his erstwhile plaything! Each new violator then went on to kneel and to copulate in the bloody mess left by his predecessor. Each was guided away from the chamber and, presumably, into some adjacent lavatory by one of the guards, as if exhausted in the course of a wholesome athletic exertion. Through all this my mind seemed to me to float outside of my body, rejecting what it could not tolerate.

The next entertainments of the evening involved no direct participation from the gathered feasters. We were, this time, to be spectators only. But for me the ensuing sights were scarcely less easy to bear. The supply of local females was not exhausted, but this time they were made the unwilling partners, not of our own number, but of a series of rutting brutes whose nature was at no time clear to me. Were they hairless hogs such as I had never seen among our squealing pens? Were they heavily-muscled dwarves from some countryside circus troop? Their priapic skill, albeit soul-upheaving in its crudeness, was efficient enough, and directly after penetration, they were taken firmly in hand by weapon-bearing guardsmen and led away. The young women, passed out from their ordeal, then received the amorous attentions of the line of robed diners adjacent to my own flank of the board. I was, of course, uneasily aware that some hideous behavior would be expected of me at some moment not long distant, but I could not actively consider what it might be as long as my attention was commanded by terrible sights such as these. The masked revelers, some with the help of their burly attendants, lifted the dead weight of the women's legs to facilitate their own thrusting. The physical condition of some of these men, both long-given to idle vice and in some cases subject to astonishing and unparalleled anatomical deformities, made the oblivion of the supine females a blessing indeed. I would, shortly thereafter, be made aware, by the local authorities, that what I had witnessed must have been the process by which the degenerate de la Poers replenished both their noble line and their meat larder, depending upon which seed should take hold. This is why these wasted females were not, like their predecessors, butchered at once.

This, I say, I learned later, but at the time my senses were assaulted anew by the realization that a pair of these women were not after all unknown to me. They, unlike the rest, had been brought in and laid down wearing hoods like those of the diners. When I saw this, I instinctively glanced at a corner where I had seen two female feasters, only to confirm their absence now. But as, first, the semi-human brutes, then the human ones, had their way with the passive, degraded forms, the veil of one unresisting woman fell aside, and I recognized *the once-sweet face of my sister Elisabeth*, now foully enraptured in a manner I dare not picture.

It came home to me that I must be next, and that whatever rite of initiation they had engineered must be of such especially foul nature that, having descended to such depravity, I should have seared my conscience forever, unable to tolerate any degree of guilt or qualms henceforth, lest I loathe myself to the point of suicide. In such fashion was the absolute loyalty of the de la Poers secured, one generation after another. I claim no credit for what I will now report. Indeed, in what I did next I only compounded the guilt of my hitherto passive presence in that inferno of horrors. But I did what I must. First I reached for the dagger I had donned, out of habit, along with some underclothes to protect myself from the cold of the night beneath the light texture of the ceremonial garb I had donned. I rose from the table and approached one of the guards, who, preoccupied with the depraved spectacle before him, was scarcely anticipating my assault. I stabbed his fat neck with my dagger, at once seizing the haft of his antique halberd, which he and his fellows carried for some purely ornamental purpose. Still, in the confines of that room it proved a deadly weapon. As he gagged on his own blood, I ran for the other two or three armed men, dispatching them easily, half-drunk as they seemed. Next I made for the door through which I had entered, bolting it. And then I set about butchering all who remained. Like stupid cattle, they moaned plaintively, scarce able to comprehend the due recompense that was at last overtaking them. None made more than half-hearted attempts to fend off my deadly blows, offering less resistance than a tree being hacked up for kindling. Dripping with their foul blood and none of my own, I turned over the heaped corpses and stripped off the hoods that remained, recognizing beneath the distorted and purpled visages of father, brothers, uncles, aunts, cousins. No pang of remorse did I feel just then, though later I knew myself a murderer, albeit of murderers and worse.

I rose from my finished work, then remembered the hallway through which the doomed women had been led. I found a better weapon, a sword, in the belt of one of the slain guards and headed for the dark aperture. There was but the feeblest of light to illuminate the silence with shivering shadows. Of armed men I saw no more. In fact, the only ones I did discover cowering in tears were my sisters Elisabeth and Rosamond, both of whom, I now realized, had taken their turn on the blood-soaked mattress. Their glazed eyes pleaded silently, but I showed them no mercy. They were no longer the kind, I judged, on whom mercy can be shown, any more than a poisonous serpent may be forgiven.

Ascending the stairs with renewed vigor, I passed trough to the residential levels of Exham Priory. My hand was firm upon my borrowed blade, and I searched the place, room by room, with vengeful stealth, but found no one. Perhaps alerted by one or two who had managed to flee before me, all servants, remaining relatives, and visiting tradesmen had made their hasty exit as if from a sinking ship. Satisfying myself that no other human being now populated these haunted halls, I packed the few clothes and papers I needed and left the old heap of stones for once and all. When I reached the village below, news of my deeds had preceded me, and I fully expected to be executed on the spot. But instead I found myself hailed as liberator and benefactor.

Thanking the villagers with a full heart, I remained with them long enough to put my affairs in order and to make ready for my final journey to these shores where, after long years during which no horrible detail has faded from my memory, I have decided to set the events down, hoping that the act may exorcise them from my mind, waking and sleeping, where they have never yet ceased to plague me. Future generations of the de la Poer line may shudder at the knowledge of the rock from which they were hewn, but they may also comfort themselves with the knowledge that, with me, the family has cleansed itself of its terrible guilt, which no future de la Poer ever need bear again.

Pettijohn felt that the shocking legacy of the Delapores or de la Poers might finally be laid to rest by a return trip to the caverns beneath Exham Priory. What difference did it make, Thomas de la Poer being dead two years? Neither Trask nor I asked this question. The de la Poer madness was so singular, opening up new lines of inquiry into the much-debated question of ancestral memory, that no men of the psychological sciences could in good conscience fail to try to resolve it. And in no better conscience could Trask, an anthropologist, and I, an archaeologist, continue to pretend deafness to the sirens of lost knowledge that had tempted us since that initial descent. We would return to the Priory, come what may. With luck we would find our colleague. As men we could hope no less. But as scientists we could hope for a great deal more.

◆

The initial entry into Exham Priory was not half the obstacle we had anticipated. Though I am loathe to trade on the modest fame my work has earned me, the rehearsing of my credentials, plus the implication by Dr. Pettijohn that his investigations were aimed at the final extirpation of the de la Poer blight, proved sufficient to gain the limited cooperation of the local authorities as the missing folklorist Thayer had been unable to do. We retraced our steps with a shiver of *deja vue*,_recalling too vividly our first expedition with Thomas de la Poer. The series of sub-cellars reminded me of the circles of Dante's Inferno, but I knew we traversed but the antechamber of Hell. The cleverly hidden altar stone designed to mask the netherworld of the de la Poers still stood tipped open. None of us had thought to restore it to its original position in our precipitous departure nearly a year before. As we crouched to pass this portal into Pandemonium, I understood another piece of the Priory's puzzle. Local lore spoke of an "inner cult" to which only certain even of the tainted de la Poers would be initiated. I now knew that whatever blasphemous revels of defilement occupied the demented clan as a whole, they must have been restricted to the Roman-era chambers we were now quitting. Only the inner initiates would be informed of the twilit grotto below - else why disguise the doorway to it beneath a secret altar stone which none outside the family might see in the first place?

Had the parricide Walter de la Poer known of the secret cult and its netherworld? No doubt the "outer" Attys and Cybele cultus with its orgies of castration and infanticide would have been enough to provoke his desperate act. But we were going deeper, to those levels of nightmare the visitation of which had driven Thomas de la Poer to cannibalistic insanity.

Beneath us stretched away the skeleton-scattered plain dotted with architectural stragglers from Roman, Celtic, Saxon, and Jacobean times. All this we had seen, and despite our best efforts, we had all of us failed to forget a single detail of it. Trask and I had come prepared with cameras and as many photographic plates as we might accommodate in our rucksacks, hoping to gather enough evidence to persuade the government authorities, in the name of science, to delay the planned destruction of so singular a site. So we paused to record as much of the unearthly scene as we might, then headed for terra incognita. On our first trip we had not penetrated the deeper recesses of the place as we had nothing approaching adequate lighting. The dim twilight of the place was supplied by the unseen cliff-fissures that let in the cool breezes that alone made the place sufferable. But out of range of that faint luminescence we had not dared explore further. This time we were prepared. High intensity chemical torches, plus an ample supply of matches, should more secretive illumination prove advisable, now made further descent practicable.

I will not tax the patience of readers who may not share my own scholarly pedantry with all the details of our exploration. These may be found in the official reports. Suffice it to say that we found a series of once-inhabited caverns, all connected by well-worn, sometimes almost-effaced stone steps. Given the curious mix of architectural styles evident on the topmost layer we did not know what to expect below. If I had had to guess, I would have predicted that the structures on the lower levels would have been of more recent design the deeper one went. The variety of styles up top would have reflected the continuous use of the area through the ages, with the lower levels reflecting a gradual tunneling descent as more space became necessary (for whatever blasphemous ends). Hence, each lower level ought to show more recent style. In fact, though the evidence was not altogether unequivocal, the very opposite seemed to be the case! The further down one went, the earlier in style the structures, or their ruins, became! This finding comported well with my tentative observation on our initial exploration, that the tunnelling seemed to evidence stroke-marks from *below*. At that time I assumed the unusual effect to be the result of some ancient and inefficient constructional technique. Now I began to see the evidence in a bewildering new light.

Stranger still were the apparently contradictory indications of more decadent, secondary workmanship that became more inept, almost appearing hurried and careless, as one descended. The secondary character of what seemed to be renovations was evident from the plain contrast with the finer work that prevailed generally on every level. My only guess was that the more recent reworking reflected a route of *retreat back underground*. Stray relics such as cups and utensils anachronistically scattered on the "wrong" levels tended to confirm this hypothesis. Actually, the general interpretation of the data seemed fairly clear, but the tendency of it equally seemed scarcely capable of belief. From whence could these ancient tunnelers have come?

Often we came upon stretches of tunnel wall that had once, I am sure, been hung with tapestries. All that now remained, thanks to the corrosive effects of the salt sea air that penetrated the cliffs, were discolored shreds. Yet it could be seen that the intricately woven arras had once borne complex and detailed scenes which presumably enshrined stories important to and informative of the weavers, whoever they may have been.

Trask had stayed behind, attempting to catalogue some of the queer semi-human skeletons and skeleton-fragments that thickly littered the topmost cavern floor. Now, sketches and photographic plates tucked away, he caught up with Pettijohn and myself. Without living subjects to interview, poor Pettijohn had had no research with which to busy himself while Trask worked on his skeletons and I studied the various ruins and artifacts. But soon his patience was rewarded.

At first the three of us thought we were becoming the prey of de la Poer's auditory hallucinations: we seemed to hear the scuffling of animal feet from further down the tunnel. We gave our lights a rest, following the ghostly radiance of phosphorescent fungi which coated the nitred walls on this level. If such plant life existed here, it was not inconceivable that there were animals of some sort as well. After assuring each other that we all heard the sounds, unlike the case of poor de la Poer whose rats only he could hear, we agreed to creep slowly forward to spy whatever animal might be grazing on the fungi.

We were not quiet enough, for instantly we heard the confusion of a group of apparently clumsy animals lumbering away out of sight.

But their herdsman remained.

Directly before us, half turned as if to follow his fleeing charges, stood a stooped and skeletal figure. His dirty white hair hung in strings from face and head, penetrated by the startled gaze of red-rimmed eyes. The clothes were filthy rags that hung precariously from his spare frame, and his shepherd's crook was a walking stick that revealed him to be, like ourselves, a visitor from the upper world. His pallid, almost translucent skin implied he had been here much longer than we, however. He looked alarmed, but more than that he stared in disbelief. He made no move.

I spread my hands to show I meant no harm and began to speak. I hardly knew where to begin. Could he have been a shepherd in the Anchester area who followed lost animals through one of the hypothetical hidden entrances to the caves? But then how to account for his apparent at-home-ness here? I thought it better to explain our presence first and let him react to that.

I told him that a family called the de la Poers had once lived here, or above here, intending to tell him of our former and present missions. But at the mention of the syllables "de la Poer," the ancient herdsman's rheumy eyes widened fully to perfect circles, and, spewing spittle, he unbottled a verbal torrent.

"*Used* ta live here, ye say? Hee hee hee! Ye don' know the 'alf of it, ye don'! Why, I knows all *about* them de la Poers, knows *too* much, I do! More'n ye might expec', f'm the look o' me! Them devils been stealin' babies and young girls f' centuries hereabouts! And ain't nobody that don' know that! But *I* (here he tapped his head and squinted one eye) knows plenty more'n *that*, I does! I knows what they did aforetime in these 'ere caves, all the *breedin'*, and the *killin'*, and the *victualizin'*! Regular epicures, them de la Poers! (I noted mentally how the mad oldster had begun to use words with which I would not have thought him familiar given his crude and wild demeanor.)

"I knows all about the *livestock* they raised in them pens up there! And where they'd go betimes t' *fatten* that herd! And I knows what they begat on the village girlies, I does! An' *rats*! Knows all about 'em, I does!"

Here the tottering graybeard began to prance erratically from foot to foot, breaking forth into a child's ditty I had heard for years concerning one Bishop Hatto who in a time of famine had invited the poor into his huge barn ostensibly to distribute provisions while actually luring them into a deathtrap. Locking them in, his grace set fire to the barn.

> "Then, when he saw it could hold no more,
> Bishop Hatto made fast the door,
> And while for mercy on Christ they call,
> He set fire to the barn, and burnt them all."

Soon after, divine justice overtook the wicked bishop in the form of a plague of famine-starved rats who swept down upon his estates and devoured all in their path, pointedly including Bishop Hatto.

> "They have whetted their teeth against the stones,
> And now they pick the bishop's bones;
> They gnawed the flesh from every limb,
> For they were sent to do judgment on him.

"No fairy-tale, me kind sirs! It *'appened!* Roight 'ere! But that bishop weren't no Christian bishop, *no* sir! Served the Old Gods, 'e did! A de la Poer! He roasted them people right enough! But *one by one* ... f' *supper!*"

In his delvings the unfortunate Thomas de la Poer had become acquainted with a whole cycle of legends concerning the rat-plague and had informed me of these when initially recruiting my efforts. The gnaw-marks we found on the skeletons on the topmost level seemed conclusive evidence of a link between the story of the rats and the evil of Exham Priory. But how could this senile old rustic be expected to make such a connection? Trask, Pettijohn, and I were all too amazed to think of interrupting the crazed old swineherd.

"But the worst 'orror is wot most folk don' know–but I knows!– Them devil de la Poers still live 'ere! They never died–just went back underground after young Walter's deed back in 1610. 'E killed the sire, an' his *legal* family, but them devils bred like rats... bred *with* rats of a kind! And they wuz plenty of 'em as had never seen th' outside o' the Priory. Just went down below, 'n they been goin' *deeper* ev'ry generation.

"But 'taint really the de la Poers, ye know! Any more'n it was the Romans! They jus' got sucked inter it, like all the res'."

I could resist no longer: "Who, then? Who was it that tunneled up from below, that built this place?"

The old man paused, savoring my rapt attention, as if considering whether to divulge this bit of information for free.

"They wuz the *Little People*, the Old Ones o' the hills!"

Trask broke in: "Of course! Miss Murray speaks of them in *The Witch-Cult in Western Europe*! Most anthropologists dismiss her theories as wild conjectures, but..."

"But," finished the mad old herdsman, "she' *right*, ain't she, Doctor Trask? Hee, hee, hee!"

Our jaws dropped as one. We had found Andrew Powys Thayer, retired professor of folklore studies, University of Sheffield. In his seeming insanity he had reverted to the plebeian accents of his childhood but the filth-clad old spectre's memory still served him. Of the long conversation which followed let me report only the gist.

Thayer hailed originally from the Anchester countryside himself and, despite his later intellectual achievements, had never quite forgotten his humble origins. Indeed it was the rich if frightening lore of his village that had first inclined him to the science of comparative folklore. Mastering the tools of the discipline, he had returned to the massed mythology of his home region and had actually founded his academic career on the Anchester-Exham legendry, systematizing and cataloguing it in a dissertation still regarded as a classic in the field. No wonder Thomas de la Poer had found him so inexhaustible a source of information, albeit disturbing, about his ancestral seat.

Hearing, as we had, of the impending demolition of the Priory, Thayer had resolved to get a second, closer look at the caverns below it. He realized that the wealth of local legends to which he had dedicated his professional life was but the tip of the iceberg. Once inside the cliff-face and its caverns, he had taken pretty much the same path we had mere hours before. He had found what he sought, but much more as well. For the de la Poer clan, as he now mumbled, still lived, more degenerate, more terrible, and more secretive than ever.

When Thayer had penetrated into their lair he had first been seized and bound in one of the butcher's sheds which were familiar to him from our first, common descent in the company of de la Poer and Norrys. Weeks passed in this captivity before (as he supposed) the stock of flabby albino anthropoids ran thin and the swathed and hooded butcher picked him to die. He was rudely stripped and tied to the block, dull-bladed axe about to descend on his scrawny turkey-neck, when the downward arc abruptly halted and the muffled tones of the butcher grunted something in a semi-coherent decadent patois. Hastily led into the presence of several other carefully shaded and mantled figures, Thayer's spare, nude form was inspected with rude jabs and close peering through masked eyes.

After much whispering and grunting, the dazed Thayer was at length made to understand that through the presence of some obscure birthmark or anatomical configuration, the furtive figures had recognized him as a distant relation! In his own veins flowed a sluggish stream of impure de la Poer blood, tainted with the infection of unguessable, doubtfully human ancestors. Instead of a livestock pen he was given his own dwelling.

Thayer had adjusted with difficulty to his new petty-aristocratic status in the unsuspected underground realm. Communicate with his newfound kin he could not, as their speech had decayed beyond any surface dweller's grasp. Nor would his hosts unveil themselves in his presence. He received the impression, from what seemed intimate scenes stumbled upon, that the netherworlders neither uncovered themselves in each other's presence. Whatever deformity resulted from centuries of inbreeding, perhaps the reemergence of the recessive traits of prehuman ancestry, it seemed to be shared by all, yet universally regarded with a repugnance that must be the only surviving vestige of surface, human existence.

Anthropologist Trask listened with renewed fascination as Thayer began disjointedly to explain what he had been able to understand of the social structure of the cavern world. It was a system of class privilege, but not of law. It was apparently a fairly small society, though even Thayer had not had occasion to find out the full extent of the subterranean world. The concept of prescriptive law had been alien to the original founders of the mysterious race. They, it appeared, lived in harmony with the inner laws of their species, these natural laws forming the basis of custom and ritual. However these customs of incest and cannibalism might clash, had clashed, with the mores of surface dwellers, whether Cymric, Roman, Saxon, or English, they were deemed wholly natural by the denizens below Exham Priory. The tiers of this society were organized on the basis of racial purity. The more direct one's descent from the founders, the higher the status one held. Those whose blood contained more or less admixture with the various races assimilated over the millennia were more or less inferior in the social scale. Class privilege was largely a matter of initiation into inner circles of the cult. Of these, there seemed fully as many as are rumored among the Masons.

Only the outermost fringe of the concentric initiation system was visible in the affairs of the surface-dwelling de la Poers. The first level involved nameless feasts of human and semi-human flesh, that of the flabby beasts nourished on the coarse vegetation harvested from the gardens of the Priory. It was "merely" this that had spurred Walter de la Poer to murder his accessible family and flee to America in 1610. These feasts, with their orgies of mutilation and carousal had been preceded by rites and liturgies in the Attys temple below the Priory.

The second level involved not just the slaughter of, but the blasphemous interbreeding with, the awful fungous beasts in the twilit grotto below. The innermost circle of the cult known to Thayer involved the consumption of the well-preserved and seasoned corpses of the mummified progenitors of the cult (here even Pettijohn, inured as he was to the aberrations of the insane, blanched and nearly fainted). In some vague way this process was held to reincarnate the original Elder Ones. Of these, only one remained in the flesh. It was called the Faceless God. Thayer had glimpsed this entity but once during a high festival when it appeared for a moment upon its dais flanked by two of the mindless, flabby subhumans which had somehow been trained to play what must have passed for melodies on two cracked, shrill flutes. The Faceless God derived its title from the bulging mask of yellow silk it wore, which, from the asymmetrical protrusions beneath it, must have veiled a physiognomy not only inhuman but positively non-Euclidean in its dimensions. To the presence of this numinous monarch the only response was immediate prostration, so the awed Thayer had caught only a glimpse before the indescribable form retreated again into occultation.

Thayer had clearly been transfigured by his experience. He seemed to view it now as an exaltation never experienced by lesser mortals, now as equally unparalleled degradation, depending upon the random mood of the moment. In any case, he refused to leave his "sacred duties" as a herdsman of the fungus-fattened cattle. Besides, if he tried, he would surely be found by agents of the cult who still foraged on certain nights among the young females of Anchester. He would take his chances with the dynamiting of the Priory, feeling confident that no harm would come to those who lived so far beneath the surface.

Pettijohn, Trask, and myself, however, he admonished to leave now and not come back. This warning put the three of us in a quandary. On the one hand, we had accomplished our humanitarian goal of finding the missing Thayer; if he wanted to stay where he was, even if it was in a hell inconceivable to sane minds, that was his decision. On the other hand, how could we turn back without verifying even a little of the wild tale Thayer had told us? Yet if it were even half true, we would be placing ourselves in extreme danger if we explored further. Thayer assured us he would not try to stop us, but it would be on our own heads.

The tattered form turned down the passageway into which his fungoid flock had lately vanished. We took the other path. After another mile or so of gradually sloping descent we began to notice certain changes in the environment. There appeared to be no fungus growing here (hence no ghostly illumination, so we reluctantly reactivated our torches), probably because it had grown less moist. I began to think I could discern the echoes of faint and distant piping. In view of Thayer's mad ramblings, I was not eager to happen upon the echoes' possible source. At the same time, the darkness began to lighten almost imperceptibly with a misty purplish radiance. Surely we must be nearing another level of the underground labyrinth.

Soon we exhausted the supply of steps. A cave mouth yawned before us. Tentatively we crept to its rim and looked out. What I saw gave credence to the whispered legends of a flight of seven thousand onyx steps that led to the gate of deeper nightmare. For there stretched out what seemed to be a featureless, windowless city of black basalt, a collection of weed-grown terraces, collapsing towers, crumbling minarets, cracked domes, and tenuous bridges suspended over oily black rivers of unwholesome ooze. This could be none other than the primal and ultimate citadel of the awful entities from whose evil roots the poisonous mushroom of Exham Priory had sprouted.

As none of the inhabitants seemed to be in evidence, we bade prudence goodbye, yielding to Pandoran curiosity as we made for the nearest building. Of furniture the place had none, so it was difficult to assess whether it was momentarily or permanently untenanted. The sole decoration in the rather large domed hall was a huge mural tapestry which I judged to correspond to that whose mere shreds I had discovered earlier in the day (or on the previous day?). By our flickering light the three of us studied the scenes, trying to make sense of the images which reflected no known culture or artistic style. The reader will recall that my professional judgment on such a matter, however extravagant it may sound, is to be accepted. To my bafflement was added the disturbing insight of Dr. Pettijohn, whose analytical techniques include the inference of personality type and psychic health from a patient's drawings. He whispered that some subtle aberration in the style suggested a characteristic state of mind wholly without parallel among the common run of mankind. His judgment is all the more unsettling when it is recalled that what we were viewing was apparently a conventionalized representational style, not the idiosyncratic manner of a single individual.

Dr. Trask, too, was hard-pressed to make sense of the physical forms represented in the arras before him. Not only were they but vaguely suggestive of Homo Sapiens, they could scarcely be placed at any conjectural point in the known cycle of terrestrial evolution.

At last we came upon another tapestry which suggested unavoidably the answers our minds had tired themselves in suppressing. I believe that what we saw depicted the arrival at some time in the remote dawn-era of our planet of these Elder Ones, the parent stock of the hellish de la Poers, from another world altogether. By piecing together various equivocal hints from this and that scene, we inferred that these beings' home world had been slowly rendered uninhabitable. First the surface grew contaminated in some unspecified way, represented by layers of piled up dots surrounding natural features, whereupon all survivors took refuge underground. Thus began their troglodyte existence. When that shelter, too, became unlivable some years or epochs later, they had somehow gained the capacity to travel through space (or so this, their myth, said). This earth was their destination. Though the surface of the planet would have accommodated them, they had grown so accustomed to underground life that they shunned the clean sunlight for the inner darkness.

There was more, much more, recorded in that arras, which I supposed must be a standard household relic, much as a crucifix or religious statue is in many of our familiar households. (Or perhaps, it occurred to me later, it was something of a port of entry at which novice abductees or initiates to the cult were shown the nature of the new and horrifying world in which they must henceforth dwell.) We had time to decipher but a small fraction of the mad revelations, indeed I suspect far madder than the little we could interpret. But inevitably we were interrupted. I should have realized we were left unmolested only as long as our unseen hosts chose to study us from concealment. For suddenly a rustling behind a section of tapestry indicated the rush of air from a hidden door swiftly opening.

The doorway was at once seen to be full of curious and threatening troglodytes, all eager to get a look, like the ancient men of Sodom, at these improbable interlopers into their sunken realm. That we had not noticed the clumsy footfalls of the shambling herd, for none of whom stealth could conceivably have been an option, is to be credited to our utter absorption as we sought to decipher the hanging mural. Absent minded professors in truth! We had but moments to stare at the looming figures, even as they dumbly scrutinized us, before they roughly took us in hand and marched us away. But in those moments I took in more than I wish now that I had. All were swathed in shapeless garments, coarse sacks, really; faces were one and all veiled, albeit protruding asymmetrically, leaving only deep-set blazing eyes visible if the feeble light chanced to catch them. The stench was unimaginable, and I shall do you no favors if I try to describe it. But the worst thing, I think, was the irregularity of the limbs, insofar as they could be distinguished from the general mass. For no two seemed to form a good match, and I could have sworn one of the mute vigilantes possessed a rudimentary *third leg*. Or perhaps a tail. I averted my glance, having for the moment lost all sense of scientific objectivity. But even the most pious missionary may, I suppose, be forgiven for forgetting his concern for souls while he is being prepared for a cannibalistic dinner. And that, I assumed, was now to be our own fate.

The paths we trod along cavernous ledges were worn smooth from uncounted centuries of foot traffic. So many millennia of path-beating had given the path a degree of reassuring concavity, leaving a curb along the outer edge, so that there was no urgent danger of losing one's footing and falling headlong into the abyss, past honeycombed hive-walls embedded in the cone-like pit. Souls crushed by despair, frames past feeling from hours of strenuous descent, we moved along like the obedient beasts which we had earlier seen old Thayer shepherding along the tunnel shafts.

It could not have been unduly long before my colleagues and I were ushered into a holding cell of sorts, a dug out chamber similar in its plainness to the residential chamber we had previously entered. There were moth-eaten, faded hangings here, too, only these were given entirely over to the depiction of cruel tortures and dismemberments the like of which, we supposed, we should anticipate for ourselves. The fiendishness of some of these damnations, though shown as inflicted by mortals, rivaled in their degree of sadistic horror the nether hells of the Tibetan Buddhists, far surpassing the dull imagination of the monkish Catholic inquisitors of more recent times. More disturbing yet, however, was the implied anatomy of the poor wretches whose tortures were here represented. Were the unlikely contortions and freakish angles into which bare limbs were twisted the product of hellish torments or, worse, the natural state of their naked bodies *before* the engines of cruelty were applied?

Fear yielded to utter and absolute exhaustion at that point. I doubt that the torture devices under whose likenesses we slept could have kept us awake. I cannot venture a guess how long we slept, but to my surprise we were allowed to awaken naturally. When my eyes opened, my friend Trask was watching me amid a circle of equally patient guards, while Pettijohn was nowhere to be seen. I never caught a glimpse of him again, nor could I find an opportunity to ask the mysterious Thayer about him. He is henceforth absent from this narrative, I am sorry to say. I hope and trust he now rests in peace.

Of our captors, a single visage was not covered, and it was of course that of our former companion Thayer. It was he who had seen to our clemency, the prerogative of the minor noble rank which he possessed in this peculiar society. Might this treatment portend more of the same? I could tell by the discomfited state of my clothes that they had been removed and put back while I slept so deeply. They had not been washed. My captors must have searched me, as they had Thayer, looking for any identifying arcana. But there would have been nothing for them to find. Momentarily I wished I might have indulged in a youthful desire to acquire a tattoo. Who knows what sort of royal crest the poor savages might have seen in that? But, alas, my wrinkled skin was pure as the driven snow, and I gather the same must have held for Trask.

Though our old colleague now counted as one of "them," it was impossible to bear Thayer any ill-will, much less hostility. He was, after all, our only life-line here. Any benefit, any amelioration of our predicament he might seek could undermine his own position among these strange denizens of the shadow realm. It was thus with the most sincere gratitude that Trask and I received our verdicts, actually, our assignments to new lives in this alien society into which we had stumbled as hapless immigrants. Needless to say, we would never be allowed to leave it. Whether opportunity might one day present itself, who could say? But, despite my physical soundness, my years were sufficiently advanced as to reduce my potential for heroics to a minimum, and any such options were, I am sorry to say, to be ruled out for the more fragile form of Trask. I think he knew this, for I saw his facial lines sink into a posture of resignation from which I dare say they never again lifted. Was he even grateful to be left alive in such circumstances? I never got the chance to ask him, for the pair of us were split up and taken to different cave-cells separated by an unknown distance. Some cryptic utterance of Thayer's gave me to believe that Trask should henceforth have some assigned task in the kitchens of our district of the sparsely populated cavern world.

Its populace appeared to survive on the most meager of sustenance. The monotonous menu consisted primarily of the bloated and strangely colored (though in this odd light, who could tell?) fungi. The loathsome meat of the flabby creatures of Thayer's herd was seemingly reserved to a more elite class of epicures, higher up the aristocratic chain—for which I may say I was devoutly grateful. Caste duties dictated the activities of the largely silent denizens who resembled, in their behavior, nothing so much as the instinct-driven drones of an insect hive. If there remained (or had ever existed) any wider cultural life, I saw no sign of it. Occasionally, a look over the protective curb of the curving path of descent offered a glimpse of silent, shambling figures headed to unknown destinations on unguessable missions, and with all the enthusiasm of a surface-world chain gang. Clearly, it was a ghost of a civilization lost even unto itself, its pointless existence maintained strictly by force of inertia. I stress this so that you may see how little inclined the shadowy rulers of the place were to close supervision. When things move predictably and without variation, one eventually comes to cast a sleepy eye over the inevitable, like a sleepy nightwatchman. As a new variable in the equation, I found myself doubly conspicuous: not only was I the only new thing to scrutinize, but I was also the only occasion to revive the atrophied exercise of scrutinizing anything. And, once I understood this, I began to think there might be a way to escape what little notice was taken of me.

It was some months before I chanced to see again my friend and fellow prisoner Trask, and when I did, I saw with alarm how he wielded a crudely-wrought crutch, more of a stick or a club, to compensate for a newly missing left leg! That his health and physical soundness should have failed did not surprise me. Indeed, I could imagine that, while recoiling from the easy prospect of suicide in this place, Professor Trask might yet have relished the prospect of death coming to relieve his trials sooner rather than later. I only hoped that whatever passed for medicine or surgery in these precincts was not too similar to the methods of torture whose depiction I had once seen on the tapestry.

What was my own role in this bizarre society to be? An old man, I might have seemed good for little, but I can only suppose that Dr. Thayer had made the hierarchs to understand something of my work as a scholar, for I found myself delivered to a great chamber of peculiar sanctity. Mere moments revealed the character of the place as an ancient archive, though I could tell the nature and function of the deep halls had been forgotten by the very people who most revered it. Their superstitious ignorance only served to increase the degree of holiness which they assigned to the place.

I had already seen an ample number of the wall-hangings whose most common theme looked to be an epic rehearsal of the history, such as it was, of these people. This cavern housed, as might be expected, a far greater number of these tapestries and in a state of much better preservation. That did me little good, though, as I had no historical measuring stick, nor any lexicon for their recurring symbols. At least there were frequent depictions of asterisk-like things which I felt sure could not be intended as visual representations of any known life form, at least none habituated to dry land. I found a vast number of documents rendered in numerous media, including parchment sheets, clay tablets not unlike those so recently discovered in the Library of the Assyrian potentate Asshurbanipal, even, I would swear, books of some type inscribed upon flayed human hide. Did the wide range of materials imply an unthinkably vast history of the collection itself? Had it been supplemented over long millennia? Or did the rich diversity and volume of holdings denote rather some long-ago period of antiquarian zeal during which manuscript treasures of various ages had been surreptitiously gathered by the surface-dwelling de la Poers from far and wide, outside the tunnel world below Exham Priory? Who knew? I should note that, among these records, I found new variant versions of the *Gilgamesh Epic* and even older sagas of a similar type, of which knowledge was long ago lost in the surface world. One was, as I judged it, a kind of paleo-Sanskrit common basis for both the *Odyssey* and the *Ramayana*.

Another text I conjecturally identified with the half-legendary *Pnakotic Manuscript*. Portions of it were written in an old Hyperborean dialect. Of this I could make little sense, but my eyes widened as I believed I deciphered something suggesting that the earliest inhabitants of this shadow-realm had been refugees from the lost land of Lomar, of which ancient legend hints, and that their blasphemous traffic with, and cultivation of, the white, flabby brutes stemmed from their ancient subjugation of the hairy, cannibal Gnoph-kehs, their blood-enemies. Still other antediluvian records contained what I took to be maps of the world, albeit with the continents in different relative positions, and certain interlineations implied the Exham settlers had first come, via unthinkably vast tunnel passages, from much larger cavern worlds far off to the west— across the Atlantic? If only I had been able to salvage such riches!

But my job extended only so far as the dull imaginations of the people I now served. No one expected me to do anything beyond custodial tasks, preserving the library (whose use they no longer understood) from simple physical disintegration. My predecessors in these tasks had not been very skilled at it, and, to tell the truth, antiquarian that I am, I performed my duties with genuine concern for the treasury which had come under my care. I think my hosts understood this on some level and even appreciated my efforts. I might be a priest chanting a litany in a sacred tongue unknown to them, but my performance was all the more sacred as a result. I will not go so far as to say I found these poor creatures kind; it may be closer to the truth to say that they lacked any more the imagination to be cruel. They shared an endless burden of life as rote repetition and knew nothing else. Mere life was Sisyphean futility, made more easily bearable by the tragedy that they knew no better. Accordingly, I soon ceased to fear for my own safety and began worrying instead for my sanity. I knew I must escape and take it with me, or I should surely lose it here. The threadbare cloak I wore would surely become a capacious straight jacket if I did not contrive to leave.

Every such thought brought the sudden red pain of guilt, for that I knew I should never be able to take with me the hobbled Dr. Trask. I did once risk taking the trouble of venturing a bit farther from my appointed section of our dreary warren in order to gain another glimpse of my friend. Would that I had not, for now I saw that he merely sat in his chamber, minus both legs, waiting for death. His mind was, I could see with a single look, gone for good. Closer scrutiny told me that his amputations were not after all medical in nature. They were *cooking and eating* him, piece by piece. I had allowed myself for a time to forget the sadistic degeneracy of the de la Poers. Now I remembered. And I resolved to endure their hospitality no more.

Of my escape there is little to tell. It was no great adventure. I have said both that attentive supervision was largely beyond the capacity of these light-shunning automatons, and that they came to appreciate, and therefore, to trust me—at least to take for granted that my behavior was and would remain quite as predictable as their own. The place seemed filled with a miasmic atmosphere of will-paralyzing lethargy which, I confess, sapped my resolve as one day passed indistinguishably into the next. I am ashamed to say that things had reached such a pass with me that I might well have given in and awaited death, which should have come without my takingmuch notice. I was fairly sure that both Thayer and Trask, not tomention poor Pettijohn, were dead by now. Who was I to think I had anything to risk or any real reason to think myself deserving of a better fate than theirs? In the end, it was something I chanced to read, or to think I read, among the half-translated and contradictory histories of the de la Poer cult and race. Let us just say for the moment that it was quite sufficient to jolt me out of my shadow-fed ennui and send me racing, old knees a-knocking, old lungs a-wheezing, up and out from that place with only a reluctant few pursuers rousing themselves to a sudden chase that more annoyed them than alarmed them. Their zeal to recapture me was never very great and flagged swiftly once we began to near the slightly brighter light of the surface-leading passages...

My ascent was slow; I am an old man. Though kept in sound physical health by my many archaeological delvings, my energy is quickly spent, and I had pressed on far too long in this day's mad quest. On my Orphean ascent I was overcome once or twice by sleep, hoping resignedly that the devils from below would not decide after all to pursue me. Obviously they did not.

But the knowledge I gained below Exham Priory has pursued me like an avenging spirit, like de la Poer's ghostly rats, and who knows that it will not succeed in hounding me finally to death?

For the pictographs and manuscripts I examined while under house arrest made rather too clear the mocking resemblance I discerned in the too-familiar lineaments of Thayer's flabby beasts. What the records showed unmistakably was not a devolution from humanity's true eidolon to the quadrupedic, slope-browed imbecility of the fungous beasts. Rather it indicated that unspeakable miscegenation between the Elder Ones (whatever their ultimate origin) and their vaguely hominid livestock was no innovation of the de la Poers. No, it was by such soul-upheaving bestiality that the first human beings were created in earth's dawn age.

APPENDIX I

THE RATS IN THE WALLS

THE GREATEST HORROR STORY EVER WRITTEN

H.P. LOVECRAFT

HOWARD, WHAT'S A NICE GENT LIKE YOU doing in a place like this? Of course I refer to the appearance of HPL's "The Rats in the Walls" in a slightly abridged and revised form in the dubious (now disintegrating) pages of the debut issue of *Zest Magazine for Men* (January 1956). It appears here in facsimile, because, to get the full effect, you really have to see what sort of company Lovecraft found himself in. You have to see his genteel prose cheek by jowl with cheesecake shots of buxom models and flanked by typical sucker ads. These "Men's Adventure" mags were aimed at readers of the caliber of Dale Gribble and Cliff Clavin, though they are most enjoyable when approached from an ironic remove. But it remains a bizarre experience to encounter bogus "expose" articles ("Is Your Daughter a Sex Film Star?") and then to behold, not a story about Nazi sex slaves or rabid bear attacks, but Lovecraftian horror! Don't say you weren't warned!

ZEST

MAGAZINE FOR MEN

JANUARY 25 CENTS

Is Your Daughter a Sex-Film Star?
PAGE 30

THE PRIVATE WAR OF SERGEANT GALLAGHER
PAGE 14

BEAUTIFUL, LONELY AND LOADED
PAGE 36

"The Rats in the Walls"
PAGE 20
THE GREATEST HORROR STORY EVER TOLD

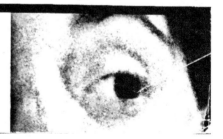

EXTRA!
A New Michael Avallone
Short Novel
THE GLASS EYE PAGE 73

The Rats in the Walls

By H. P. LOVECRAFT

■ ON July 16, 1953, I moved into Exham Priory after the last workman had finished. The restoration had been a stupendous job. The place had been uninhabited for 400 years. When a tragedy had struck down the master, five of his children, several servants and had driven out his third son Walter, who had fled to Virginia and changed his name from de la Poer to Delapore. It was from this Walter de la Poer that I was descended.

During the Civil War my great grandfather had been killed by the Yankees and my father had come North with his mother to Massachusetts where he later became a wealthy manufacturer. I knew nothing of my family since an envelope that had been passed from father to son telling of our background had been burned when McClellan's men had sacked our old family plantation in Virginia.

Then in 1941 my only son Alfred went to England with the Air Force and met a Captain Norrys of the RAF who became friendly with him and told him about our old property which adjoined the Norrys'.

Apparently the place had a colorful and sinister history and Norrys related to my son some of the wild superstitions about Exham Abbey which, of course, neither Norrys nor my son took seriously.

In fact just before the end of the war I decided to buy the old place which I was able to get for a surprisingly low figure and being about to retire thought I might go over and fix it up.

Then my son was maimed and came home to die. This left me a childless widower and in 1951 I went to England to see the property I had bought and to take some steps to fixing it up.

Visiting Anchester in December, I was entertained by (Continued on page 55)

217

What was the nameless
horror that lay buried under
the foundations of
the Abbey and
lived only by Night?

wind until they were fifteen miles out from the old military post. Here Garret halted them. He picked Lee Hall, Tom Emory, and Jim East.

"You fellows come with me," he told them. "Rest of you stick here with your horses."

The four crept up the gully, silent as Apaches until they saw the little rock house outlined against the sky. Dawn was just beginning to show. They worked their way on their bellies up the bank until they lay just beneath its brink within ten yards of the building.

The place had no windows; the door was the only opening. They watched it while the cold bit them to the bone.

Three horses were standing near the threshold, hitched to the vega poles; now and again one stamped or blew loudly. The door opened. A man came out carrying a nose-bag. It was Charley Bowdre.

"Hands up!" Pat Garret was calling. Bowdre's right arm was dropping toward his revolver-holster as the sheriff and Lee Hall fired.

"Got him," the former said quietly. "Save your ca'tridges boys."

Pat Garret spoke.

"Boys, we got to shoot those picket-ropes in two." The Winchesters spoke slowly, and the horses snorted in terror. When two had galloped away, the sheriff shot the other down before the doorway.

Garret nodded to Lee Hall: "Go and get the rest of the boys."

When the others had come, they surrounded the little building.

"You fellows may's well surrender now. We've got you," Garret called.

Billy the Kid flung back profane defiance. Then silence came. It lasted through the day. Dusk was settling down when one of the posse caught sight of a flutter of white above the roof-tree. The beleaguered men had tied a handkerchief to a pole and raised it through the fireplace chimney. Pat Garret crept up the brink of the bank beside Charley Bowdre's frozen body.

"All right," he called. "When you come out, come with your hands up, all of you."

"Give us your word to take us safe to Santa Fe." The promise was given. The door was opened, and Billy the Kid stepped out. Then the outlaws came on with upraised arms.

They took Billy the Kid and his 3 men to Las Vegas through a blinding blizzard. They locked them in the adobe jail that night, but no man on the posse slept. Someone might try to liberate the outlaws. But no one came. Until the next day when 50 armed men bore down on the station and tried to get the men from the train which would take them to Santa Fe and jail. The attempt failed. The train jerked to a start. The prisoners settled back in their seats.

It was spring when Jim East rejoined the wagon crew at San Ilario. He told them of the fighting and the capture. There was one more thing they wished to know. The reward.

"Five hundred dollars in gold," he said. "What did we do? Why danced, and ate and fiddled a whole week. Then I went scouting Apaches." He was quiet a while, and then he spoke like a man who is saying what lies heavy on his mind.

"I wonder," he said, "if they have got a real saloon in Tascosa yet." ■

A WICKED EYEFUL!

That's what confronted *this* lucky male! "He forgot that he was a porter and had only one eye . . . He availed himself of those rights which his calling gave him to act like a brute. Brutal he was accordingly — and happy!" . . . Thus begins a gay evening session of THE PLEASURE PRIMER. Thousands are now enjoying *Rollicking Bedside Fun*, and you will too, when you possess this ideal bedside companion. Here's entertainment for open minds and ticklish spines. Here's lusty, merry recreation for unsqueamish men and women. Here's life with apologies to none. Collected, selected from the best there is, this zestful Primer is an eye-opener. . . YOU ARE INVITED TO EXAMINE THE PLEASURE PRIMER 10 DAYS AT OUR EXPENSE. IT IS GUARANTEED TO PLEASE OR YOUR PURCHASE PRICE WILL BE REFUNDED AT ONCE!

The Pleasure Primer — ONLY 98¢ — THE IDEAL PLAYMATE

10-DAY TRIAL OFFER

PLAZA BOOK CO., Dept. P-1212
109 Broad St., New York 4, N. Y.

Please send THE PLEASURE PRIMER on 10 day trial. If I'm not pleased, I get my purchase price refunded at once.

[ ] Send C.O.D. I'll pay postman 98¢ plus postage.
[ ] I enclose $1. You pay all postage.

Name
Address
City ___ Zone ___ State ___

RATS IN THE WALLS   (Continued from page 21)

Capt Norrys, a plump, amiable young man who had thought much of my son, and secured his assistance in gathering plans and anecdotes to guide in the coming restoration. Exham Priory itself I saw was a jumble of tottering mediaeval ruins covered with lichens and honeycombed with rooks' nests, perched perilously upon a precipice, and denuded of floors or other interior features save the stone walls of the separate towers.

As I gradually recovered the image of the edifice as it had been when my ancestors left it over three centuries before, I began to hire workmen for the reconstruction. In every case I was forced to go outside the immediate locality, for the Anchester villagers had an almost unbelievable fear and hatred of the place. This sentiment was so great that it was sometimes communicated to the outside laborers, causing numerous desertions.

My son had told me that he was somewhat avoided during his visits because he was a de la Poer, and I now found myself ostracised for a like reason until I convinced the peasants how little I knew of my heritage. Even then they sullenly disliked me, so that I had to collect most of the village traditions through the Norrys. What the people could not forgive was that I had come to restore a symbol so abhorrent to them; for they viewed Exham Priory as nothing less than a haunt of fiends and werewolves.

Piecing together the tales which Norrys collected for me, and supple-

55

menting them with the accounts of several savants who had studied the ruins. I deduced that Exham Priory stood on the site of a prehistoric temple; a Druidical or ante-Druidical thing which must have been contemporary with Stonehenge. That indescribable rites had been celebrated there, few doubted, and there were unpleasant tales of the transference of these rites into the Cybeleworship which the Romans had introduced.

WIERD TALES

Inscriptions still visible in the subcellar bore such unmistakable letters as "DIV . . . OPS . . . MAGNA MAT . . ." sign of the Magna Mater whose dark worship was once vainly forbidden to Roman citizens. Anchester had been the camp of the third Augustan legion, as many remains attest, and it was said that the temple of Cybele was thronged with worshippers who performed nameless ceremonies at the bidding of a Phrygian priest.

These myths and ballads, typical as they were of crude superstition, repelled me greatly, and were unpleasantly reminiscent of the one known scandal of my immediate forbears—the case of my cousin, young Randolph Delapore of Carfax, who went among the negroes and became a voodoo priest after he returned from the War. A few of the tales were exceedingly picturesque. There was, for instance, the belief that a legion of batwinged devils kept witches' sabbath each night at the priory and, most vivid of all, there was the dramatic epic of the rats—the scampering army of obscene vermin which had burst forth from the castle three months after the tragedy that doomed it to desertion—the lean, filthy, ravenous army which had swept all before it and devoured fowl, cats, dogs, hogs, sheep, and even two hapless human beings before its fury was spent. Around that unforgettable rodent army a whole separate cycle of myths revolves, for it scattered among the village homes and brought curses and horrors in its train.

EXHAM

Such was the lore that assailed me as I pushed to completion the work of restoring my ancestral home. When the task was done, over two years after its commencement, I viewed the great rooms, wainscotted walls, vaulted ceilings, mullioned windows and broad staircases with a pride which fully compensated for the prodigous expense of the restoration. I looked forward to redeeming at last the local fame of the line which ended in me. I would reside here permanently, and prove that a de la

Poer (for I had adopted again the original spelling of the name) need not be a fiend. Although Exham Priory was mediaevally fitted, its interior was in truth wholly new and free from old vermin and old ghosts alike.

I moved in on July 16, 1953. My household consisted of seven servants and nine cats, of which latter species I am particularly fond. My eldest cat, Black Tom, was seven years old and had come with me from my home in Bolton, Massachusetts; the others I had accumulated while living with Capt. Norrys' family during the restoration of the priory.

For five days our routine proceeded with the utmost placidity. I had now obtained some circumstantial accounts of the final tragedy and flight of Walter de la Poer. It appeared that my ancestor was accused with much reason of having killed all the other members of his household, except four servant confederates. This deliberate slaughter, which included a father, three brothers, and two sisters, was cheered by the villagers, and so slackly treated by the law that its perpetrator escaped honored, unharmed, and undisguised to Virginia.

On July 22 occurred the first incident. It was so simple as to be almost negligible. What I afterward remembered is merely this—that my old black cat, whose moods I know so well, was alert and anxious. He roved from room to room, restless and disturbed, and sniffed constantly about the walls which formed part of the Gothic structure. I realize how trite this sounds—like the inevitable dog in the ghost story, which always growls before his master sees the sheeted figure.

UNREST

The following day a servant complained of restlessness among all the cats in the house. He came to me in my study, a lofty west room on the second story, with black oak panelling, and a triple Gothic window overlooking the limestone cliff and desolate valley; and even as he spoke I saw Black Tom creeping along the west wall and scratching at the new panels which overlaid the ancient stone.

I told the man that there must be some strange odor from the old stonework, imperceptible to human senses, but affecting the delicate organs of cats even through the new woodwork. This I truly believed, and when the fellow suggested the presence of mice or rats, I mentioned that there had been no rats there for three hundred years, and that even the field mice of the surrounding country could hardly be found in these high walls, where they had never been known to

stray. That afternoon I called on Capt. Norrys, and he assured me that it would be quite incredible for field mice to infest the priory in such a sudden and unprecedented fashion.

That night I retired in the west tower chamber which I had chosen as my own, reached from the study by a stone staircase and short gallery —the former partly ancient, the latter entirely restored. This room was circular and very high.

Seeing that Black Tom was with me, I shut the heavy Gothic door and retired, sinking on the carved and canopied four-poster, with the cat in his accustomed place across my feet. I did not draw the curtains, but gazed out at the narrow window which I faced.

DREAMS

At some time I must have fallen asleep, for I recall a distinct sense of leaving strange dreams, when the cat started violently from his placid position. I saw him in the faint glow, head strained forward, forefeet on my ankles, and hind feet stretched behind. He was looking intensely at a point on the wall somewhat west of the window, a point which to my eye had nothing to mark it, but toward which all my attention was now directed.

And as I watched, I knew that Black Tom was not vainly excited. I heard a low distinct scurrying as of rats or mice. In a moment the cat had jumped on the screening tapestry, bringing it to the floor with his weight, and exposing a damp, ancient wall of stone; patched here and there by the restorers, and devoid of any trace of rodent prowlers.

Black Tom raced up and down the floor by this part of the wall, clawing the fallen tapestry and seemingly trying at times to insert a paw between the wall and the oak floor. He found nothing, and after a time returned to his place across my feet. I had not moved, but I did not sleep again that night.

In the morning I questioned all the servants, and found that none of them had noticed anything unusual, except the cook remembered the actions of a cat which had rested on her windowsill. This cat had howled at some unknown hour of the night, awaking the cook in time for her to see him dart out of the open door down the stairs. In the afternoon I called on Capt. Norrys, who became exceedingly interested in what I told him. We were genuinely perplexed at the presence of rats, and Norrys lent me some traps and Paris green which I had the servants place in strategic places.

I retired early, being very sleepy but was harassed by dreams of the most horrible sort. I seemed to be looking down from an immense height upon a twilit grotto, knee-deep with filth, where a white-bearded swineherd drove about with his staff a flock of fungous, flabby beasts whose appearance filled me with unutterable loathing. Then, as the swineherd paused and nodded over his task, a mighty swarm of rats rained down on the stinking abyss and fell to devouring beasts and man alike.

BLACK TOM

From this terrific vision I was abruptly awaked by the motions of Black Tom, who had been sleeping as usual across my feet. This time I did not have to question the source of his snarls and hisses, and of the fear which made him sink his claws into my ankle, for on every side of the chamber the walls were alive with nauseous sound—the verminous slithering of ravenous, gigantic rats. I was not too frightened to switch on the light.

I saw a hideous shaking all over the tapestry, causing the designs to execute a singular dance of death. This motion disappeared almost at once, and the sound with it. Springing out of bed, I poked at the tapestry with the long handle of a warming-pan and lifted one section to see what lay beneath. There was nothing but the patched stone wall. When I examined the circular trap that had been placed in the room, I found all of the openings sprung, though no trace remained of what had been caught and had escaped.

Further sleep was out of the question, so, lighting a candle, I opened the door and went out in the gallery toward the stairs to my study, Black Tom following at my heels. Before we had reached the stone steps, however, the cat darted ahead of me and vanished. As I descended the stairs myself, I became suddenly aware of sounds in the great room below; sounds of a nature which could not be mistaken.

The oak-panelled walls were alive with rats, scampering and milling, and Black Tom was racing about with the fury of a baffled hunter.

I now heard steps in the corridor, and in another moment two servants pushed open the massive door. They were searching the house for some unknown source of disturbance which had thrown all the cats into a snarling panic and caused them to plunge down several flights of stairs and squat, yowling, before the closed door to the sub-cellar. I asked them if they had heard the rats, but they replied in the negative. And when I turned to call their attention to the sounds in the panels, I realized that the

noise had ceased.

With the two men, I went down to the door of the sub-cellar, but found the cats already dispersed. Later I resolved to explore the crypt below, but for the present I merely made a round of the traps. All were sprung, yet all were tenantless. Satisfying myself that no one had heard the rats except the cats and me, I sat in my study till morning, recalling every scrap of legend I had unearthed concerning the building I inhabited.

I slept some in the forenoon. Later I telephoned to Capt. Norrys, who came over and helped me explore the sub-cellar.

Absolutely nothing untoward was found, although we could not repress a thrill at the knowledge that this vault was built by Roman hands. Every low arch and massive pillar was Roman—the walls were covered with inscriptions familar to the antiquarians who had repeatedly explored the place—things like "P. GETAE. PROP . . . TEMP . . . DONA . . ." and "L. PRAEC . . . VS . . . PONTIFI . . . ATYS . . ."

THE CRYPT

The reference to Atys made me shiver, for I knew something of the hideous rites of the Eastern god, whose worship was so mixed with that of Cybele. Norrys and I, by the light of lanterns, tried to interpret the odd and nearly effaced designs on certain irregularly rectangular blocks of stone generally held to be altars, but could make nothing of them. On one of the blocks were some brown stains which made me wonder. The largest, in the center of the room, had certain features on the upper surface which indicated its connection with fire—probably burnt offerings.

Such were the sights in that crypt before whose door the cats howled, and where Norrys and I now determined to pass the night. Couches were brought down by the servants, who were told not to mind any nocturnal actions of the cats, and Black Tom was admitted as much for help as for companionship. We decided to keep the great oak door—a modern replica with slits for ventilation—tightly closed and we retired with lanterns still burning to await whatever might occur.

The vault was very deep in the foundations of the priory, and undoubtedly far down on the face of the beetling limestone cliff overlooking the waste valley. That it had been the goal of the scuffling and unexplainable rats I could not doubt, though why, I could not tell. As we lay there, I found my vigil occasionally mixed with half-formed dreams from which the uneasy motions of the

57

222

cat across my feet would rouse me.

These dreams were not wholesome, but horribly like the one I had had the night before. I saw the twilit grotto, and the swineherd with his unmentionable fungous beasts wallowing in filth, and as I looked at these things they seemed nearer and more distinct—so distinct that I could almost observe their features. Then I did observe the flabby features of one of them—and awaked with such a scream that Capt. Norrys, who had not slept, laughed considerably. Norrys might have laughed more—or perhaps less—had he known what it was that made me scream. But I did not remember myself till later. Ultimate horror often paralyses memory in a merciful way.

Norrys waked me when the phenomena began. Out of the same frightful dream I was called by his gentle shaking and his urging to listen to the cats. Indeed, there was much to listen to, for beyond the closed door at the head of the stone steps was a nightmare of feline yelling and clawing, while Black Tom was running excitedly around the bare stone walls, in which I heard the same babel of scurrying rats that had troubled me the night before.

ROMAN WALLS

An acute terror now rose within me, for here were things which nothing normal could well explain. These rats, if not the creatures of a madness which I shared with the cats alone, must be burrowing and sliding in Roman walls I had thought to be of solid limestone blocks . . . unless perhaps the action of water through more than seventeen centuries had eaten winding tunnels which rodent bodies had worn clear . . . But even so, the horror was no less; for if these were living vermin why did not Norrys hear their disgusting commotion? Why did he urge me to watch Black Tom and listen to the cats outside, and why did he guess wildly and vaguely at what could have aroused them?

By the time I had managed to tell him, as rationally as I could, what I thought I was hearing, my ears gave me the last fading impression of the scurrying; which had retreated *still downward*, far underneath this deepest of sub-cellars till it seemed as if the whole cliff below were riddled with rats. Norrys was not as skeptical as I had anticipated, but instead seemed profoundly moved. He motioned to me to notice that the cats at the door had ceased their clamor, while Black Tom had a burst of renewed restlessness, and was clawing frantically around the bottom of the large stone altar in the center of the room, which was nearer Norrys's couch than mine.

My fear of the unknown was at this point very great. Something astounding had occurred, and I saw that Capt. Norrys, a younger, stouter man, was affected fully as much as myself—perhaps because of his lifelong and intimate familiarity with local legend. We could for the moment do nothing but watch the old black cat as he pawed with decreasing fervor at the base of the altar, occasionally looking up and mewing to me in that persuasive manner which he used when he wished me to perform some favor for him.

Norrys now took a lantern close to the altar and examined the place where Black Tom was pawing. He did not find anything, and was about to abandon his efforts when I noticed a trivial circumstance which made me shudder.

THE LANTERN

It was only this—that the flame of the lantern set down near the altar was slightly but certainly flickering from a draught of air which it had not before received, and which came from the crevice between floor and altar where Norrys was scraping away the lichens.

We spent the rest of the night in the brilliantly-lighted study, nervously discussing what we should do next. The discovery that some vault deeper than the deepest known masonry of the Romans underlay this accursed pile would have been sufficient to excite us without any background of the sinister. As it was, the fascination became two-fold; and we paused in doubt whether to abandon our search and quit the priory forever, or to gratify our sense of adventure and brave whatever horrors might await us in the unknown depths.

By morning we had compromised, and decided to go to London to gather a group of archaeologists and scientific men fit to cope with the mystery. Before leaving the sub-cellar we had vainly tried to move the central altar which we now recognized as the gate to a new pit of nameless fear. What secret would open the gate, wiser men than we would have to find.

In London Capt. Norrys and I presented our facts to five eminent authorities, all men who could be trusted. We found most of them intensely interested. It is hardly necessary to name them all, but I may say that they included Sir William Brinton, As we all took the train for Anchester I felt myself poised on the brink of frightful revelation.

On the evening of August 7 we reached Exham Priory, wher the

servants assured me that nothing un-usual had occurred. The cats had been perfectly placid; and not a trap in the house had been sprung. We were to begin exploring on the fol-lowing day.

I myself retired in my own tower chamber, with Black Tom across my feet. Sleep came quickly, but hideous dreams assailed me. There was a vision of a Roman feast like that of Trimalchio, with a horror in a cov-ered platter. Then came that damn-able, recurrent thing about the swine-herd and his filthy drove in the twilit grotto. Yet when I awoke it was full daylight, with normal sounds in the house below. The rats, living or spectral, had not troubled me.

At 11 A.M. our entire group of seven men, bearing powerful electric searchlights and implements of exca-vation, went down to the sub-cellar and bolted the door behind us. Black Tom was with us, for the investi-gators found no occasion to despise his excitability. We noted the Roman inscriptions and unknown altar de-signs only briefly. Prime attention was paid to the central altar, and within an hour Sir William Brinton had caused it to tilt backward, bal-anced by some unknown counter-weight.

THE HORROR

There now lay revealed such a horror as would have overwhelmed us had we not been prepared. Through a nearly square opening in the tiled floor, sprawling on a flight of stone steps so worn that it was little more than an inclined plane at the center, was a ghastly array of human or semi-human bones. Those which retained their form as skele-tons showed attitudes of panic fear, and over all were the marks of rodent gnawing. The skulls denoted nothing short of utter idiocy, cretinism, or primitive semi-apedom.

Above the hellishly littered steps arched a descending passage seem-ingly chiseled from the solid rock, and conducting a current of air. This current was not a sudden and noxious rush as from a closed vault, but a cool breeze with something of fresh-ness in it. We did not pause long, but shiveringly began to clear a passage down the steps. It was then that Sir William, examining the hewn walls, made the odd observation that the passage, according to the direction of the strokes, must have been chiseled *from beneath.*

I must be very deliberate now, and choose my words.

After ploughing down a few steps amidst the gnawed bones we saw that there was light ahead; not any mystic phosphorescence, but a filtered daylight which could not come except from unknown fissures in the cliff that overlooked the waste valley. A few steps more, and our breaths were literally snatched from us by what we saw; so literally that Thornton,

CHESTY

Sabrina, the girl who is bending over, is one of our favorite people. When Sabrina straightens up she is an English girl who is on the stage, in fact she is sort of the talk of London. In case you are worried about Sabrina having lumbago or something, don't. She just likes to go around town in a half crouch.

60

the psychic investigator, actually fainted in the arms of the dazed man who stood behind him. Norrys, his plump face utterly white and flabby, simply cried out inarticulately; while I think that what I did was to gasp or hiss, and cover my eyes.

The man behind me—the only one of the party older than I—croaked "My God!" in the most cracked voice I ever heard. Of seven cultivated men, only Sir William Brinton retained his composure.

It was a twilit grotto of enormous height, stretching away farther than any eye could see; a subterraneous world of limitless mystery and horrible suggestion. There were buildings and other architectural remains —in one terrified glance I saw a weird pattern of mounds, a savage circle of monoliths, a low-domed Roman ruin, a sprawling Saxon pile, and an early English edifice of wood —but all these were dwarfed by the ghoulish spectacle presented by the general surface of the ground. For yards about the steps extended an insane tangle of human bones, or bones at least as human as those on the steps. Like a foamy sea they stretched, some fallen apart, but others wholly or partly articulated as skeletons; these latter invariably in postures of frenzy, either fighting off some menace or clutching other forms with cannibal intent.

BONES

When Dr. Trask, the anthropologist, stopped to classify the skulls, he found a degraded mixture which utterly baffled him. They were mostly lower than the Piltdown man in the scale of evolution, but in every case definitely human. Many were of higher grade, and a very few were the skulls of supremely and sensitively developed types. All the bones were gnawed, mostly by rats, but also by others of the half-human drove. Mixed with them were many tiny bones of rats—fallen members of the lethal army which closed the ancient epic.

I wonder that any man among us lived and kept his sanity through that hideous day of discovery. Each stumbling on revelation after revelation, and trying to keep from thinking of the events which must have taken place there three hundred, or a thousand, or two thousand, or ten thousand years ago. It was the antechamber of hell.

Horror piled on horror as we began to interpret the architectural remains. The quadruped things—with their occasional recruits from the biped class

—had been kept in stone pens, out of which they must have broken in their last delirium of hunger or rat-fear. There had been great herds of them, evidently fattened on the coarse vegetables whose remains could be found as a sort of poisonous ensilage at the bottom of huge stone bins older than Rome. I knew now why my ancestors had had such excessive gardens—would to heaven I could forget! The purpose of the herds I did not have to ask.

Sir William, standing with his searchlight in the Roman ruin, translated aloud the most shocking ritual I have ever known; and told of the diet of the cult which the priests of Cybele found and mingled with their own. Norrys could not walk straight when he came out of the English building. It was a butcher shop and kitchen—he had expected that—but it was too much to see familiar English implements in such a place. I could not go in that building— that building whose activities were stopped only by the dagger of my ancestor Walter de la Poer.

SKULLS

What I did venture to enter was the low Saxon building whose oaken door had fallen, and there I found a terrible row of ten stone cells with rusty bars. Three had tenants, all skeletons of high grade, and on the bony forefinger of one I found a seal ring with my own coat-of-arms. Sir William found a vault with far older cells below the Roman chapel, but these cells were empty. Below them was a low crypt with cases of formally arranged bones, some of them bearing terrible inscriptions carved in Latin, Greek, and the tongue of Phrygia.

Meanwhile, Dr. Trask had opened one of the prehistoric mounds, and brought to light skulls which were slightly more human than a gorilla's. Through all this horror my cat stalked unperturbed. Once I saw him monstrously perched atop a mountain of bones, and wondered at the secrets that might lie behind his yellow eyes.

Having grasped to some slight degree the frightful revelations of this twilit area, we turned to that apparently boundless depth of midnight cavern where no ray of light from the cliff could penetrate. We shall never know what sightless Stygian worlds yawn beyond the little distance we went, for it was decided that such secrets are not good for mankind. But there was plenty to engross us close at hand, for we had

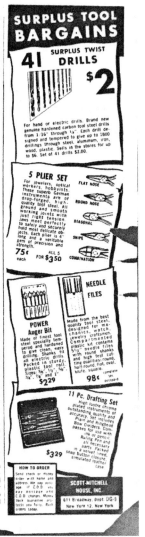

not gone far before the searchlights showed that accursed infinity of pits in which the rats had feasted, and whose sudden lack of replenishment had driven the ravenous rodent army first to turn on the living herds of starving things, and then to burst forth from the priory in that historic orgy of devastation which the peasants will never forget.

NIGHTMARE

God! those carrion black pits of sawed, picked bones and opened skulls! Those nightmare chasms choked with the Celtic, Roman, and English bones of countless unhallowed centuries! Some of them were full, and none can say how deep they had once been. Others were still bottomless to our searchlights, and peopled by unnamable fancies. Once my foot slipped near a horribly yawning brink, and I had a moment of ecstatic fear. I must have been musing a long time, for I could not see any of the party but the plump Capt. Norrys. Then there came a sound from that inky, boundless, farther distance that I thought I knew; and I saw my old black cat dart past me like a winged Egyptian god, straight into the illimitable gulf of the unknown. But I was not far behind, for there was no doubt after another second. It was the scurrying of those fiend-born rats, always questing for horrors, and determined to lead me on to those grinning caverns of earth's center.

My searchlight expired, but still I ran. I heard voices, and yowls, and echoes, but above all there gently rose that insidious scurrying; gently rising, rising, as a stiff bloated corpse gently rises above an oily river that flows under endless onyx bridges to a black, putrid sea.

Something bumped into me—something soft and plump. It must have been the rats; the viscous, gelatinous, ravenous army that feast on the dead and the living. . . . Why shouldn't rats eat a de la Poer as a del la Poer eats forbidden things? . . . The war ate my boy, damn them all . . . and the Yanks ate Carfax with flames and burnt Grandsire Delapore and the secret . . . No, no, I tell you, I am *not* that daemon swineherd in the twilit grotto! It was *not* Edward Norrys' fat face on that flabby fungous thing! Who says I am a de la Poer? He lived, but my boy died! . . . Shall a Norrys hold the lands of de la Poer? . . . It's voodoo, I tell you . . . that spotted snake . . . Curse you, Thornton, I'll teach you to faint at what my family do! . . . 'Sblood, thou stinkard, I'll learn ye how to gust . . . wolde ye swynke me thilke wys? . . . *Magna Mater! Magna Mater!* . . . *Atys . . . Dia ad aghaidh's ad aodaun . . . agus bas dunach ort! Dhonas 's dholas ort, agus leat-sa! . . . Ungl . . . ungle . . . rrlh . . . chchch . . .*

That is what they say I said when they found me in the blackness after three hours; found me crouching in the blackness over the plump, half-eaten body of Capt. Norrys, with my own cat leaping and tearing at my throat. Now they have blown up Exham Priory, taken my Black Tom away from me, and shut me into this barred room at Hanwell with fearful whispers about my heredity and experience. Thornton is in the next room, but they prevent me from talking to him. They are trying, too, to suppress most of the facts concerning the priory. When I speak of poor Norrys they accuse me of a hideous thing, but they must know that I did not do it. They must know it was the rats; the slithering scurrying rats whose scampering will never let me sleep; the rats that race behind the padding in this room and beckon me down to greater horrors than I have ever known; the rats they can never hear; the rats, the rats in the walls. ∎

FIRE

(*Continued from page 23*)

ning bolt crashed into a dried out fir tree—somewhere beyond my vision in the valley. There had been no rain for ten weeks in the mountains and, in the forest spreads, the twigs and fallen pine needles crackled underfoot.

By late evening—when my day was about to end—the fir tree began to smoulder. A strong wind blew up during the night. It fanned the sparks eating into the sere wood of the tree. Suddenly, it burst into flame and stood for a brief instant like a solitary, red-orange torch in the middle of the forest.

I didn't know this, either, for I was asleep in my bunk. Nor could I imagine what was to happen next.

I felt the stiff breeze funnelling through the valley the next morning. It was while I was repairing a torn window screen that I looked out over the valley—and saw the shroud of blue-white smoke lazing into the sky far away.

Instinctively, I knew what this meant. Forest fire! With the woods dry as tinder, the blaze would spread rapidly!

Although I was certain that forest rangers would have spotted the blaze from their observation towers located throughout the area, I decided to get to a telephone and call in the report —just in case. I marked the general region of the fire in my mind and closed up the cabin.

The engine of the jeep started without any trouble and, within minutes, I was bumping and slewing down the road to the home of Hank Barton, my chicken-farmer friend. His was the nearest telephone.

"What? Need more eggs so soon?" Hank kidded as I pulled up in front of his frame cottage. "Or have you been having hungry company?"

"No—no eggs today," I replied. "Wanna use your phone. Fire up the valley . . ."

A grim look passed over Barton's leathery face. "Sure. Right inside."

He followed me into the house. I grabbed the receiver of the old-fashioned phone hanging on one wall and cranked the handle. I was put through to the State Forestry Service instantly when I told the operator my business.

"Thanks," a voice at the other end of the line said after I identified myself and made my report. "We've got it taped. There's a crew on the way there now. We'd appreciate it if you'd let us know if you observe anything unusual though, Mr. Stiefel."

As long as I'd driven to Hank's place anyway, I figured I might a well make an outing of the day. His wife cooked up a batch of fried chicken for lunch—and we spent the afternoon swapping old yarns.

"Keep us posted, Jim," Barton asked. I was started back an hour or so before dark. "We can't see much of the valley here . . ."

The smoke cloud had appeared to have grown no bigger by the time I got back to my place. I guessed that it was under control, ate a cold supper and turned in.

The roar of an airplane engine passing overhead woke me a few minutes before my regular time. The sound of a plane was unusual enough in that part of the country and I ran outside to see what was going on.

It was still almost dark. The first tinge of pink were appearing in the east, but I was able to see only the red and white marker lights of the ship which was headed out over the valley.

My radio explained the presence of the aircraft. I listened to the announcer read off the bad news . . .

"Forest Service parachute firefighters have been dispatched in an effort to control a forest fire raging in the Shasta National Forest northwest of Redding. The blaze, which was origi-

226

APPENDIX II

Introduction to
THE WHIPPOORWILLS
IN THE HILLS

AUGUST W. DERLETH

THIS STORY (WHICH FIRST APPEARED IN WEIRD TALES, September, 1948) is an obvious homage to Derleth's mentor Lovecraft's classic tale "The Rats in the Walls." The scale is a bit smaller, but the syntagmic axis is exactly the same. Which story are we talking about here? A man moves to an ancestral home where he finds himself at once the object of hostile suspicion by all the locals. They seem to fear his arrival signals the revival of the evil perpetrated by his mysterious ancestors. His slumber is disturbed by the sounds of creatures and noises within the house. At length, thanks to the residual unwholesome influences of the old house, he lapses into atavistic insanity, attacking others in a bestial manner. Ending his autobiographical account in the confines of a cell, he still cannot believe himself guilty of the bloody depredations with which he is charged. And he notes in closing that he remains tormented by the mysterious sounds of the ____s in the _____s! When it is this close, I think it inappropriate to speak of borrowing, much less plagiarizing. The one story must be intended as a salute to the other. And a fine tribute it is! Derleth's narrator maintains a committedly mundane, hard-headed realism with a combined toleration for the rustic's tight-lipped mores and a healthy suspicion of them. We do get the feeling that his narrator's self-reassurances are whistling in the dark rationalizations by a man who dares not face the truth he uneasily suspects. No, he will have none of this superstition. Even once he has been through the ringer, he just will not credit what we readers know must have happened to him. The result of all this is a firm control of narrative mood, without which his tale would seem like the merest fanzine pastiche. Often Derleth's tales are skillful remixes of elements from Lovecraft's stories, and "The Whippoorwills in the Hills" is no exception. But the choice of Lovecraft elements is particularly interesting, for though the basic skeleton is surely "The Rats in the Walls," Derleth has spliced it with "The Shadow out of Time," and with interesting results. When the "Whippoorwills" narrator experiences psychic displacement and finds himself in a primeval age, in the time of the Old Ones' occupation of the earth, the description is highly reminiscent of Lovecraft's portrayal of remote, archaic Australia inhabited by the cone race. And the *Necronomicon* passage the narrator reads makes a new connection. If I read it right, Derleth's Alhazred is equating the "invisible whistling octopi" (as Edmund Wilson derisively called the subterranean foes of the coneheads) the same as the Great Old Ones. It was the eruption of the brethren of Cthulhu and Yog-Sothoth that prompted the Yith-minds to voyage into the far future. Of course, "The Whippoorwills in the Hills" owes a debt to "The Dunwich Horror" as well, what with the eponymous avians and the mention of those darn Whateleys, but the dependence is much less significant than that found in "The Shuttered Room," which almost counts as a sequel.

HIEROPHANT OF THE HORDE

Photo by Andrew Migliore. RMP performing the wedding of Kat and Joe Pulver

ROBERT M. PRICE discovered H.P. Lovecraft in 1966 thanks to the Lancer paperback editions. Weird fiction became a life-long obsession. Fastforward to 1981, Price discovered S.T. Joshi's journal *Lovecraft Studies* and submitted his first article to it. Joshi then invited him to attend the NECon (New England Fantasy Convention), where he was introduced to the Providence Pals including Joshi himself, Don and Mollie Burleson, Marc Michaud, Peter H. Cannon, Ken Neilly, and Jason Eckhardt, who christened him "the Hierophant of the Horde" and urged him to join the Esoteric Order of Dagon Amateur Press Association. It was a pivotal year in which he earned his first Ph.D, and met his future wife, Qarol.

The price of admission to the E.O.D. was a 'zine of a few pages four times a year, so Price began to issue his soon-to-be-renowned *Crypt of Cthulhu* which before long grew to 40, then 60 pages and appeared eight times yearly. Many contributed articles, reviews, and humor pieces. Its letter column served as a discussion forum for readers including Robert Bloch, Ramsey Campbell, Brian Lumley, and L. Sprague de Camp.

Nine Years later Price was invited to compile Lovecraftian anthologies for Fedogan & Bremer. A few years after that, the lords of Chaosium, Inc., approached him to do the same for them in order to provide the classic stories on which the role playing game Call of Cthulhu was based. He has produced others for publishers including Arkham House, Hippocampus Press, and Celaeno Press. He received an achievement award, "the Howie," at the Lovecraft Film Festival (2006). At the 2015 NecronomiCon Price was given the Robert Bloch Award for his contributions to the Lovecraft community—and promptly banned from ever again speaking at the event!

Robert M. Price is also a noted Bible scholar and theologian, though he lacks a belief in God. He frequently explores the deep connections between religion, myth, and horror. He is the author of many books in the field and serves as editor of the *Journal of Higher Criticism* and the host of The Bible Geek podcast. He has taught at Drew University, Montclair State College, Bergen Community College, Mount Olive College, the Johnnie Colemon Theological Seminary, and the Unification Theological Seminary. He and his wife Qarol host Heretics Anonymous discussion groups.

RMP confers with Tom Kuebler's H.P. Lovecraft, created for Guillermo del Toro

Blasphemies &
Revelations

Robert M. Price

❖Other Anthologies
Curated by Robert M. Price❖

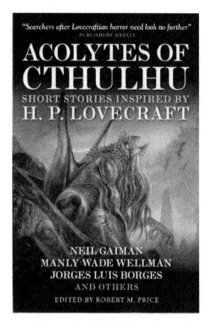

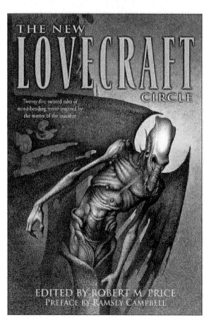

❖Other Anthologies
Curated by Robert M. Price❖

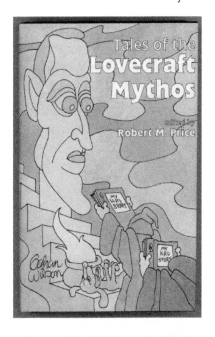

❖Other Anthologies
Curated by Robert M. Price❖

❖Other Anthologies
Curated by Robert M. Price❖

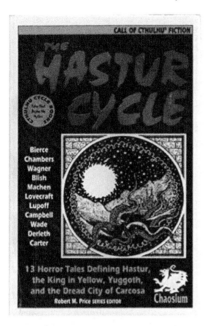

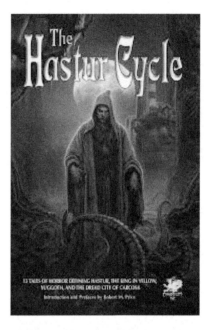

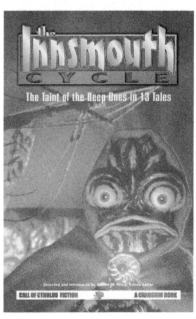

❖Other Anthologies
Curated by Robert M. Price❖

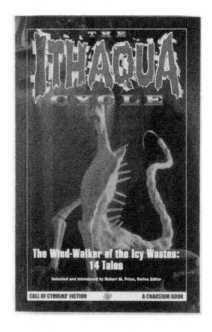

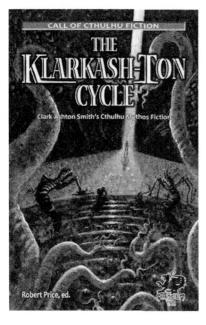

❖Other Anthologies
Curated by Robert M. Price❖

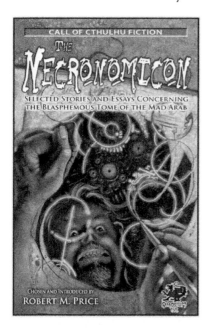

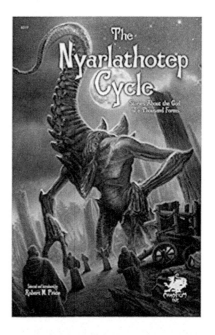

❖Other Anthologies
Curated by Robert M. Price❖

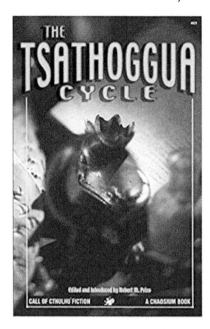

Printed in Great Britain
by Amazon

41788562R00138